CW00411172

JULIET

"The Alex and Juliet Series"

Book Two

JOANNE HOMER

Copyright © 2018 Joanne Homer

The right of Joanne Homer to be identified as the

Author of the Work has been asserted in accordance with

the Copyright, Design and Patents Act 1988

Visit my website and subscribe for your free

EBook – Find out how it all started

www.joannehomer.com

Facebook – joannehomerauthor

Instagram – joanne.homerbooks

Chapter 1 – The Proposal

So did Juliet say yes?

Life is never easy, far from it and it had been especially hard for Juliet. She loved Alex, there was no doubt about that but love is the most complex of emotions. It is not clear-cut it is not black and white it is greyscale with blurred lines.

They had spent a turbulent nine months together since they had met up again in Paris on that fateful January day last year. And then they had spent another nine months apart. And now here he was in her little flat on a lovely July day asking her to marry him. She had been through so much and much of that alone without him by her side. She was unsure about his question and therefore unsure about her answer.

Yes all girls grow up with the ideal fairytale romance in their minds and they all want happy endings but right now Juliet was contented. Contented is not happiness but being content is good. Juliet was stable and had built herself a new life. There were so many unanswered questions in her mind, questions that needed answers before she could decide whether or not to accept Alex's proposal.

"Alex," Juliet said, "you know that at one time there was nothing I wanted more in the world to say yes to a proposal of marriage from you. But things are not easy. It is difficult and my heart wants to say yes, yes, yes but I know in reality that to make it work, things have to be right. I left you in the cottage because you couldn't handle the situation with me losing Guy and you withdrew from me and became depressed. It was so hard for me to see you like that and it cut me to pieces. I left not because I didn't love you but because I thought you didn't love me anymore. That was so hard, so fucking hard to think we had gone through all that we had only to find that you didn't love me. So I left. I have questions that need to be answered and things that need to be sorted out. I see you standing here before me and I want to throw my arms around you and welcome you into my bed and love you like before but to be honest, I don't know whether I should. I am a broken woman Alex. You should have been there for me and you weren't."

Alex looked stunned and Juliet could see anger beginning to build in his eyes and then he spoke. "That is just what I expect from a slag like you. I suppose you have been up to your old tricks haven't you? Just who have you been fucking Juliet? Baker? Hamilton? It wouldn't have taken you long to get in touch with Baker would it? This flat is too nice for you to have done it all on your own. And how have you managed to pull off seeing Guy? I presume you are giving Hamilton something in return for seeing him. I want a paternity test. I don't think Clara is mine."

Juliet's jaw dropped. She was speechless and she stood there shocked beyond belief. She certainly hadn't been expecting this little outburst. He had suddenly changed and had become a monster again. She simply couldn't believe what he was saying. But she knew, she knew it was because he was mentally ill.

When Juliet had left Alex and returned to Oxford to live on her own she had spent many days in the library searching for answers to Alex's behavior. Deep down she knew his behavior was not normal. In the cottage she had been conditioned and her love for him was so deep that she was blind to his faults. She thought his rages to be a consequence of the messy situation they were in. She had refused to allow him to push her away.

4

At first she had thought his sudden rages and change in character could be a sign of schizophrenia because he had used cannabis heavily in previous years. But as she read and studied the characteristics of schizophrenia she realized that it wasn't that. However she read more and one particular mental condition ticked all the boxes. Borderline Personality Disorder fitted Alex's behavior down to a 'T'. In an attempt to understand him she had bought two books on the subject and read about it. She knew that his sudden anger was in retaliation for her not saying yes to his proposal of marriage. The insults and request for a paternity test were his childish, mentally ill way of coping with her rejection. Most sensible people would have thought that what Juliet had said was entirely reasonable but not Alex. He had taken what she had said as a straight rejection and he was lashing out to hurt her.

Juliet remained calm. She really wanted to lash out at him herself. To tell him he was being bloody stupid but she knew from what she had read that this was counterproductive.

"Alex," said Juliet, trying to remain calm. "You are entitled to your opinion and I can do nothing about what you think but I know the truth and I have not been sleeping with anyone else. As for the paternity test, I feel very upset that you want one. We were holed up in that cottage miles from anywhere and anyone and we hardly left each other's side. It is quite obvious that Clara is your child as she looks just like you. But if you want to waste your money on a paternity test then go ahead. You have quite clearly been watching too many episodes of Jeremy Kyle. But I will have no part of it." As soon as she had said the words about Jeremy Kyle she knew she shouldn't have done so. It was inflammatory, to say the least and not what you should do with a BPD sufferer but she was hurting from the accusation hurting very badly after all she had gone through alone.

She really wanted to tell him to get the fuck out of her little flat but she knew he was ill and she wanted to help him. If they stood any chance at all of having a relationship he needed to get well. She owed it to Clara to try.

There was a stony silence as Alex stood angrily eyeing Juliet. Juliet regained her composure and broke the silence. She knew that she should behave in a very cool and detached fashion. "Anyway Alex," she finally said, "how long are you here for and where are you staying?"

Alex softened and said "I have a month off. I need to go back to the cottage. I am going to give notice on it and although the rent is not a lot I am not going to use it and it seems a waste of money to keep it on. I thought I could stay here tonight if that is ok with you?"

Juliet sighed. Just typical of him that he wanted to doss down at her house. He hadn't thought this through, he hadn't figured she might reject him and he was manipulating her. But after the display of anger she had just witnessed she really did not want to sleep with him. She could not risk being sucked down into that whirlpool of emotions that she knew would so easily return if she was intimate with him. She thought about it and then said. "Ok Alex, you can stay here but you can sleep on the sofa. Clara wakes in the night and she will disturb you when I have to feed her." By way of a get out clause that she hoped would not offend nor enrage him.

"That's fine by me," replied Alex and he gave her one of his mischievous little boy smiles.

You stupid fool, thought Juliet to herself. He is not going to sleep on that sofa and you know it. He is going to try and seduce you. The look on his face had just told her that. I am just going to have to resist him, she thought to herself.

Juliet cooked dinner and sent Alistair a text to ask him to stay with one of his friends tonight. It wasn't that she wanted to be alone with Alex. She just didn't want Alistair witnessing them having a row because she feared another. To outsiders it looked toxic but Juliet had to try and help Alex get better. Besides he had really given her very little choice. If Juliet had said he couldn't stay it would further enrage him and look petty but she knew what he was doing. She just had to be strong and not give in.

Juliet knew that she had to be strong and not bend to accommodate Alex. She had done so in the past and it was just what he expected. From what she had read BPD sufferers expect you to go the extra mile for them. It was a game, an attention seeking act and one that Juliet had all been too ready to fall for before desperate to make their love work. But now she wasn't going to bend over backward to please him. Now it was on her terms.

"I am sorry Alex but I haven't got anything vegetarian. I eat meat now. I need to eat meat. I was so thin when I left you in the cottage. Val said it was not good for me. But you are welcome to have the food I have." said Juliet.

Alex sat on the sofa with a straight view of Juliet in the galley kitchen of the ground floor flat, he looked relaxed and at home on her sofa. "Oh, I am not a vegetarian anymore. I gave that up ages ago."

Well that was typical, Juliet thought to herself. She had gone through hell for nothing but then she knew that was part of his illness. The constant changing things about the way the borderline lives in order to try and improve their lives, not realising the source of their unhappiness is their mental illness.

Juliet cooked a pulled pork meal, ready -made. She and Alistair enjoyed it with spicy wedges and sweetcorn and it was what she had planned they would eat that night. She certainly wasn't rushing out to get anything special for her uninvited guest. He would just have to make do with it. They sat on the sofa and ate their meals from trays. Juliet certainly

7

wasn't going to lay the table and make it look like she was making an effort for him as she would have done in the past.

Alex's mood had changed again and he was on a charm offensive. "Juliet, that meal was delicious. You haven't lost your touch. I have missed your cooking. You worked marvels in the cottage on JSA. I am so impressed with the way that you have made a life for yourself. This flat is really lovely and you are doing wonders with Clara. She is really adorable." Juliet was flattered but she knew he was trying to cast his spell on her and she must resist. And what had happened to the "you couldn't have possibly done this on your own?" remark. She ignored his comment but his charm was hard to resist. She had been so deprived of attention, so lacking in love when she had needed it, and God did she need it now. She had been on her own for nine months, battling alone without anyone and she soaked up his praises like a sponge takes up water.

Clara had her last feed and Juliet put her to bed in the cot in her room and went into the kitchen to tidy up. Alex was having a bath. Juliet stood with her hands in the soapy water contemplating what was happening. Why did he have to come back? She had been alright on her own but she had missed him. She had missed his touch and although, there was no denying he had some problem mentally, all she wanted right now was for him to kiss her again and to tell her he loved her. It was all she had thought about for months on end when she was alone but the thoughts had slowly abated and she had become accustomed to being without his love, although the memory was still there as fresh as yesterday. Juliet put these thoughts to the back of her mind. It was just her hormones talking, she rationalised with herself but then she felt the pull and she wondered if she could resist.

The time had slipped by whilst Juliet had been in thought in the kitchen. She suddenly realised that Alex had been in the bath for what seemed like ages. Juliet went to the bathroom. The door was open and he wasn't in the bathroom anymore. She went into the bedroom and there he was, naked in her bed.

There was no point in telling him to get out, he would just laugh and ignore her. He would think it even more of a game to try and stay put, so she said nothing. She took her pyjamas into the bathroom, changed, and brushed her teeth and went back into the bedroom and climbed into bed next to him "Goodnight Alex," she said, as she turned off the light and turned away from him.

It didn't take long for his arms to find their way over to her and he put one around her. Juliet froze. What should she do? "Alex, given that you think I have been sleeping with all and sundry, I don't think it is a good idea if we are intimate with each other. I am tired so I would like you to remove your arm and let me go to sleep please." He did as she instructed and didn't say a word. It had taken every bit of self-control to do that. She had managed to resist him but for how long? Every inch of her body wanted him. The months she had missed his touch and she lay there in the darkness wide awake, in torture. Her mind and heart in conflict with each other.

She finally drifted off to sleep and awoke the next morning. Clara had slept through the night, thank goodness and Juliet fed her silently whilst Alex slept. She looked at his sleeping face and was lost in time, if only for a moment. She put Clara back in her cot and went and made herself some tea and a coffee for Alex. He was awake when she returned to the bedroom. "Good morning Juliet," he said.

"Good morning Alex," replied Juliet, and sat in bed next to him. She could smell his manliness. His own particular scent and she was transported back in time. All the memories came flooding back. She could feel tears welling up in her eyes and she tried to fight the urge to let them flow but it was too late and a solitary tear rolled down her cheek.

"Hey, what's the matter?" he said.

"Oh, nothing," she replied, "my hormones are all over the place still and I cry for no reason whatsoever."

"Juliet, I am so sorry for everything, and I am sorry about what I said to you yesterday. I was angry you hadn't said yes to my proposal but you are right, it is not the right time to get married. But why don't you let me hold you. I want to and I am sure you would like to be held?"

Juliet tried to resist. "That is very kind of you Alex but I am ok honestly. I was very damaged by everything that went on last year and I think we should take it slowly don't you?"

"It wouldn't hurt. I am not asking for anything else. I have missed you and I want to hold you."

It was too late, she had crumbled and she let him spoon her, feeling safe in his arms, if only for now.

He left the flat to travel by train back to Wales and the cottage. Juliet breathed a sigh of relief when she closed the door behind him. He had bought a paternity test with him and had taken a swab from the inside of Clara's cheek. It was not a rash act. He had clearly been planning it for a while. Was that the reason for his impromptu visit? Had the proposal just been because he felt it was the right thing to do? Was it just part of the manipulation? And if she had said yes maybe he would have never got angry and blurted it out about the paternity test. If that had happened, would he have conducted the test on the sly when she wasn't watching? There were still so many unanswered questions about him but for now, he was gone and she was safe.

Chapter-2 Gilfach Cottages Revisited

It had been just over a week since Alex's visit and he and Juliet had been emailing each other. Despite her reservations Juliet had to admit to herself that she missed him and they had been getting on well with each other. Just like old times. They were the best of friends when they wanted, he was sympathetic and she was caring and they melded with each other so easily.

It was a Sunday and Charlotte had come to stay for the weekend and they had just eaten Sunday lunch. Juliet turned on her computer and opened her emails. There was one from Alex

"Hello Juliet

I miss you and Clara and it seems a waste for me to have a month off and not spend it with you both. I had the paternity results back yesterday and Clara is indeed my child. I am sorry I ever doubted you, can you forgive me?

Would you like to come and stay here for a week or so?

Alex x"

Juliet was angry about the paternity test. It had really rankled with her. It seemed stupid in the extreme and it had cost him 100 quid. But the truth was, she missed him and she did want to see him. What harm would it do to go and see him? It would be good for him to bond with his daughter. After all she was doing this for Clara, she told herself, not acknowledging that she was also doing it for herself.

She told Charlotte about his invite. "I think you should go Mom. What harm can it do?" Oh the young are so foolish.

They do not see things the way age and wisdom see them. All the pitfalls and all the potential for error but Juliet was just looking for reassurance from someone else that her decision was the right one even though she doubted it was right herself.

"I suppose you are right," said Juliet and then she had an idea. Charlotte was travelling back to the Midlands that afternoon and she could get a lift to the station at Wolverhampton and catch a train from there to Wales. It would halve the travelling time and the expense. She no longer had a car as it hadn't passed the MOT and she had weighed it in last November. She hadn't bothered replacing it as she had no need for one in Oxford. She opened the website and looked at the train times. "Look Charlotte, can I cadge a lift with you? Would you drop me at Wolverhampton? I can catch a train from there. I can quickly pack a bag and be ready within the hour."

Charlotte laughed, "Oh mom, you are mad there is no doubt about it. But yes, if that is what you want." Juliet flew around packing bags, and getting ready and loaded the car. They were on their way in no time, Clara asleep in her car seat and Juliet and Charlotte chatting happily away. Charlotte wanted her mother to be happy and she was doing her best to convince Juliet that she was doing the right thing.

She had emailed Alex with the news that she would be on her way before she had left so he knew she was coming. She got off at Newtown station and found a taxi to take her to the cottage. She was nervous but excited as they drove along the winding road through the valley to the cottage. Nervous because she had been left so scarred from the events of the last eighteen months. She still loved Alex but she didn't want to see his rages again, ever but she knew she would. She knew that lurking around the corner in the dark would be his rages his alter ego. What and who exactly was the real Alex?

Alex was waiting at the back door to the cottage when they pulled up. He came over and helped unload the taxi. He paid the taxi driver and hugged Juliet. She was pleased to see him and he was clearly pleased to see her.

The cottage hadn't changed at all apart from the fact it seemed very empty without Juliet's furniture in the lounge which was bare. Alex had made a little sofa out of the camp bed mattress on the floor, folding it in half, with half up the wall but you had to sit on the floor. It looked like student digs. Juliet had to laugh, forty-three and he still lived like a student when he was on his own. "Would you like a drink of wine?" Alex asked "we made that Elderberry wine last year and it was in the cupboard when I got back. I have had a taste and it is really rather good." Juliet had never tasted decent home-made wine. In her opinion it had always been rather poor. Syrupy and odd tasting but she agreed to try a glass and to her surprise it was comparable with a good merlot. Clara had been fed and was asleep in her pram. It would double up as a cot for the next week or so and it was still big enough for her. They sat on the floor on the makeshift sofa.

"I knew Clara was mine when I saw her," said Alex, "but I had worked myself up into such a state over the last month, about why you hadn't told me about you were pregnant, I felt unsure whether she was mine. I had ordered the paternity test and thought I might as well use it as I had paid for it. Then I would have no doubt in my mind whatsoever. I am really sorry, I hope you understand." Juliet sighed, she didn't understand, she would never understand the way his mind worked.

Near the end of their relationship the previous year, before she had left Alex she had gone to see Bill. Alex had been in Newtown and he had asked her to pick him up at Bill's, and she had arrived before he had. Bill had joked and said "Alex is stark raving mad."

Juliet had laughed at the time and said "we are all nuts."

But then Bill, with a very serious face had gone on and said, "no Juliet, he really is mad. He can philosophize with the best of 'em but he can't think his way out of a paper bag. I have seen how thin you have got Juliet, You must have lost two stone since you have lived with Alex. Do you want to be beatified? I told my daughter that if Alex came and lived with me I would get a gun and shoot myself. He won't change, he is not right in the head and he is wearing you down." At that time Juliet was planning to get out and so she said nothing to Bill about leaving, she didn't want him to tell Alex. Although she doubted he would, she couldn't be sure so she kept quiet.

"I am not sure I do Alex, but it is done now and you know for sure that Clara is your daughter, so let's just leave it at that." They sat and sipped their wine, and Alex talked about his work in Iraq. He was entertaining and charming and he knew what he was doing. He said the teaching was awful but he liked his students and he had made friends with some of them. This was something Juliet thought foolish to say the least and crossing the professional line. Surely no good would come of that. He was sharing a flat with a Lebanese man called Maher and he obviously liked Maher a lot. Maher was newly married but his wife was back in Lebanon and Juliet knew that it would have been an arranged marriage. Love was not part of the decision. Alex said he was very handsome. Juliet thought it odd that Alex should describe another man as handsome and what was even stranger was the way he said it. Juliet had to admit that she was not sure about his friendship with Maher but she put it to the back of her mind.

The elderberry wine was going to her head and Juliet was falling under his spell again. She had been deprived of eligible male company since she had left Alex last September and she was feeling drawn to him again. The question of

14

entering into a sexual relationship with Alex had entered her head more than once over the last week. In fact, it was something she had found herself contemplating quite a lot when she had moments alone with her thoughts. She had concluded that it was futile to resist, she wanted to sleep with him and that was all there was to it so if the opportunity came up she would not resist. Although she was worried about it as she had torn when she had given birth to Clara and it had not been stitched as she had given birth at home. It did not feel quite right down there when she washed herself. She should have done something about it but being busy with a new baby she hadn't bothered.

It was growing dark outside and Alex lit some tealights and lit the fire in the wood burner then he sat down next to Juliet and topped up their glasses with wine. "Can I kiss you?" he said. Juliet went weak at the knees. Before she had time to reply he took her in his arms and kissed her passionately on the mouth.

"I didn't say yes," said Juliet.

Alex laughed, "no you didn't but the amazing speed with which you got here, told me all I needed to know. I didn't expect you to come for a couple of days and yet within an hour of me asking you, you were on your way," and he laughed heartily.

He is cocky, thought Juliet but she had to see the funny side of it, she had been transparent. "Life is too short," said Juliet "and Charlotte was travelling up to the Midlands. It meant that it would save me changing trains and you can see what I have had to bring with me; a car seat, two bags, and a pram. The journey wouldn't have been easy."

"I suppose so," said Alex, "but you did want me to kiss you, didn't you?" Juliet looked into his sea blue eyes. She felt like a drowning woman. It was too late, it was futile to

15

resist even though she knew she should but in true Juliet style she threw caution to the wind and gave in.

They climbed the narrow winding stairs to the bedroom. It hadn't changed but he had moved the bed so his side was against the wall. The bedroom was small and the only way it could accommodate a king-sized bed was if one side was against the wall. It used to be her side but now he had moved it. In no time at all Alex was naked. Juliet was still undressing, "look Alex, I am very nervous about this, I have not long had a baby and my body is still recovering. I am not sure what I am going to be like down there," and she pointed downwards to her crotch. "I tore when I gave birth to Clara so please be kind," and she continued to undress and got into bed. He took her in his arms and she was again transported back in time. How she needed this, to be held by him, to be kissed by him. It was just the best feeling in the world. All the times when she had been on her own and needed to be comforted and he wasn't there. She had missed his arms around her and had cried. It was always when she was alone. She never let anyone else know what she was feeling, they wouldn't have understood. No one would understand just how powerful their love had been, to most people it was incomprehensible what it felt like when they were together.

They made love tenderly but Juliet knew that her vagina was not as it used to be. Alex had difficulty coming when he was inside her and Juliet had made him come with fellatio. Although that was not unusual as during 'part one' all those years ago he often had difficulty achieving orgasm. Something which Juliet had put down to the very late hour when they made love and to the amount of red wine he had consumed. He had been drinking that evening. Perhaps that was the cause but even so it was not what Juliet had hoped for. When they lay together afterward, she turned to Alex "What was it like?" "Fine," he said, "I could tell no difference, you only gave birth a few months ago. I don't

16

know about these things Juliet." Juliet knew it wasn't fine, but she shrugged it off, happy to be in Alex's arms once again. He didn't say he loved her though and she hadn't said she loved him and he had not attempted to give her an orgasm. Let's just not rush it this time she thought to herself. She didn't want him to go into a downward spiral like before and they fell asleep.

Juliet woke before Alex and lay in the early morning light, thinking. It was strange to be back in the cottage and she never thought she would ever be here again. But so far so good. Alex seemed overall to be more settled and happier, perhaps it was because he was working and earning money. The poverty, lack of employment and money the year before had certainly helped pile on the misery to an already complicated and troubled situation. Clara stirred in the makeshift cot in the corner of the room and Juliet went to make her a feed and tea for herself. When she returned to the bedroom Alex was still asleep and she picked up Clara and sat in bed feeding her. When she had finished and Juliet had changed her nappy the sound of a noisy infant had woken Alex. "Does she always wake up so early?" he said rather crossly.

He has no experience of babies at all, thought Juliet "I'm afraid she does. Would you like a coffee?"

Alex mumbled, "I would like some more sleep but seeing as I am not going to get any then yes a coffee would be nice." Juliet was irritated as she went downstairs to get him a coffee. What did he expect? He wasn't there for the birth, he hadn't seen what she had gone through and he hadn't bonded with his daughter. No he had just turned up and he had not had to bother his arse one little bit. Then Juliet softened, she hadn't given him the choice had she? So it was not entirely his fault.

She went back upstairs with the coffee. "I'm sorry Alex if we are an inconvenience and you hadn't realised what having a baby entails. If we are getting on your nerves then we can go home but you did invite us here and I thought you wanted to spend time with your daughter and get to know her? I think it is important, don't you?"

Alex turned over in bed to look at Juliet. He smiled at her "sorry I was such a grump, my sleeping is all over the place at the moment after living in Iraq. There was nothing to do there when I wasn't teaching and it was so hot. I would often stay up late at night and sleep during the day when I could. I did the evening shift for teaching and it has mucked about my sleep patterns. I am glad you are here Juliet and I am very happy to be with Clara. Please don't go, we have so much to catch up on."

Juliet bent and kissed him on the lips. "Good," she said.

Juliet was determined that she was not going to bend over backward to appease Alex. She had done so in their relationship before as she had so desperately wanted it to work but now the balance had shifted and if they were to ever have a relationship together it had to be equal in order to make it work, she knew that much.

"We need to go and get some groceries today," said Alex. "I hadn't expected you so soon, and I have very little food but first I should phone mom as I know she would like to see Clara. Is that ok Juliet? She can give us a lift into Newtown to Tesco where we can get some food. It would save the hassle of the bus." Juliet did not really want to see Jean, she really didn't like the woman and there was always an undercurrent that Juliet couldn't quite put her finger on. The woman was nice enough to Juliet's face but she felt that underneath it all Jean didn't like Juliet. She had hoped for someone who was more innocent than Juliet and preferably someone who had not been married before as a partner for

Alex. But she had been forced to accept Juliet as Alex was looking like he would never get married and he had lived with her on and off over the years so Juliet was better than nothing. Alex had confided to Juliet during the previous year that the reason why he had suddenly ended their affair all those years ago was because his mother had advised him against Juliet. She had said to Alex, "she has been unfaithful to her husband with you and if you have a relationship with her then she will ultimately be unfaithful to you with someone else." Juliet had been very angry about this when she had found out. It had not helped Alex's insecurity, of that she was certain and it all stemmed from the fact that both her ex-husbands had left her for other women, something from which she had never recovered. Although Juliet pointed out to Alex that it was rather odd that she never did any self-reflection, or felt she had been at fault. But Alex had taken his mother's advice all those years ago even though he had been nearly thirty years of age at the time. The woman had some kind of hold over him and she was a very strange person to say the least, thought Juliet. But she had to let her see her granddaughter. "Yes, that is fine Alex. I have a load of unused Tesco vouchers in the kitchen, as I haven't bothered changing my address on my club card yet."

Chapter 3-Jean

It was nearly eleven o'clock when the sound of tires crunching on the gravel driveway signified that Jean had arrived in her little KA. It was one of several that she had owned over the years and they had all been driven into oblivion and this was her latest. Jean came in the back door of the cottage. "Hello Jean," said Juliet.

"Where is she then? My grand-daughter."

"In the pram in the lounge," replied Juliet. And Jean walked straight past Juliet into the lounge.

Alex came down the stairs on hearing his mother's voice. "What do you think Mom?" Alex said to Jean, as they stood by the side of the pram. "Isn't she lovely?"

"I can't understand how you managed to make something so beautiful," said Jean sarcastically, and then added, "yes, she is gorgeous." Jean didn't behave like a doting grandmother. She didn't even pick up Clara and she didn't really say anything to Juliet. They are a weird bunch, Juliet thought to herself but then she knew they were. "I don't know how we are all going to fit in the car," said Jean.

"I don't take up much space, thank you for the lift Jean it is greatly appreciated." They all piled into the car and were soon on their way to Newtown. Alex sat in the front with his mother and Juliet sat in the back with the car seat. Once at Tesco Juliet loaded Clara into a trolley and they set off around Tesco.

It was one of Jean's peculiarities that she couldn't help but make fun of Alex. There had never been a time when they had been in her company that she hadn't taken a pot shot at

Alex for something or another. To her, he was a failure. Jean liked to brag about her children. Nicola was her pride and joy and had become a primary school teacher and was the epitome of middle class with two children and a successful Conservative voting husband. One of her other daughters lived far away in the north of England and Jean had fallen out with her many years ago because she hated her husband. They did not speak and hadn't for some years. The other daughter had got herself pregnant at sixteen and was quickly married to the poor man who had made her pregnant. They had two children together and according to Alex she was as domineering as Jean and was also very overweight. Alex said that she had suffered from eating disorders when she had been a teenager but seemed happy enough now. Jean liked Jenny and her husband because she could rule the roost with them. But Alex, no, she was definitely ashamed of him. Giving up a professional career as a solicitor to go and teach English as a foreign language was not something she could brag about to anyone and appearances were everything to Jean. She had said so to Juliet on more than one occasion.

They were all getting on fine until Jean made some remark to Alex. Making fun of him as a father and that was it. Juliet had learned not to laugh at these jokes even though they were spot on and extraordinarily funny. She had done it once last year on meeting Jean and Alex had instantly raged. She had never laughed since at Jean's jokey put-down comments of Alex. Alex's mood changed instantly and he went sulky and brooding. They got to the checkout and unloaded their goods onto the conveyor belt. Juliet assumed that Alex was going to pay for the groceries but when the time came to pay he did nothing. "I thought you were paying?" said Alex to Juliet.

Juliet was dumbfounded. She was on benefits and he had invited her to stay with him. "I thought you invited us to stay with you?" she said "I have no money, I am on benefits as you know. You can have all my Tesco vouchers. There is £15 off there."

Jean was outraged and for once stuck up for Juliet. "Alex, pay the bill, Juliet is right. You are earning. I cannot believe that you are expecting Juliet to pay. I am ashamed of you." Alex looked angry but got out his card and paid for the groceries. He said nothing after but both Jean and Juliet knew he was fuming. He had been made to look small at the checkout and like his mother appearances were everything to Alex.

They got outside of the store and Jean just couldn't let it go. "Alex, I am ashamed of you. That was appalling in there. I can't believe you expected Juliet to pay."

Alex turned viciously on his mother, "I give her maintenance."

"And so you should my lad because she is your daughter." Alex went quiet and Juliet wished Jean would say nothing else. It was not good to enrage him further and she was only making it worse.

They loaded the car and set off. Then all hell broke loose. "How dare you make me out to be in the wrong mother," shouted Alex, "she is a whore and has been sleeping around. God knows what she has been up to since she left the cottage." Juliet was stunned. Did he have no sense of decency? Why was he behaving like this in front of his mother? It was attention seeking at the very worst and all because Jean had sided with Juliet. He felt left out and like a child wanted to discredit Juliet in front of his mother, to make himself look good.

"Alex, don't talk about Juliet like that! She is the mother of your child."

Juliet started to cry in the back of the car, "please stop. I don't want to argue, I really don't. I am sorry Alex I didn't know you wanted me to pay for the groceries, you should have made that clear before I came. I would not have come if I had known. I will go as soon as I have benefits on Wednesday, or I will phone Charlotte and ask her to lend me some money." But Alex kept up his rant, going on and on about Nigel Baker, and raking up all the old dirt from Juliet's past. Even Jean said nothing. By the time they got to the cottage, Juliet was sobbing in the back of the car.

"Do you want to come to my house and stay with me Juliet?" said Jean "I am sorry about Alex. His behavior is appalling,"

Juliet was scared. It had been one thing being subject to Alex's rages when she had been on her own and had a car and thus a means of escape but now with a baby and all the luggage and no money, she was effectively trapped. Alex showed no signs of calming down as he angrily retrieved the shopping from the boot. "Thank you Jean, I will take up your offer if you are sure that is alright," said Juliet. She wasn't going to let him beat her down. Whilst she didn't relish being with Jean, she had never been alone with her, and it would be good to hear Jean's perspective. In any case, she didn't want to stay at the cottage. Jean helped her collect her things and the pram which they just about managed to wedge into the KA.

By the time they arrived at Jean's cottage, Juliet felt much calmer. Jean got out the wine. "I don't think it will be one glass of wine night tonight Juliet," she said. After Jean had cooked dinner and Juliet had washed up they sat down to watch TV. "He has always been the same Juliet," said Jean "he has made a scene at family occasions more times than I care to remember. He will suddenly take umbrage at something for no apparent reason and we will all sit there flabbergasted at his sudden rage. I blame the skunk he smoked for years myself. It has messed with his mind." Juliet was shocked but then she shouldn't have been. So it wasn't just her, he was like that with everyone he knew well. She thought of Alex in the cottage and wondered if he was feeling remorseful yet although the phone hadn't rung, she expected it wouldn't. There was no signal at the cottage for a start and the landline had been cut off ages ago. Alex had not wanted the expense. She still couldn't believe he had been so tight as to expect her to pay for the groceries. However it was peaceful at Jean's house and the woman actually seemed to be pleasant for a change, even if it was only pity.

Jean was a good hostess and away from Alex she adored Clara, she talked to her and genuinely liked her. "Your daddy is a fool," she said to Clara the next morning "he has something so wonderful and he behaves like an idiot." Juliet laughed softly. "Let him stew on his own Juliet. I will take you to the station at Aber when you are ready to go home, but stay a few days please, I would like to spend some time with Clara."

Juliet said "yes, thank you Jean" but she really thought that she ought to go and see Alex once he had calmed down, as she knew he would.

Jean was good company and she had given Juliet the guest bedroom which was pleasant and cosy. The large bed was comfortable and Clara slept with Juliet. The room was full of antiques, a legacy from the days when Jean had an antiques shop and it was full of photos of her family. Juliet noted that there was a picture of Alex as a baby and he looked very similar to Clara. There was also a photo of Jean and her father on her first wedding day and Alex was definitely like his grandfather. Juliet learned a great deal about Alex's family and in particular his grandparents, Jean's parents. Her father, Alex's grandfather, had adored his grandmother. Often asking Jean as a child to take a flower into her mother when he was in the garden, and kissing her mother passionately on the lips at the kitchen sink. They had married relatively late in life. They had both been in their early thirties but the arrival of two children had been something he had resented, taking his beloved Emma away from him. Jean said she had adored her father but he could be a tyrant and a little unkind to her and her brother. Juliet wondered if this was also a problem for Alex, as he had clearly adored her, like his grandfather had adored his grandmother.

They went out that day to Rhyader as Jean wanted to browse the charity shops. "I need to phone Charlotte and ask her to lend me some money when I can get a mobile signal as I need to buy some formula milk for Clara." Juliet had swapped Clara over to formula in the last couples of weeks as she could not keep up with her demands for milk, she just wasn't producing enough herself. "I can lend you some money," said Jean and Juliet gratefully accepted the loan.

That evening after dinner they sat and talked again. "Look Juliet, I would rather see you go back with your ex-husband, than be with Alex. He is no good." Juliet was shocked that Jean was actually suggesting this. Surely she would want Clara to be with her father? "That will never happen Jean, I could never go back to him even though he has Guy, whom I adore. Our marriage was hell and toxic and he would use my leaving him as a stick to beat me with. I was just a slave and I would be miserable. I owe it to Clara to try and give Alex a chance. I know his faults and his rages but I don't want Clara turning to me when she is older and saying I never tried. She would resent me for that."

Jean sighed "I suppose you are right," she said. "But what about Baker?" Juliet knew now that she was being questioned about her past as Alex had surely given his mother the not very nice version of the story.

Juliet laughed, "Oh Jean, what can I say? I didn't love the man. Sure, I could have married him. He wanted me to but I didn't love him. It is as simple as that. He had lots of money and yes that was a big draw, but I would have turned into an alcoholic if I had lived with him. He was boring and I didn't fancy him."

Jean laughed, "yes, but you wouldn't be grubbing around in your purse for the money to buy a packet of sausages for dinner." Juliet knew that she didn't understand. She had never had money and she couldn't understand how Juliet had turned it down. She had never had to sleep with someone who was just so repulsive that she had to get drunk in order to do it. It wasn't as if he was a bad person, he wasn't but Juliet needed true love not some fake love to be happy. Juliet questioned Jean's motives behind this statement. Did she herself not want Alex to be with Juliet? Juliet knew that she had frowned upon Juliet as a suitable partner for Alex. Was this her real motive? Or was she genuinely acting out of concern for Juliet? Juliet thought it was probably the former as even though Jean criticised Alex, he was her son and blood is thicker than water.

"I do love him Jean. I know that the sensible person should just leave him alone and I was determined to do so, but I can't. I have to do it to the death. For so many years I wondered 'what if?' I cannot go on with that thought. I need to try," said Juliet.

"Well you are a grown woman Juliet, and you know your own mind." replied Jean.

"Can I use your computer please Jean, to access my emails, I need to know whether he has contacted me?"

"Yes, of course, you can Juliet," said Jean.

Juliet logged onto her emails but there was nothing from Alex. She didn't send him a message. It was another two days before she received an email from him and she was overjoyed.

Juliet

I am sorry I behaved so badly. Will you come back to the cottage please? If you are still at moms. I can't believe you went with that old harpy. I miss you and Clara.

Alex xxx

Jean took her back to the cottage. "You know where I am if you need me Juliet," she said on the way to the cottage.

"Thank you Jean," said Juliet, but there was no way she would be calling on Jean again. She had heard enough.

Alex was sweetness and light and was back to his charming self. "That old bag just wanted to have Clara to herself," he said once they were all safely in the cottage, and Jean had left. He laughed "you know she prefers girls to boys. She treats her granddaughters differently to her grandsons and she treats her daughters better than her sons."

" She said she would rather see me back with my ex-husband than with you," said Juliet.

"It doesn't surprise me in the least," said Alex, "she doesn't want me to be happy."

"Well, I was shocked by it to say the least Alex and I told her in no uncertain terms that it would never happen," said Juliet.

"Her second husband was an alcoholic and she was besotted with him. That is why she doesn't see it is a problem. But I am so glad you came back. I really am sorry. My mother had wound me up and I took it out on you." And he took Juliet in his strong powerful arms, and kissed her passionately on the lips. "I want to take you to bed properly and give you an orgasm. You deserve one. You work so hard and I know you have looked after Clara on your own. I have a chicken in the oven."

Juliet laughed, "So that is why you wanted me back. You need me to cook your dinner."

Alex laughed "no Juliet, I don't. I am quite capable of cooking a chicken although it won't compare with one of your dinners." Now Juliet laughed, he was a charmer.

"Flattery gets you everywhere," she said as she started to look for veg to prepare.

Alex got out his tobacco and then he took out a little plastic bag with weed in it. "You don't mind if I have a joint do you Juliet? I will smoke it outside. There is a new neighbour called Jay in number one and he sells weed. There is a bottle of wine in the fridge for you. It is my holiday and I think I deserve it."

Everything suddenly fitted. What could Juliet say? But then she thought that he would be in a better mood if he was stoned. She had never seen him smoke cannabis before. It would be interesting she thought to herself. In any case, there was no point in voicing an objection, he clearly had already started to roll the joint and he wasn't really asking for her approval. To voice an objection would only cause an argument. "Be my guest," said Juliet "just please do it outside. I don't want Clara anywhere near it."

Chapter 4-Love again?

Smoking weed certainly had a calming effect on Alex and he was easy going and relaxed although Juliet was still very wary of him. He had been too stoned on pot to give her an orgasm like he had promised. In fact, his sexual performance was decidedly lack lustre whilst he was stoned. For the next few days he was under the influence and he was good company but Juliet had decided to go home on Tuesday. She had had enough of being in the cottage, there was nothing to do and she missed her little flat. They had enjoyed each other's company although there was something missing. There was not quite the emotional intimacy they had once had but it was more settled and at least after Alex's initial outburst the day after she had arrived, it was ok now. Bill was travelling up to the Midlands and he offered Alex and Juliet a lift to Wolverhampton Train station where Juliet would catch the train back to Oxford.

Juliet was glad to arrive at Oxford Station and to get a bus home to her flat. She liked being on her own and for now she felt it was just what she needed. She had been very damaged by Mark and by Alex and the events of last year, and her life was stable now. She didn't know if she could ever love Alex the way she had loved him before and there were too many problems. He worked abroad which would make it unsustainable. If he had been jealous before when they lived together constantly, how would it be if he was abroad for most of the time? Then there was Guy. Whilst Mark was ok with her at the moment, it was because Alex was not on the scene (or so he thought). But Mark hated Alex so much that he would turn very awkward again over Guy and would stop Juliet seeing him if he thought Alex was around. Juliet had still not taken Mark to court to get a proper order sorted out for Access, she just couldn't face it, she needed to be stronger and her hormones were still all over the place. Then there was Alex's mental health. She knew he really needed treatment if he was to make any progress. He was very wearing when he went into a rage although Juliet was trying not to get provoked by these rages and not take them personally. However Alex was off work for a month and then he would be going back to Iraq. As usual and like most men Alex did not explain what he was going to do. They emailed each other daily and they were getting along fine.

About a week and a half after she had left the cottage Alex said that he would like to spend time with Juliet again before he left for Iraq. He had booked himself a break in Amsterdam for three days and he had finished packing up anything he had left at the cottage and could he stay with her? Again Juliet felt as though she had been handed a 'fait accompli' and had very little choice in the matter so she said yes. He no doubt wanted to go on a weed binge in Amsterdam but she had to admit to herself that she had missed his company. She was virtually isolated and had no friends apart from Val to speak of. Life was lonely for her.

Bill was bringing Alex down to Oxford on Saturday. How she was going to hide him from Mark was another matter. She would just have to tell Mark that she was going up to the Midlands for a week or so. He never had reason to venture down to the little cul-de-sac where she lived but it didn't stop her worrying.

Juliet was excited at the prospect of seeing Alex. He had been most charming in his emails and she knew what he was doing but it didn't stop her falling under his spell, no matter how hard she tried to resist.

It was Saturday morning and Bill was bringing Alex to Oxford. Juliet wondered how he had managed to swing this but Bill was curious and he did have a soft spot for Juliet. Juliet also suspected that Bill was combining the trip with a visit to Birmingham and an old flame who lived there. He did like the ladies although he had never been anything but a gentleman with Juliet, he was old enough to be her father.

Juliet had decided to cook roast lamb. Alex would no doubt love it and Bill may stay for lunch. As usual, Alex hadn't specified but she had to ask, it was only polite. They arrived a little after midday and Alex was his charming self. He kissed her lightly on the lips as he walked into the flat, "something smells lovely," he said to Juliet, "and whatever you are cooking smells wonderful too."

They both laughed at his cheesy comments, but he was very good at flattery and it worked. Usually a cynic and a sceptic, he didn't lavish his praise all of the time and on everyone but he knew when to do it and how to deliver it to maximum effect. It just made the flattery more special and he knew it. "It is roast lamb," said Juliet with a flourish. She knew he loved his lamb since he was no longer vegetarian. "Would you like some lunch Bill?" Juliet said.

"I would love to Juliet, but I have an appointment to attend," said Bill. Alex winked at Juliet and she knew he had a date with his old flame.

"Well, maybe next time," said Juliet, although she doubted there would be one. Bill said his goodbyes, and hurried off to see his woman. It must run in the family though Juliet to herself.

When Bill was gone Alex came into the kitchen and took a bottle of red wine out of his rucksack. Just like old times thought Juliet but she was secretly pleased. Juliet had already had a glass of her own that she had purchased. Alex uncorked the wine to breathe and took Juliet in his arms and kissed her with a passion that he had not done since the day he had turned up on her doorstep. The passion had returned! "I can taste wine on you. Have you already had a glass?" Alex laughed.

"I was nervous," Juliet replied.

"Nervous of what?" Alex said, intrigued.

"Seeing you again," she replied. As soon as she had opened her mouth she realised that she shouldn't be so open with him. It was what had got her into a lot of trouble before with him. He would prey on every little vulnerability that she had. It was not fair. One of the reasons she had adored him to begin with was the fact she could be herself and now, knowing he had BPD and knowing she should be guarded, had taken the joy out of it all. She wanted as we all do, to be loved for herself, for who she was, not to have to hold back, to say what she felt. If she had to do that she could have a relationship with almost anyone but that was not the kind of relationship she wanted. She wanted someone to know her intimately and to love her for herself, as she loved Alex for himself, flawed as he was, warts and all. But she had to be careful although having had two glasses of wine made her careless.

The meal was delicious and Alistair soon went out to see his friends. Clara was asleep for her afternoon nap. The wine had taken effect on both Juliet and Alex and thankfully Alex was smoking nothing more than tobacco. He took out his pouch and rolled a cigarette for Juliet and handed it to her. It was smooth and perfectly formed, unlike the ones Juliet rolled for herself. Despite the years of rolling her own she still couldn't roll one like Alex. It was the way he moved his fingers and thumb so dextrously and twiddled the paper, filter and tobacco together, Juliet was mesmerised, and it reminded her of how dextrous his fingers could be on her clit and she began to feel very hot. He took the roll up to his lips, and lit it in a very casual sexy way and deeply inhaled, looking Juliet in the eyes as he exhaled the smoke. "You know what I want to do this afternoon?" he said with a deep slow sexy voice. Juliet wasn't paying attention to his words. She was fascinated by his face and his lips drawing on the cigarette. "I don't know," she said breathlessly, suddenly realising the implication of what he had said. He was propositioning her.

He finished his cigarette and said "I need to have a nap. Care to join me?" She knew what he was really saying, although a nap would have suited her better at this precise moment.

"Ok," she said nonchalantly, "Clara may wake at any minute though." Just to warn him and put him off seducing her.

It made no difference to him, he was carefree and careless and he had lust in his eyes. They walked into the bedroom and he shed his clothing. Naked he climbed into bed. Juliet was not quite so uninhibited and she kept on her pants and a vest top and climbed in next to him and pulled the duvet over and lay on her side prepared to sleep. Alex pulled her close to him in one fell swoop and was spooning her. Gently stroking her stomach and thighs, and kissing the back of her neck. No matter how much she tried to not succumb to his touches, she was drawn there. He knew how to touch her, and where to touch her, and it was futile to resist. The months of intimacy in the cottage had taught him how to be master of her pleasure and how to get her to give in to him. Months of longing for his touch and battling with her mind gave way in an instance when he touched her where he knew she would like it best. It was overpowering and intoxicating and she felt herself giving way to let him pleasure her. She made no move to touch or kiss him yet the more she denied his touch, the more he kept up his onslaught. She was being taken out of her consciousness, into a dreamlike state. It was hard for Juliet to comprehend whether this was because she had drunk wine, or because he was so good at touching her but Juliet could not deny her body was revelling in his touch. She allowed him to continue, her mind powerless to override her body and its responses.

He turned her over and kissed her passionately. Her body was already aching with desire for him and she had already submitted to the inevitable. How could she not? It had all she had desired for the last nine months. All she had dreamt about, even though she had told herself a thousand times that it was no good for her. She drowned in his kisses and his embrace and his hands wandered over her body but in a gently familiar way. She was dripping for him and aching with desire and there was no turning back.

They touched and kissed each other in intimate places, and he was as eager for her as she was for him. The beads of come on the tip of penis told her how much he desired her, and her wetness told him, how much she wanted him. They worshipped each other's bodies before Alex finally made love to her and she floated high as he brought her to climax with his fingers before making love to her with a passion.

They dozed for a while before Clara woke them, or at least Juliet. Alex dozed and Juliet was annoyed. However much pleasure he had given her that afternoon, she knew not to trust him and he was there sleeping, like the hedonist that he was whilst she, feeling groggy from the sex and the wine, got up and cared for Clara and cleared away the remnants of the meal. Indeed, he didn't wake up until 7pm that evening when she had put Clara to bed. To say she was annoyed was an understatement.

She said very little to him when he came into the lounge. He was hungry. Juliet just said "help yourself to whatever you want, I am off duty for the evening. The chef has finished for the day." In previous times she would have rushed around to make him something but she had a child now and so did he, but he was not taking care of her, Juliet was. And there was something about his arrogant cocky

34

manner that Juliet didn't like one bit. Did he really think that just because he had given her an orgasm she would be his slave? The balance of power had shifted, he just hadn't realised it yet.

Chapter 5– Revelations

Alex was off to Amsterdam on Monday and whilst Juliet had accepted him in her bed on Saturday she still wasn't sure of him, and she didn't trust him. There was a barrier between them, a barrier that Juliet had placed there but Alex hadn't noticed it. He was still under the effect of a two-week long pot fest and Juliet knew it. He was like a teenager and his sleeping habits were erratic to say the least. She would be glad of the break.

He left for Amsterdam on Monday morning. Juliet breathed a sigh of relief but then much to her dismay, she actually found out that she was missing him. You bloody fool she said to herself, why, oh why did you let him give you an orgasm? She was fine having sex with him if she didn't allow herself to come. She knew she was slipping down into the whirlpool, she was getting hooked again. Like some drug addict who thinks they can handle just one little hit and they won't get hooked but then the old familiar feelings come back and they find themselves wanting more.

Alex sent her a text on the Monday evening.

"Missing you like hell," he said, then *"I am done with travelling alone, it is no fun without you"*, then *"I miss Clara, give her a kiss from me."* Then she received an email from him

Juliet

I am really sorry I came on this trip. When I booked it, I didn't think you and I would be together and I didn't think things would work out with us the way they have. What a waste of money and time! I wished I was with you and Clara. The accommodation is awful and I feel old. I am on a

houseboat that has been turned into a hotel and the woman in charge is a dragon! My fellow guests are all young and it makes me realise how old I have got. I can't wait to come home.

Love

Alex xxx

Well that was a turn up for the book thought Juliet as she laughed to herself when she read the email. Perhaps he was genuine after all and he had put love on his email. But it was an easy emotion when you typed it at the end of an email. It was not like being spoken. There was no intonation there to signify the import of the word. Or perhaps he was maturing for the first time in his life?

The next morning Juliet was in the bath and her phone rang. She had to get out of the bath to answer it. Ordinarily, she wouldn't have bothered but she thought it may have been Alex and she knew how suspicious and jealous he was, and he would probably accuse her of having another man in the house if she didn't answer. It was him and she took the phone back into the bath. Clara was still asleep.

"Hello," he said in a deep sexy voice.

"I have had to get out of the bath to answer this phone," Juliet said rather tersely.

"I wish I was there with you, I would soap your back and other parts," he said, full of charm and soon he was charming her again. It was as though he relished the challenge of getting her to fall for him all over again.

They chatted for a while, flirting but Juliet had to remain in control, "Look, this is really decadent, talking to your lover on the phone whilst in the bath in a morning but my bath water is going cold, and Clara will wake up any minute. So I am going to say bye.

"Oh, don't go yet," said Alex.

"But I must Alex," replied Juliet.

"Bye, love you," Alex said, and Juliet hung up on him. She placed the phone on the towel beside the bath and then pulled the plug on the now tepid bath.

What the hell was going on? Did he just say he loved her? She couldn't be sure. He was up to something of that she was certain. And what was all that "I am tired of travelling alone crap?" He loved it, he was a nomad and he would never tire of travelling alone. Juliet gave up thinking about it. It will come out in the end she thought to herself and then her phone pinged with a text message.

"Marry me," it said. It was from Alex. Her heart fluttered with excitement. She laughed out loud to herself and she was annoyed. He was asking her to marry him by text! Well she thought to herself, I suppose I bruised him a little when he asked me a few weeks ago and I turned him down even though it was reasonable in the circumstances.

She picked up her phone. *"If you want to ask me to marry you, then I want to hear you say it. I am not going to reply to a text message asking me to marry you"* she text back. She admitted to herself she was very flattered and she did want to say yes to him but she also doubted his motives. She had been thinking about the reasons why he had been keen on marrying her for a few weeks now and she still wasn't sure what they were.

Her phone started to ring. It was Alex. "Will you marry me?" he said.

"Yes," said Juliet.

Juliet laughed to herself when she came off the phone. He is stoned, she thought to herself and when he is no longer stoned he will find a way to wriggle out of this. Let's test him to see if his motives for marriage are true. She was joining in his game. He would never commit she knew that now, he never had. How many other women had he got engaged too? She knew of one but there may be more. Juliet had always wondered what had really gone on in his relationships, not the carefully edited version he told Juliet.

Whilst in the cottage Alex had been very careful when talking about his previous relationships never to give out a surname. He had told Juliet about the relationships, about the women, what they were like, what they looked like and what they did for a living. He had even gone on to describe the relationship he had with each of them. Of course they were all slags as he put it, all except for Bernadette but then he had not loved Bernadette and she wasn't his usual professional intelligent woman. When Juliet had left Alex she had plenty of time on her hands alone to think over all of the things he had said. It struck her as particularly strange that of the many women he had purported to have had significant relationships with they had all been unfaithful and lacking in morals when it came to their fidelity. Juliet had even called him out on it once and had said, "I don't believe all of these women were at fault. They are intelligent, professional women. It seems highly unlikely to me that they were all unfaithful. However, the one common denominator in all of this is you." Of course he strenuously denied it and called Juliet mad and said that of course she would say that, as she was as bad as them.

But Juliet really wanted, to ask one of them at least what their experience had been of Alex. If only she knew their surnames. And then one day it came to her. Alex had spoken with particular venom for a woman he had gone out with, called Marieke. She was a Barrister and she was Dutch. He sai, that he had known her and had described in detail how she had another man 'on the go' as he had put it whilst he was seeing her and that this other man was married. So on one of her trips to the library Juliet first Googled 'Dutch

39

women's names' in order to identify the correct spelling, and then she Googled "Marieke, Barrister." Everyone had profiles on the internet these days and she waited while the little icon whirred around and around at the top of the page. And the, there it was. With a name as distinctive as that there was only one result, and she clicked on the page. There before her was a picture of a woman around the same age as Juliet, whose photo fitted Alex's description of Marieke perfectly and there on the page was an address of the Chambers where she worked. Her surname was Van der Berg. You couldn't get more Dutch than that. She made a note of the address and when she went back to her little bedsit on the Iffley Road she wrote a letter to Marieke.

She felt a letter was better because there was always the chance it might not be the right person, or that the woman would not want to respond. In which case she could just bin the letter and forget all about it. It was also of a personal nature and not a work-related issue.

Juliet wrote a little about what she had been through with Alex and also what Alex had said about Marieke. Juliet was candid and said that she would like to hear her version of the relationship. She added her email address.

Two days later, she received an email from Marieke and as Juliet read, the more she felt vindicated. This is what Marieke wrote to Juliet:

Dear Juliet

I received your letter today, and first I would like to express my sorrow at all you have had to endure.

It is difficult to know how to begin - and really, I feel a conversation would be more appropriate than trying to write a reply.

If you feel that you would like to talk, please do send me a phone number and a suitable time to call.

If you don't wish to talk, then I can understand that too. It is difficult for me to know, not knowing you at all, but recognising that you are in some anguish, how best to help - but please do not take that as unwillingness to be of any assistance I can

You may not wish to talk, so perhaps I can tell you some brief things, which may (or may not) make things clearer for you.

I met Alex some (and here I have to stop and do some calculations) 10 years ago. Think it must have been end 2000. One of the reasons why I am rather taken aback by your letter, is that I think labelling whatever there was between us as "a relationship" is really putting it rather high. I have not had cause to think of Alex for years, and at first, I have to admit that it took me a few minutes to place his name. I am afraid that for me he was one of those that one "puts behind you" as quickly as possible, and he had little lasting memory for me. It is really with rather a lot of anxiety that I realise that 10 years later, he is (it appears) representing me as someone he had a meaningful relationship with (not to mention that there was something to be criticised about my "conduct"!). I must admit I find that more than a little creepy. The last I spoke, saw or had anything whatever to do with him must have been around August 2001. (I thought he was probably gay, he had some rather odd relationships with men - I seem to recall he had a "best friend" who had 2 young daughters, and that whole set up always seemed slightly odd to me, I mean his relationship / attitude both to the "best friend" and to the daughters)

Fortunately for me, the time that I was seeing a bit of him, I avoided your situation - in that I had my place and life in

London, and he spent most of his time in Wales. He also rented a room somewhere in London, but as I recall had a slightly difficult relationship with his landlady, so didn't like staying there much over the week-ends, although he was working in London during the week, so he had to stay there then. We did spend a bit of time together, but not very much - partly because he was constantly in a rage about something, and there is only so much time I was prepared to give over to trying to placate or rationalise. Please understand, this is not to make you feel foolish, I am trying to be honest so that you stop (if you are) blaming yourself. My situation was different, because I didn't give anything up for him (like home, family, job etc - as it sounds like you did), so I was in a better position of strength than you were. His accusations became so outlandish, his demands so ridiculous that he was just incredibly unpleasant to spend any time with. However, I can tell you that he is a deeply disturbed individual, prone to violence. I have spent the afternoon trying to recall incidents from the time when I was seeing him. They may seem rather disparate, but as I say, he was not a big part of my life even then, and I have not had cause to think of him for ages. As I recall he was pretty strapped for cash, because he was paying for the room in London and the mortgage in Wales, so he rarely asked me out. We mostly met for coffee, and sometimes lunch around Bar school. I did go to Wales to spend the weekend, but as I recall, he flew into a rage about something late at night after drinking a bottle of whisky, and ordered me to leave - and I went into a B&B. I recall the joy I felt as I drove over the border into England the following morning!! (that is the bit I remember best, I'm afraid - quite what the argument was about, or what triggered it, I don't recall, he did throw my coat around the room though, I remember that too because he smashed a much-treasured brooch that was pinned to the lapel!). We had intended to write a book together (drugs and criminal law) he had got the publishers interested, but knew nothing about drugs or forensics - I was a scientist before being a

42

lawyer - and at the time (starting out on my law career) it seemed like a good opportunity. The times I went to Wales were meant to be to work on book content, although nothing ever came of it.

Alex from the start was massively and uncontrollably jealous. I recall him flying into a temper on one occasion because a guy from work had sent me a Christmas card. It had a Madonna and child on the front - and he convinced himself that this meant the guy who sent it wanted me to have his baby. No rationalising with him (for e.g. - "Alex, he's a bloke, he probably hasn't even noticed the picture on the front of the card!") could placate him. There were countless examples of this. For example, sitting in a cafe, he would be convinced that I was looking at someone else. He went to Wales every weekend, and once term ended (or did he take sick leave for stress? something like that I think) he moved there permanently, - but he would phone the land line at my home Friday, Saturday and Sunday evenings at odd times of the evening or at night. If I didn't answer, he would demand to know where I had been and who with etc. Although he was in Wales, he seemed to think I shouldn't go out at all while I was in London. Fortunately, those rages had to be over the phone, so it had little impact on me, although it was exhausting to be constantly accused.

He used to criticise how I spent my money (which really annoyed me) and seemed to think I should fund him. I remember that he had booked a trip to the Caribbean in or around August 2001 (on his own). He then suggested that I went too - I had a few months off and was looking to get away. In the end, I did book a flight to Jamaica too, arriving around the same time as he did. But this was not a jointly planned trip, I just found a cheap flight at the last minute and thought Heck, why not. It was arranged as a purely "friends" thing - we were going to have separate beds etc, but given that transport etc is so expensive (you have to take taxis

43

everywhere - there is no public transport) we thought we would both benefit by sharing some expenses, and doing some things together (for me there was also a safety issue in Jamaica; for Alex it was more a saving expense arrangement). I had my doubts about it working, but thought I would see how it went.

A day or so into the holiday, he started accusing me of being a trollop (broadly speaking – I can't remember the details) for the first time, rather than trying to placate, I lost my temper with him for constantly having a go at me and making everything so unpleasant all the time. He hit me, I walked out but warned him that if he ever attempted to contact me again, I would bring charges, and he could forget about practising again. (I packed up, walked out, and to my very good fortune, met some new friends from France, and went on to have a fabulous holiday with them, I never gave Alex another thought) That was the last I ever saw or heard of him until I got your letter.

So that is what I can tell you. I have no wish to resurrect this, but at the same time, I want you to be under no illusions about the guy you are dealing with. Sometimes women need to help each other, even if they don't know each other.

So, I don't know if that answers your question, or even if I am quite sure what your question is. If you are asking, did you invite this behavior, or is any of it your fault? Absolutely not. This man is a deeply damaged individual, and you cannot help him, and he will never treat you as you deserve to be treated. He will find someone else to abuse. Please stop it from being you. If you would wish to talk to me further, I promise that I will call you.

Kind regards, and much strength to you

Marieke

Alex had nearly persuaded Juliet in the cottage that she was a slag and that she had no morals. But once she had left, she began to see things differently. She had been isolated and only had his voice in her ear but once free and settled, she started torealise that she had not been wholly at fault. When she received and read Marieke's email she felt even stronger as Marieke had suffered exactly the same behaviour from Alex as she had. It seemed unlikely that Marieke would exaggerate as she had nothing to gain from it. Her relationship with him had been over 10 years ago but it was interesting that she said he was "a deeply damaged individual." However, Juliet was prepared to try and help him if she could, if only for Clara.

Chapter 6– Illusions

Juliet knew that Alex would not buy her a ring, well not one of her choice. He was too tight for a start off and he had been busy saving money for the place in France. In fact she had got used to the fact that he was quite mean with his money. He had given her maintenance, yes that was true but he had decided on the sum of £200 per month and he did not disclose to Juliet how much he was earning. But Juliet did know it was tax-free. She hadn't really been made aware of his meanness when they had lived together in the cottage, they both were unemployed and neither had anything to give to the other.

Juliet decided that the measure of his commitment to marriage and his love for her would be measured by the amount of money he would be willing to spend on a ring. However she was not going to be mercenary and name a figure straight off. No, she was going to play it a little bit craftier than that. If he bought her the ring that she desired then he was genuine, if he steadfastly refused, he had motives that were not genuine for wishing to marry her. As the old saying goes 'put your money where your mouth is.'

Alex arrived back at Juliet's flat. He had bought a present for Clara, a growth chart that she could hang on the wall. It was highly inappropriate for a child just a few months old but it was the thought that counts. He bought some tulip bulbs for Juliet. Black tulips called "Queen of the Night." "When I saw these I thought of you Juliet because that is what you are; a Queen of the Night." And he gave her a little wink. She was quite flattered and at least he wasn't using her sexuality as a stick to beat her with. That made a change.

"I am glad you said yes to my proposal of marriage," he said to Juliet "we will have to buy you a ring. After all, you sold all of your jewellery in the cottage for us. It is only right."

He was going about this in a very unromantic fashion, thought Juliet to herself, which only backs up my thought, that his motives are not real but she let that thought slide.

"Wonderful Alex," she said, as he opened up his computer.

"What sort of a ring would you like?" said Alex.

"Well," said Juliet. "What is your budget? You do know that you should spend 10% of your annual salary on an engagement ring. It signifies your love and it has to last a lifetime. It is something you look at when the chips are down and we are cross with each other and then you look at the ring and melt thinking of how much you love each other." She knew he wouldn't buy into this and tell her how much his salary was but she was trying to draw him on this one.

"I don't earn that much Juliet and I am saving for a place in France that will be ours."

Juliet knew he would come up with a remark like this but she kept her cool. "Oh Alex, I didn't say that was what I wanted, I just said that was what was recommended. I know you don't have a lot of money otherwise I would ask for a one-carat solitaire, old rock cut and set in platinum. If I know how much you want to spend I am sure I can find something that is suitable."

Alex looked annoyed, this ring buying discussion wasn't going the way he wanted. He sat for a while in thought, and then he said "£250."

Juliet spluttered on her wine. "Alex, that is as much a cheapskate as Mark and you scoffed at him for buying a wedding ring out of the Argos catalogue, and his engagement ring which he reluctantly bought after our affair was about that price. And now you want to do the same. I love you Alex but that is such a token amount of money, you might as well not bother. I am quite happy to have an antique ring which

47

will be cheaper than a brand new one out of a high street store but I doubt £ 250 will buy anything of significance." The conversation went on all afternoon, whilst they searched the internet for an antique ring but he still hadn't settled on paying more and it was annoying the shit out of him. But Juliet held firm, she was enjoying annoying the shit out of Alex too.

She cooked dinner and they ate in silence. So this was it. This was how much he loved her thought Juliet. It all came down to money and for once she didn't care. Since the time when they had met she didn't give a fuck, she was holding fast. He had already said enough that afternoon to tell her he had other motives for marrying her than true love. So she said nothing.

They went to bed that night but didn't make love. Well Alex stayed up and Juliet went to bed. He stayed up into the small hours and she didn't miss him. She had grown accustomed to being alone and quite frankly she didn't give a damn. She loved him, that was a given but now she wasn't going to bend over backward to appease him. If he had let a small thing like money come between them, it wasn't much of a love,was it? It wasn't even the money for Juliet. If he had gone out and bought a ring and presented it to her with love in his eyes she would have swallowed it hook, line, and sinker. But he hadn't. He had sat there with a cold heart and negotiated the shit out of it. It wasn't love he was doing it for something else. But for what? She had no idea. There was no question that she wouldn't let him see Clara, even if they weren't in a relationship. She wasn't going to do to him what Mark had done to her. She really couldn't fathom his behaviour at all.

She woke in the night to feel his hands all over her. Gently caressing her at first but then with a roughness that she had not previously known. But it was good, very good, once she had shaken the sleep from her eyes and had drunk some water, she soon returned his fervent kisses and grasps. They fucked roughly and quickly, and as they parted, he said: "you had better get your vag sorted out, because no man will want to fuck you, the way you are now." She lay there in the darkness with tears streaming down her face. Was this the truth? Or was it his fucked-upness and her rejection that had prompted this outburst. She knew it was both. Her vag did need sorting out and it was not for another man. But how could he be so unkind? He could have been kind about telling her but he hadn't been. He was truly fucked up mentally, she knew he was but how much more of this torture could she take? She lay in the darkness, tears rolling down her cheeks, not letting out a sound but her heart was slowly hardening and growing cold, to Alex at least.

In the morning he left. Juliet had walked him to the bus stop with Clara in the pram. He said he would come back for Christmas. Juliet was happy even though she had reservations, but they had never spent a Christmas together and it was long overdue, especially as they had Clara. They sat on the bench waiting for the coach, talking. It was what they were good at besides sex, when they were both of the same minds, when he wasn't being a self-absorbed wanker. Alex was in a different mood, more sombre. Was last night the withdrawal effect of weed? After caning it in Amsterdam? But today he seemed to be calm, reflective and genuinely sad at parting. "Thank you, Juliet, for everything. I have enjoyed my few weeks holiday more than I had expected. Keep looking for a ring, and let me know when you have found one."

Juliet was truly sad at his leaving. They had had their ups and downs over the last few weeks but their relationship was growing and at least she was standing her ground, unlike before. "I shall miss you, Alex," she said. "Keep in touch please, and I will make Christmas truly magical for you." The coach rolled into the stop and they stood up. Alex loaded his minimal luggage into the coaches hold and then he took Juliet in his arms. He kissed her tenderly on the lips. For all of her misgivings she was still in love with him although she sorely wished she wasn't. Still, there was no going back. Do it to the death, she thought. But she vowed to make Christmas magical for him. He had experienced enough shit Christmases and she would show him what a good one was.

But as the coach rolled out of view, Juliet breathed a sigh of relief. She would go to the doctors and get her vag sorted out. He wasn't ever going to speak to her like that again. No one, but no one would ever speak to Juliet Grosvenor like that and fucking hell, no way was she going to marry that conceited fucked up dick unless he had a complete mental makeover!

Chapter 7 – Life Continues

Juliet made an appointment at the doctors. It had been long overdue. They hadn't picked it up, the problem with her vag at her six weeks check-up but then they didn't examine your vag as they used to when Juliet had had her older children. They just asked whether everything was fine and Juliet was a single parent and was so besotted with Clara that she hadn't really realised that there was something wrong. Given that she wasn't about to have sex in the foreseeable future at that time it was the least of her problems.

She saw a young female doctor and she voiced her concerns. The young woman examined her. "I don't see much of a problem down there," she said. "You have a slight prolapse but given your age and the fact you have had six children it is only to be expected."

Juliet lay on the couch with her knees up in the air and her legs splayed and felt mortified. How could the woman say that? Wait until she was 45 and then tell her that. Why do the young think that sex ends when you are forty? Juliet closed her legs and pulled on her clothes. "Well, I am quite aware that I have had six children and how old I am but I do not think I should put up with it. I am far from dead yet and I want to be referred to a consultant."

The young female doctor sighed. "I don't think they will be able to do anything for you," she said.

Still Juliet was firm in her resolve "maybe not, but I would like to have a second opinion. Thank you." She was so firm in her voice, that the doctor agreed and said that they would write to Juliet. "Thank you," said Juliet as she grasped Clara's pram and left the room. "Stupid little cow" she muttered ever so slightly under her breath as she left the surgery.

Life went on as usual in the happy way it had been before Alex's return. They were able to pay their bills and were well fed. Juliet tended the little garden and Clara grew and grew. Juliet enjoyed weaning her with homemade cooked food for her and Alistair was working. Guy and Mark came down to Juliet's little flat twice a week for food. Once midweek and once on a Sunday for a roast dinner. Guy adored roast potatoes so much that he remarked Clara should be renamed Cherry Roast Potato in honour of his favourite foods, cherry tomatoes, and roast potatoes. He played with her as she was growing more and more robust, so much so that Juliet laughed about her. She didn't shuffle on her bottom and showed no sign of crawling. She is a lazy shit like her father. Juliet thought affectionately to herself.

Alex emailed every two or three days and although Juliet had installed Skype on her mother's old computer and she had the best and fastest Wi-Fi BT could offer the internet connection was poor in Iraq and they could only just hold a voice conversation. The internet frequently went down and their conversations were disrupted or terminated and it was usually when Alex was slagging off his employer. He said in emails that he expected their conversations were being listened too. They probably were but where do you draw the line between the truth and Alex's paranoia?

The one thing that became apparent to Juliet was that Alex talked a lot about his flatmate Maher, disturbingly so. Alex had remarked that they were such good friends that Maher would bring him ice cream in bed in the morning. Juliet was reminded of how he had said Maher was 'handsome' and of Marieke's comments that she thought he had been 'gay'. It was quite disturbing. What was even more poignant was that one of the symptoms of BPD was that the sufferers were unsure of their sexual identity, i.e., they didn't really know whether they were heterosexual or homosexual. Most adults know who they are by the time they are forty. This is a psychological fact. If you are religious or not religious, you rarely change your opinion after the age of forty. By the time you are forty you have decided you are either gay or heterosexual. You have decided that you like this and that and you don't like this or that. There are minor exceptions, little things you change your mind over but the main principles of your life are generally set in stone. Not for the sufferer of BPD, they mess with their life. They perceive the way to make themselves happy is to fix the minutiae of life. They never realise that they are deeply damaged, deeply flawed. It is the little things that will make their life complete, not the underneath that needs fixing first. And that was how it was with Alex. But after what he had said and after what Marieke had said in her email, it did make Juliet wonder whether after all, Alex was gay or at the very least bisexual.

Juliet got her appointment with a consultant at the beginning of December. She went with trepidation but soon had nothing to worry about. The consultant was a lovely friendly attractive woman in her mid-forties. She examined Juliet. "You have a slight prolapse of the womb but more importantly you have a prolapse of the back wall of your vagina, no doubt caused by the forceps that were used in your fifth childbirth. Then there is the tear that was not sewn up after your sixth and latest childbirth," Juliet sighed, it sounded like a lot of messed up stuff. No wonder Alex said her vag was lacking. But then he had made no complaints on first fucking! And the problem with her back wall had obviously been there before Clara. He hadn't complained in the cottage. She got back in the room and was listening intently to what the consultant had to say. Her bedside manner was impeccable. "We can fix all of this," she said. "What traditionally has been done for a prolapse is to remove the womb but there is another procedure, one that is less drastic. We can perform a hysteropexy where we perform keyhole surgery and sling your womb up in a mesh that is stapled to your spine. This ensures that all of your pelvic floor is safe. The problem with the traditional removal of the womb is that it does not solve the problem of weak pelvic floor muscles and often a bladder prolapse follows." This all made for horrifying listening but listening Juliet was. "So we will perform that. Also, if your womb and cervix are left intact it is proven that you have better sexual enjoyment and I think after six children you deserve some sexual enjoyment." As for the back wall of the vagina, we will repair it by making an incision and repairing it. Juliet was overjoyed. At last someone was on her side. "Thank you, thank you," she said with tears in her eyes. The consultant gave her some leaflets and said she could see a video of the operation online but there was no way Juliet was going to watch that.

She couldn't wait to tell Alex but he wasn't listening, not listening exactly as she had emailed him but nonetheless he didn't make a comment. Juliet was lost. Why didn't he care? But he was a man and men don't listen to women's problems. It doesn't mean they don't absorb what you are saying, they just don't want to join in the discussion or be sympathetic. It is beyond them. The female condition. They are happy to take their pleasure, not so happy to deal with the complexities of the female physiology.

Things plodded on, week by week. Alex had left at the end of August and Juliet had emailed him every day or so and he had largely responded quite quickly. They spoke by Skype once a week and everything seemed to be going well. Juliet made plans for Christmas and soon amassed a selection of Christmas presents for Alex. His wardrobe was severely lacking and she had bought a jacket from TKMaxx and a lovely large cashmere/wool overcoat from the charity shop. It had been a steal at £10 and was worth far more. She bought other little gifts; a book, boxer shorts, leather gloves, a scarf, dark chocolate. They were all meant to make him feel loved, adored and cared for. The preparations for the food also went well. Juliet got in a store of food for the Christmas period. Lovely red wine for them to enjoy, a stock of roast chicken crisps which were hard to come by, Wensleydale cheese with cranberries, dark chocolate mints and a host of other little treats. They were all Alex's favourites. It was to be their first Christmas together.

Alex had asked for some suggestions for Clara and he had also asked what Juliet wanted. She made suggestions for Clara and said she wanted a cookbook and some CDs. Alex ordered them from Amazon and Juliet wrapped up Clara's presents. She had been busy making preparations for Christmas and couldn't wait to see Alex again. He was arriving late on the 23rd December so on the 22nd she sent him an email;

Dear Honoured Guest

We wish you a safe and untroubled journey tomorrow.

The staff here at Hotel Colwell Drive have been planning for your stay for many months, to ensure you have the most enjoyable visit. The decorations are up and the Chef has been extremely busy shopping and cooking for the festivities (we have minimal staff). There have been some delectations laid on specifically for your delight as you are a VIP guest. Please see the attached menu for the festive period. Of course, Boxing Day will be the chef's special as she has a day off then.

You are booked into our only Deluxe Room and there will be freshly laundered bed linen. You also have freshly laundered towels and your own personal toiletries. There is a full English Breakfast (unless otherwise requested) and room service is available on request (at a small charge). However, we do request that the room is made available between the hours of 11am and 12, in order for the maid to service the room. The special request you made has been taken care of.

Please be aware, however, that our manageress is undergoing extreme stress at the present time (due to the unprecedented amount of work and the early starts she maintains) and she is very, very volatile. Please approach her with extreme caution, as she may explode at any time.

Look forward to seeing you tomorrow
Best Wishes

The Management

Christmas Menu 2011

Friday 23rd December

French Farmhouse Pate with

wheat meal toast

Boeuf Bourguignonne accompanied by

French green beans and miniature new potatoes

Tiramisu

Coffee and mints

Christmas Eve

Homemade Leek and Potato Soup

with assorted tiny bread rolls

Special marinated Roast Chicken
accompanied by, pigs in blankets, sage and onion stuffing
creamed potato, peas,and sweetcorn

Blackcurrant cheesecake/ cheese and biscuits

Coffee

Christmas Day Luncheon

Prawn smoked salmon and avocado cocktail

Roast Sirloin of Beef, with
Yorkshire Puddings
Roast Potatoes, Roast Parsnips, Cauliflower Cheese
Peas and carrots

Vanilla Cream terrine with Raspberries
And Blackcurrant Coulis

Cheese and Biscuits

Coffee, liqueurs,and mints

The "special request" Juliet referred to in the email was weed. Alex had asked Juliet to ask Alistair to get him some weed. She wasn't very happy about it but she wanted him to be happy and so she agreed.

It was late on the 22nd and Juliet sat watching Dr. Zhivago on the TV and she was both nervous and excited. She had cooked a casserole which she could heat up for him if he wanted. He hadn't answered her question when she had asked him if he wanted her to make him something to eat when he arrived. Again it was typical of the thoughtlessness.

There was a knock on the door, it was just after eleven and Juliet went and let him in. He came into the lounge and sat on the sofa dropping his bag on the floor. Juliet had kissed him on the cheek when he had entered but he hadn't taken her in his arms. He seemed distant. Juliet suspected he was tired after all the travelling. "It is lovely to see you, Alex, I am so excited about Christmas," said Juliet.

"I am absolutely knackered," said Alex "You have no idea how exhausting teaching is Juliet."

Juliet admitted to herself that she didn't have a clue. It wasn't hard manual labour for goodness sake and he didn't do that many hours. He was lazy, she knew that. The times he would sit in bed in the cottage on his laptop. Playing chess online or looking at all sorts of random shit. It had infuriated Juliet when the sun had been shining outside and they were surrounded by spectacular scenery.

"Have you got the weed?" said Alex. Typical that was what he wanted most, a joint. Juliet got the little bag of green and gave it to him and he skinned up a joint. "Do you want anything to eat?" said Juliet.

"No thanks, I had a big mac on the way here."

Juliet felt disappointed. No proper kiss, or a passionate embrace and now he was turning down her food. Had he even read her email? "I could kill for a bath though," he said.

"Well go and have one if you want. Shall I bring you a glass of wine and come and talk to you?" said Juliet.

"That would be nice," said Alex. Juliet handed Alex a Christmas card that she had chosen especially for him, and had written lovingly inside a few well-chosen words about the prospect of spending their first Christmas together. Alex opened it and read the card and then put it down on the side table saying nothing. He clearly hadn't got a card for her and Juliet was a little taken aback. He just seemed weird. Perhaps it was tiredness, he might be better in the morning.

He went and ran the bath and Juliet took him a glass of wine, and sat on the closed toilet lid talking to him. The sight of his naked body filled Juliet with lust and longing. Pavlov's dogs again. She associated him with sexual pleasure and the sight of his body triggered arousal in anticipation but nothing would happen tonight, she knew that he was stoned.

The next day Juliet was up early as usual but Alex slept soundly despite Clara making a noise. Juliet bathed and got dressed, and took Clara into the lounge to let Alex sleep. By ten o'clock Juliet was beginning to get irritated. He still wasn't awake and it was Christmas Eve. She decided to walk to Headington with Clara to get a few last-minute bits for tomorrows' meal. It was good to get out into the fresh air and her irritation passed as the exercise took effect. The truth was she was sexually frustrated and whilst it didn't usually bother her with all those male pheromones hanging about it was getting to her.

When she got back to the flat it was nearly midday. And he was still asleep. She felt her irritation rising again so she made him a coffee and took it into him. "It is nearly midday, and it is Christmas Eve, sleepy head" she said, as she put the mug on the bedside table and knelt on the bed leaning forward to kiss Alex.

He seemed to sense that she was not best pleased and he made an effort to sit up and struggling to open his eyes, he took a sip of coffee. "Sorry Juliet, I am just exhausted."

"I just want you to spend some time with us over the next week Alex. It is important that you spend time with Clara and I appreciate that you have been teaching on an evening and therefore sleeping late, not to mention the time difference, but please try and make an effort." This Christmas was not turning out quite as she had hoped. But then what is new? Christmas is always a disappointment. You pin all your hopes on it, thinking how wonderful it will be and it almost always fails to live up to your expectations.

The day passed by and things picked up a little. Alex admired the tree that Juliet had put up. It was a real one and Juliet had bought lots of decorations and she had made some of her own, little felt hearts that she had sewn little applique shapes of mistletoe leaves on. She had used seed pearls for the berries. She had decorated the flat tastefully, garnering greenery from the little lane behind the flat. Everywhere, pictures and mirrors were festooned with holly and ivy. The little-paned window in the kitchen had fake snow in the corners, (a bit cheesy, but you had to have a bit if cheesiness at Christmas) and iridescent angels hung from the kitchen cabinet knobs. In the lounge, gold and red baubles hung from the central light fittings, at different levels with ribbon bows. It looked very Christmassy and then there were assorted candles on a large plate on the table.

Clara went to bed at 6pm and Alistair had gone out with his friends. Juliet and Alex were sat at the table eating food. Alex had spent a lot of the afternoon on his computer sat in the lounge. Juliet wasn't very please, as he had not played

60

with Clara at all but she tried to hide her annoyance. He had ordered himself a new hard drive. Why? Wondered Juliet; tucked up the old one with a virus from watching porn? She thought to herself but didn't say. "You really have made a lovely job of decorating the house. Mom never bothers, she fetches out a little decorated tree and puts it on the table and that is it." said Alex.

Juliet laughed "It is the best thing about Christmas for me, that and buying gifts for those I love." He had not shown her any affection whatsoever. Was this what it was going to be like? Was it going to be like every other relationship she had had, a brilliant, passionate start and then the slow descent into drudgery and apathy? She hoped not. He hadn't asked her about choosing an engagement ring after he had left in September and she had not mentioned it to him again. Content to let it slide. She knew he wasn't really serious and the subject had not come up again. Would he make a move on her tonight? It was looking doubtful.

They sat and watched TV after the meal and again, there was no sign of affection. Aware that she had a lot to do the next day, Juliet said she was going to bed about 11pm, hoping Alex would join her but he had been drinking coffee and smoking weed since dinner "I don't feel tired yet Juliet. I hope you forgive me but I am going to stay up a bit longer. It is the time difference, I still haven't caught up with it." Said Alex. What could Juliet do? Juliet went to bed and drifted off to sleep.

Christmas day came and went and although Alex got up at 10am he really wasn't there, not in spirit. Juliet had dressed up especially but Alex didn't say a word, not one single compliment. He opened his presents but didn't really seem grateful for them. He was not behaving as he should or perhaps it was because he had hardly bought anything for her. Still, Juliet was grateful for his company and overlooked this. She didn't want any gifts, she wanted his love.

The rest of the week slipped by with Alex staying up late, and getting up late. The day after Boxing day he didn't get up until 4pm in the afternoon. Juliet woke in the night at 1 am and he wasn't in bed. How could he do this? How could he waste his time with her and Clara like this? They were like ships that passed in the night. He had not been intimate with her at all. Juliet was at a loss. Was it her vag? Here he was again, making her feel shit or was he withdrawing again? She longed for some intimacy with him but it was clear it wasn't going to happen. His sleep patterns were all over the place and he was stoned most of the time.

The day before New Year's Eve, they walked to Headington together. He hadn't left the house since he had arrived and Juliet was glad of the company on her little walk and they chatted. "They turned my application down to become a member of the Quakers," Alex said. Juliet was relieved.

As part of his BPD, Alex had wanted to become a Quaker. Whilst in the cottage he had made Juliet go with him to a couple of meetings in Llanidloes. They were on a Sunday morning and everyone just sat around in silence for an hour. Religion was not for Juliet, she had decided that a long time ago and after two meetings she had said to Alex. "Look Alex, if you want to be a Quaker then that is fine by me but I am not religious and I don't want to be a Quaker, so I shall not be attending anymore meetings."

But whilst he had not attended anymore meetings without Juliet in Wales, he had started going to meetings in Iraq, much to Juliet's dismay and he had put in an application to be a bona fide member and now he was telling her this.

Juliet tried to sound sympathetic. "Well Alex, I have to say that if you have to be approved to become a member, then what kind of religion is that? I thought God welcomed everyone?"

Alex huffed "I suppose your right Juliet but I think the main reason is because of Clara."

Juliet was puzzled "What do you mean Alex, because of Clara?"

"Well, it is because we are not married. But that isn't going to happen, that will never happen." And he laughed loudly. Just what the fuck did he mean by that? Juliet thought to herself. He was obviously saying what he really thought, as he was stoned and careless. So that was the reason he had proposed. She made a mental note of this. It was another little chip off her heart.

Alex left at just after midnight on New Year's Eve. She felt sad that he had gone but was relieved in an odd sort of a way. She didn't know what was going on in his mind but something was not right. Before he had gone they had talked about a holiday together in March, and had decided on Egypt. They would meet in Cairo but first Juliet had to get a passport for Clara.

Chapter 8 – New Year

Juliet awoke on New Year's Day to an empty bed, and she thought of Alex and the time they had spent together. She would have liked more affection and had missed the intimacy but it had been pleasant enough and sometimes you cannot have everything you want, life is just not like that. The weed had been largely to blame but Juliet couldn't help thinking to herself, that he didn't really love her. Still, there was a holiday to look forward to. Later that day Juliet sent him an email;

I am glad you arrived safely and managed to get into your apartment (I presume you have).

We miss you terribly. Hope to speak to you tonight, but understand if your sleep timetable is still catching up and we miss each other.

All my Love
Juliet
XXXXXXX

The next day she had a response;

I just wanted to thank you again for providing a wonderful environment for Christmas which I enjoyed very much.

I hope to speak to you tonight

much love

Alex
xxxxxx

It made her happy when she read it, At least he had had a good Christmas.

They Skyped that evening but Alex was agitated. Juliet had asked him why he hadn't shown her any affection and he just went off on one. He was always like this a few days after they had parted or was it the withdrawal from the weed? Juliet didn't know what to make of it but he was belligerent and picking at her, dragging up the past again and accusing her of going online looking for men. There was no reasoning with him. It was as much as Juliet could do to restrain herself. After all the effort she had gone to at Christmas and he was being a dick again. She cried when she finished the call and went to her bed and she lay there in the darkness. Anger began to rise up in her. Why was she putting up with this? She had been nothing but kind and loving with him and this was how he repaid her? The more she thought about it the more she was behaving like a doormat again, before long she would be in the same situation with Alex as she had been with Mark. She got up and opened up the computer, and fired off an angry venomous email to him.

Alex

The truth is that I am fed up with your accusations. The "online in search of men" is a figment of your imagination. You have solved my dilemma for me. I will keep you "out if it" as you put it. Keep you out of everything. I no longer wish to have a relationship with you.

Just so as you get it straight in your mind, it is for these reasons
1) You are not really in love with me. Little things like not

65

even knowing the colour of my eyes. Not admitting to other people that you are in a relationship with me (no mention of me on Facebook - I bet you haven't mentioned to anyone else the effort I went to for Christmas - you certainly didn't mention it to your mother, preferring to keep the image of me as lacking and poor). Lack of attentiveness over the last few months. A lack of understanding about my situation. You are motivated only by the fact you are Clara's father

2) Your stupid, outrageous jealousy is completely off the wall and unreasonable.

3) You are selfish and self-centred

4) I have no desire to live a life of poverty for the dream you have which is wholly unsustainable and impractical given your natural inclination to be lazy and stoned, it is no good for me or for Clara

5) Your way of life and lack of self-control means you keep unsociable hours, totally unsuitable to raising a child

6) You are immature and no comprehension of responsibility or real life (once again you came here with not enough money to see to your own needs - or rather you did, but spent it on a new hard drive for yourself).

Therefore, you are no longer welcome here at no 24. I will keep your possessions safe until you collect them. You are welcome to see Clara at mutually convenient times, but I am no longer willing to put you up.

I will send you fortnightly email updates on Clara.

Juliet

It was a bit strong but Juliet was seething. After Mark and then Alex in the cottage, she wasn't going to let anyone walk all over her again.

The next day she received this reply;

Juliet

Oh, my darling! Please forgive me my moments of madness! How could I possibly ever doubt you, or suppose that you might ever tell lies or engage in any form of dishonesty? And you are so right! It's because I project my own shortcomings on to you ... I hope that you will find it in your enormous heart to forgive me! I know that I am missing you so terribly - I really should make the most of all the opportunities we have to communicate with each other and desist from this silliness.

Oh how I love you!
Alex xxxx

Juliet didn't know whether to take this email seriously. It had a ring of sarcasm to it that she didn't like one little bit. But she couldn't be sure so she just made a mental note of it. He could after all, genuinely mean it. She had to give him the benefit of the doubt. That was the trouble with emails, the language has to be precise. Flowery language without the tone and intonation of the spoken voice, left it open to ambiguity

But the next time they emailed, everything was fine and continued to be so. Albeit for a few weeks.

Juliet applied for a passport for Clara and Alex kept pressuring her to book flights to Egypt. He had already done so during Christmas but Juliet was very unsure of him and £300 was a lot of money to blow on flights. What if he went off on one again? She would not be able to get that money back but he kept on being nice and he kept up the pressure, so at the end of January she booked the flights. They were departing for Cairo on the 9th March and she would spend her 46th birthday on holiday. She was finally relaxing and getting used to the idea and she emailed Alex about her excitement. He responded:

Juliet

thank you for sending me your news. forgive me if i seem distant or brief in what i say - teaching is proving exhausting and i struggle to think of stuff to talk about because there seems to be so little that happens in my life ... but rest assured, i am counting down the days to our holiday and looking forward to a great holiday with both of you.

all my love

alex

xxxxx

It was an odd email. Rushed. No capital letters. How could he be so stressed about teaching? But that was BPD. They struggle to hold down jobs, Alex always had, and they find work relationships as difficult to handle as personal ones. Alex had said that he had got a new female boss and she was making his life hell. Juliet did her best to support him when they spoke via Skype but he was hard work.

A few days later they Skyped and Juliet had asked Alex to bring the remainder of her maintenance for Jan to March, a sum that equalled £300. It was not a great deal of money. She had also said that he should bring at least £300 for himself to cover expenses. After all, there was the accommodation to pay for, the bus fares to Nuweiba and the food they would consume. He agreed over Skype and then a few days later she received this email

68

Juliet

so when you said that i would not need to worry about spending money provided you had the 600 pounds quarterly payment in advance, what you meant was that I'd need to bring 500 in spending money? what have you done with all the money i sent since last summer, that you were going to use exclusively to facilitate our seeing each other?

the balance of clara's money for the quarter jan to march will be transferred at the end of march. i wish to have my own vacation without you. in all of the circumstances, it is better thati don't see you. i am sorry that i won't see clara. rather than throw good money after bad, i may choose to stay here rather than fly to egypt. should i come to egypt, i ask that you don't try to meet me or cause a scene at the airport.

i also do not wish to pretend that you and i are husband and wife. find some other mug who wants to play your dishonest, manipulative games. given that you tricked me into getting you pregnant to keep me on a string indefinitely, and that this strategy has now failed, you should know that i would be happy, at any time, to take her and raise her without you. it may be that she gets in your way at some future time, or that you die. in either event, i will happily raise her without you. i will not go to law with you unless it comes to my attention that clara is suffering neglect or other abuse.

should you try to create any trouble for me with anybody, you will have some explaining to do with the dole/csa as to why you have not declared the income i have voluntarily paid and will do my best to continue to pay. bear that in mind.

Alex

Juliet's head was reeling. Where the fuck had this all come from? What the fuck was going on with him? She knew it, She just knew he would back out of this holiday. What was going on in his crazy fucked up mind? She was upset and she was angry, very angry. She responded but tried very hard not to be emotional;

Alex

Oh dear. Money does strike a chord with you doesn't it.

Firstly, I have not had the £600 payment in advance. You sent me £300 (which was not in advance - you always pay in arrears). By the time I arrive in Egypt I will have spent over £700 on this holiday including the money that I bring with me. I merely asked you to bring the other £300 that will be up to the end of March, plus some money to cover your expenditure. Is that really so unfair? Am I to take it you expect for me to fund you out of Clara's maintenance?

I spent a large amount of money on Christmas with food and the such like, that was designed with your specific comfort in mind. I also gave you money to return with (plus some weed you never gave me the money for, I think it amounted to £40) although I do not count the cost with you.

The idea that we pretend to be husband and wife was for mine and Clara's safety whilst in Egypt. Not some manipulative game. All of the guidebooks advise that when you are travelling with a man you pretend to be married.

I do not think that I have been unreasonable in all of this.

I do not wish to "keep you on a string" as you put it. Indeed, our life would be a lot simpler without you. And as for the paltry £200 per month, it is hardly a king's ransom and I can do without it (it is not as if I have been living some luxury lifestyle on it, as most of it has been spent directly for you).

Either you are 1) stressed out, or 2) showing your true colours. Time will tell.

Why the fuck I should make trouble for you, I have no idea. It has always been the other way around to my mind. You are deeply insecure, I know that.

Juliet

He did not reply. Or the next day, or the day after that. In fact he stopped contacting Juliet at all. What was going on with him? He had sent that email on the 25th February, less than two weeks before they were due to go on holiday. Juliet was beyond angry, she was completely fucked off. He accuses me of wasting money and then throws the towel in on a holiday at last minute and knows I shall lose the money if I cancel those flights, she thought to herself as she walked to Headington two days later. The more she thought about it, the more she thought it was a smokescreen for something else but whatever the reason she couldn't go on putting up with this behaviour. She had had enough. It was over, she had to stop believing there could be a future for them. She had been patient, kind and loving with him but his behaviour hadn't changed, instead he was taking advantage of her just like Mark had done all those years before.

she was so busy thinking to herself and still so angry as she marched along the pavement that she didn't notice someone coming towards her, someone who she used to know quite well. "Juliet," said a voice, and she was snapped out of her daydream and she looked up to see Nigel Baker standing in front of the pushchair. Juliet didn't know whether to run or say hello. She quickly examined his face to judge his expression but before she could do anything he spoke "It is

71

so good to see you Juliet, I thought I would never see you again. Is this your baby?" He was so inoffensive. After Alex and all his fucked-upness she decided that she was really quite pleased to see him.

"Hello Nigel," said Juliet "Yes, this is Clara."

Nigel looked at Clara, "she is beautiful, just like her mother," and he turned to Juliet. Juliet stood stunned on the pavement, unable to move "How are you?" he said. Juliet had not expected to see him. He worked just down the road, and usually Juliet was on the lookout when she went to Headington. She was usually careful to avoid lunchtimes when she knew he may go to the bank but she had been so angry today she hadn't given it a second thought and yet here he was. She was so taken aback by how pleasantly surprised she had felt to see him after all the anger and sorrow of Alex, she felt tears well up in her eyes when he asked her how she was. She tried to say I am ok, but it came out croaky and a tear rolled down her cheek.

Nigel looked really sad. "Why are you crying then Juliet?" he said.

Trust him to ask a question like that. "It is a long story," said Juliet and left it at that.

"Well, why don't you come for a coffee with me and tell me all about it," said Nigel. "I want to know all about what has been happening to you. The place isn't the same without you, you know. I have missed you."

Juliet felt she should turn him down but she had no one to talk to. She had no friends and she had been careful about discussing the troubles between her and Alex with her daughters. They were not old enough to understand and they could be very judgemental.

"Thanks, Nigel, that would be nice." There was a little café in Headington called Café Bonjour. Bloody stupid name for a café but it was an okay place run by Turkish people, and there was enough space for a pushchair. The last time Juliet had been in that café was when she was on maternity leave with Guy and her mother and her aunty Pat had visited her.

Now her mother was dead. It made her sad to think of her mom again, she could still remember her sitting opposite her.

They found a little table and sat down. "Would you like something to eat Juliet?" said Nigel, "It is nearly lunchtime. I think I will have something."

"Thanks, Nigel, but I can't really afford it." She replied.

"Juliet, I want to buy you lunch. I honestly thought I would never see you again. I am so pleased I bumped into you. Do you live locally? I thought you had moved to Wales, at least that was what the Director said but he didn't give me your address for your last payslip."

Juliet blushed and felt ashamed. She had asked the old Director Ben not to let him have her address, given how absurdly jealous Alex had been for fear of him writing her a little note.

"I am so sorry Nigel, it is honestly such a long story but I owe it to you to tell you all about it. And your offer of lunch is very nice thank you, I will accept." She was beginning to relax. Clara was asleep in her pushchair and wouldn't wake for a while. She ordered a bacon and cheese panini and a cup of tea and told Nigel all what had happened.

Nigel's eyes were wide in horror as he listened to her story. "Oh God, Juliet, you have been through so much. You should have contacted me, I would have helped where I could."

"Nigel, I could never have done that. Alex would have had a fit if he had found out I was even emailing you. He made me cut off contact with all of my male friends and then when I left work he made me change my email address and close the old one down. In any case, I had caused you enough trouble and you are married."

"Well, not anymore. Jackie and I are going through a divorce. I have had my decree nisi and I am just waiting for my decree absolute. After you left my marriage really got worse and I thought about what you had said and I had a chat with Jackie and we decided to call it a day.

" Now it was Juliet's turn to be surprised. "Well, I never thought you would divorce Jackie, I honestly didn't."

"Look, Juliet, I would like to meet up with you again for a coffee or lunch. As old friends. Will you have my number? Please say yes, it would mean a lot to me."

Juliet pondered about it for a little while and then said "yes." Fuck Alex, this was only a friendship, nothing else and she was done with Alex, or was she?

Chapter 9– Hope

Juliet walked home. It was the last day of February and the sun was shining. She could feel the power of the sun as she walked along the pavement by the big beech hedge. She felt happy after bumping into Nigel. It felt good to get her problems off her chest and for someone else to say that she had had an awful time. She was glad she had accepted his telephone number and she had decided she would meet him again. She thought about her holiday. She would go. It would be good for her to have a change of scene and somewhere sunny as well!

She got home and put her key in the door and picked up her post. There was a letter with an NHS frank on it, so she opened it. They had scheduled the 20th March for her operation. Were they having a laugh? It was the day before her birthday and she would be on holiday. She phoned them up to explain and they said they would cancel and re-schedule.

After a relaxing afternoon ironing (if anyone can find ironing relaxing) and watching crappy daytime TV (well Juliet had to admit to herself, that she was rather enjoying Monarch of the Glen, which she hadn't seen the first time around and also Judge Deed. Gosh, how old Martin Shaw had got. She remembered him as a bit if a heart throb in the Professionals), she had given Clara a bath and put her to bed in the cot in Juliet's room. She poured herself a glass of wine and started to cook some food for her and Alistair. Whilst it was cooking she turned on her computer. Still no email from Alex. She had to check but she still felt very angry about what he had done. How he had let her down yet again. How many more times will he have to do that Juliet Grosvenor, before you truly give up on him? She thought to herself but she wasn't going to email him, oh no, he could stew.

What was going on with him? She thought as she stirred the pasta sauce and sipped her wine. It was almost as though he had picked a fight out of nothing to get out of going on holiday with her, and after he had been looking forward to it so much. All the emails she had received saying 'only so many more weeks to go'.......'can't wait to see you and Clara'......" it made no sense. Unless. He was having an affair. If he had someone else then that would explain why he suddenly wanted to get out of going on holiday with her. The distance at Christmas, the lack of intimacy, it would fit. She didn't have any proof though and anyway there was only his boss and the wife of a colleague who attended the Quaker meetings that were female. She ruled out the wife of a colleague because she gathered she was in her late fifties, but his boss? Well, it could fit. He was after all charm itself. Juliet had witnessed his power over women first hand on numerous occasions. There had been some old colleague they had once met in the park in Newtown. She had stayed chatting for a long time, so long that Juliet had wished she would just fuck off but she saw Alex working his charm on her, making her laugh, laughing his deep sexy laugh and the glint in his eyes. Then there was the stern woman down at the job centre. He had her eating from the palm of his hand. Juliet had remarked to his mother Jean that he could get women to throw their knickers at him. Yes, the boss could fit. He could have turned his charm on with her if he had been having a hard time. It was a game to him, a challenge. Still there was nothing Juliet could do about it, even if she could prove it was true so she put it to the back of her mind. She would find out about whatever the reason was eventually.

The next day Juliet felt much happier when she woke up. At least if Alex wasn't communicating with her she didn't have that awful sense of fear about his emails. Would they be nice or nasty? One never knew with him, what you were going to get. One of the books she had read about BPD was called 'Walking on Eggshells.' and it really was like that, having a relationship with a BPD sufferer. They can be immensely pleasurable and satisfying at times but pure hell at others. She dug her phone out of her bag and messaged Nigel.

It was nice catching up with you yesterday. See you soon. Juliet.

It hadn't gone long before her phone pinged with a message in reply.

How about lunch again today? Nigel

Juliet had to laugh to herself, he was keen. She knew she was perhaps not doing the right thing by accepting his invitation, or by giving him her number but he was controllable and she was not going to sleep with him. He was just a friend. It was a free meal and a little company if nothing else.

The night before, Juliet had done some internet research. She couldn't waste those tickets to Cairo. Alex and she had planned to travel by bus to Nuweiba but she could hardly do that with Clara on her own. Thankfully they had not booked up any accommodation. Cairo was not going to be suitable. The current political climate was too dangerous. There were Militant uprisings in Cairo as the President had been imprisoned and the military were ruling. The fundamentalists wanted to gain control. She couldn't stay there. She could go to Luxor. She had been there many times with Mark and she could remain mostly in the hotel. She wouldn't want to see any monuments with Clara and she had visited them all many times before in the early years with Mark, before he didn't

77

work. She looked at the accommodation. She could get the out of town Sofitel cheaply, £30 quid a day but she would have to arrange internal flights and they were £70 each. Then there would be two nights in Cairo one at each end of the holiday as the plane arrived at midnight. Looking at it she was short of money. She could just about do it if she had access to her benefits whilst there but without some cash it was not going to be possible, she would have to cancel. Of course, Alex had promised £300 at the end of the month but would he pay it? She could borrow it from her daughters and pay them back. That is if they had the cash. She decided to sleep on it.

Later that morning she and Clara walked to Headington to meet Nigel at the Café Bonjour. He was as usual punctual. He wouldn't let you down Juliet thought to herself. "Hello, Juliet, I am glad you could come for lunch," said Nigel.

Juliet laughed "Well it is not like I have anything else to do Nigel," said Juliet. Clara was awake.

"She is lovely Juliet. I can't believe Alex wanted a paternity test. I would be overjoyed at having a daughter." said Nigel.

"Well, as I told you yesterday Nigel, he is not right in the head." They perused the menu. It was the standard fare; panini's, jacket potatoes and the like. Nigel settled on a jacket potato with cheese. Juliet went for another panini, this time chicken tikka with a salad.

"How did you get on last night with accommodation for your holiday?" said Nigel.

"Well, if I can't borrow £300 from the girls I am stuffed and I will have to cancel the tickets and lose 300. No win situation really. To say I am furious with him is an understatement and he had the audacity to accuse me of wasting money. Shame because I was looking forward to a break away somewhere warm just lounging by the pool."

"I will lend it to you," said Nigel suddenly.

Juliet froze, she didn't want to accept money from him, she knew he still fancied her; that was obvious. "That is very kind of you Nigel, but I can't accept it. I had money from you in the past, and I regret what I did," said Juliet. "Well, I would like you to have it. It is a loan, not a gift. And I don't regret giving you any of the money I gave you, you were worth it,"

That eased Juliet's conscience and she said, "I will think about it Nigel, thanks." It was good to have company again and it made her realise how lonely she had been. He wouldn't set the world on fire would old Nigel and no woman would ever throw their knickers at him but he was steady and reliable. They passed a pleasant hour and he told her all about his divorce and how Jackie had moved out taking the furniture with her. He needed help with getting the place ready to sell. "If I can be any help advising on soft furnishings and the like Nigel then please ask. If you are putting it on the market you want it to look like a home and not a box without much furniture." said Juliet.

"I will take you up on that offer but first you need a holiday and to get your operation out of the way." Juliet had told him that she needed an operation but had just said it was for 'women's stuff' and had left it at that. She certainly hadn't gone into the finer details. She didn't want to think about the operation now, she would have to face that when she came back. They finished their lunch and Juliet had decided she would accept his offer of the loan. "Nigel, I will take you up on your offer, if you don't mind," said Juliet.

"I am only too glad to help," said Nigel "write down your bank account details and I will set you up as a payee when I get home later this afternoon and transfer it and then you can book up your accommodation and internal flights. I wish I was coming with you."

Juliet gave him her bank account details and when he had paid for the meal she kissed him on the cheek. "Thank you so much, Nigel for everything." She said. "It's ok Juliet, it is just lovely to see you again."

79

Juliet walked home. It was a grey afternoon and it was about ¾ mile to her flat and she always made a point of walking to Headington every day, rain or shine. Clara liked to be out and about and it was exercise for Juliet and it kept her weight down. She looked forward to getting home and booking up her holiday as soon as Clara had gone to sleep.

Later that day when Clara had gone to bed Juliet turned on her computer and logged into her emails. Still no email from Alex. What the fuck was he playing at? Still she didn't care anymore. She was going on holiday and she had soon booked up the internal flights and the accommodation. Once there she knew that they could live cheaply, probably cheaper than at home. For the first time in a couple of weeks she was looking forward to having a holiday and she didn't mind being on her own. What was that stupid statement about turning up at the airport and making a scene if Alex decided to go to Egypt? Was he on crack? He was seriously deranged? She didn't even know what flight he had booked and didn't care. But why say that? She thought he had cancelled his flights, unless he was going there with someone else. None of it made any sense and she decided that she wasn't going to waste her time trying to make sense of it. He was nuts like Bill said. Nuts, that was all there was to it.

She sent Nigel a text.

Thank you for the loan. I have now booked everything up. Once again thank you for your help. Juliet

She met Nigel a couple of times before her holiday and he was pleasant company and it was a free lunch. He had asked her out for dinner but she had said she couldn't leave Clara with Alistair. He was pleasant with Clara and he could rock the pushchair in a crisis but looking after her for a few hours was beyond his skill level. So she politely declined. Nigel understood but she could tell that he was disappointed. She certainly didn't want to get beyond friendship level with him again, she was still in love with Alex no matter how much she tried to deny it to herself although he was chipping away at her love, little by little, there was no doubt about that.

The day soon arrived for her holiday. Juliet had prepared everything down to the last detail. It was not going to be easy travelling alone with a child aged 11 months but she had travelled with small children before and she would do it again, it was about time she did something outside of her comfort zone, she had grown soft in her quiet little life. It hadn't helped that herself-esteem had taken a bashing from both Mark and Alex and she felt quite timid. Her little flat at Colwell Drive had become a sanctuary, safe, secure, hers but she needed to broaden her horizons once more.

Alistair walked with Juliet over to the coach stop dragging her wheelie suitcase. It was quite convenient where they lived as it was only about half a mile away from a major coach stop on the outskirts of Oxford, the Park,and Ride. From there you could catch a coach to London (every ten minutes), a coach to Gatwick (every fifteen minutes) and a coach to Heathrow (every fifteen minutes). It really was very convenient thought Juliet to herself as she sat waiting for the coach. It didn't take long for it to arrive and Juliet soon took Clara out of the pushchair and collapsed it. The driver was helpful and she found a seat on the coach after paying. They set off but for some reason Clara started crying. She cried all the way to Heathrow. A fine start to my holiday thought Juliet as her stress levels rose. But perhaps it was because Juliet was anxious to begin with that had set off Clara crying. Juliet was embarrassed for other people, and when she got off the coach there was a couple standing there with their two children, who were aged about 10 and 12. Juliet struggled with the pushchair alone to assemble it whilst holding Clara. No one offered to help and then the miserable looking woman from the couple said "Good luck with your holiday."

That did it. Juliet was really annoyed. What kind of a woman says that and did not offer to help? Juliet just shot her a look down her nose and said: "I have five other children, I am sure I will cope." And turned away. She felt triumphant and she was not going to fail on this holiday. She loved nothing more than someone throwing her a challenge.

Once in the airport Juliet began to relax, it wasn't going to be so bad, it was going to be fun. Clara had stopped crying and was looking in awe around her. Heathrow is wonderful and it had been many years since Juliet had travelled from there and then that was not alone. She took a deep breath and relaxed. You have plenty of time Juliet Grosvenor, you are 45 and there is nothing, but nothing to this, you have seen some shit, and you can travel with an infant alone to some place where there is civil unrest. And then she let out a nervous laugh. Who's fucking idea was this anyway? Alex's! That said it all, and she laughed again as she made her way through security.

Once on the plane she settled in her seat. She had booked herself in online and had got a seat where there were fold down infant cots in front, although they looked more like tray tables with a restraining strap on. She wondered if Clara would ever sleep on that or whether she would have her on her lap for the whole of the flight. There was some lone Egyptian woman next to her with two kids, or was she alone? No, Juliet concluded she had a nanny. How lovely to be rich, thought Juliet.

The flight went well and Clara did manage a little sleep on the tray table cot, which allowed Juliet enough time to go to the toilet and to be chatted up whilst in the queue for the toilet by an Egyptian doctor from Cairo. Well he was too upper class to chat her up but chat with her he did all the same. They talked about the political climate in Egypt and how he feared for his two westernised teenage daughters, and he asked about Juliet and Clara. Upper-class Egyptians are a lot more cosmopolitan and subtler in their flirtations than the ordinary waiter in Hurghada. Juliet had consumed two gin and tonics was relaxed and could face the departure from Cairo airport at midnight with confidence even though she would have to find a taxi, but she was prepared for that.

She cleared passport control with Clara and her bags and was soon inundated with Egyptians in Gallabiyah's asking if she needed a taxi. She refused the first few and then one stuck to her like glue, he seemed ok, not too pushy but the Egyptians are the masters of selling. They were a nation of shopkeepers long before the British ever were but then they had been occupied by us so perhaps they had picked up a thing or two and they were the masters of imitation. "How much to the Holiday Inn Maadi?"Juliet said. She knew it was on the other side of the City, right around the massive ring road that encompassed Cairo. When she had booked it she had reasoned that it would be midnight and the ring road would be quiet at this time of night whereas the centre of Cairo would still be buzzing. She got more hotel for her money this way and the taxi should only be around £10. The trouble was that when you started thinking in Egyptian pounds you thought they were real pounds and at that time the exchange rate was about 9 Egyptian pounds to 1 British. The tout started his opening shot 150 Egyptian (16.50 GBP). "La" (means 'no' in Egyptian) was Juliet's firm response shaking her head but not looking at him, she just carried on walking, getting nearer to the taxi rank outside. Taxi car park more like as the car park had many taxi's waiting. The Egyptians knew when the BA flight from Heathrow was landing. "120," said the Egyptian. He was lowering his price. "70," responded Juliet. He threw his hands up in the air. "Madam, I cannot possibly do it for that." He said. "Well, I will find someone who will," said Juliet, not stopping or slowing her stride. Clara in the pushchair, looking dazed at being woken in the middle of the night to witness this strange sight of a man in a long dress. Then he said "100." Juliet did not wish to rob them, she merely wanted a fair price and not to be ripped off. Petrol was cheap here.

She turned to the Egyptian "What is your name?" She asked, looking him in the eye

. "Gamal," he said.

"Well, Gamal, you have yourself a deal," said Juliet "100 Egyptian it is," and proffered her hand to shake. The greasy young devil kissed it. They just can't help themselves can they, Juliet thought to herself and laughed. This holiday was going to be fun but she hadn't got in the taxi yet, there may still be skulduggery at foot and Juliet had to be on her guard.

Sure enough when she got to the taxi, the tout handed her over to a taxi driver who didn't have such a good command of English as Gamal. She heard Gamal say 120 to the local taxi driver, as he loaded the pushchair into the boot. Juliet rounded on the two men with a sharp look in her eye. "Gamal, we agreed 100," the other man was shaking his head. Juliet looked around and shouted, "taxi" and immediately 20 men looked and started to walk over. Juliet was asking how much to the Holiday Inn Maadi and telling her originally engaged taxi driver to get the pushchair out of the boot.

The poor man looked crushed and knew he was beaten. "Ok Madam, 100 Egyptian." I will have to watch him thought Juliet but she had dealt with Egyptians before and they were okay really. She would come to no harm they loved and adored children, and whilst young women scantily dressed might fall prey to the unscrupulous as long as Juliet maintained the respectful look and demeanour of some respectable woman she would come to no harm. When they finally arrived at their destination, he had been a good driver and Juliet tipped him an extra 20. She knew he would have that tip, and the greasy tout Gamal would know nothing about it. He smiled and said, "Thank you, Madam."

It was after 2 am when she got to the hotel room. Thankfully Clara soon fell asleep in the bed next to her Tomorrow they were catching the 12.15 to Luxor, so back to the airport they would go but Juliet was glad to be here. Driving around the ring road at night with the taxi windows open and the warm air blowing in seeing the monuments illuminated from below was delightful. The clear night sky with the stars being nearer the earth in this part of the world had restored her joy, restored her reason to live and she turned off the lamp on the bedside table and cuddled Clara close and fell fast asleep.

Chapter 10– Egypt

Juliet awoke. The light was streaming in through the floor length net curtains. She hadn't drawn the proper curtains the night before even though there was the glow from the street lights. They were on the fifth floor way above the street and she hadn't wanted to oversleep. Juliet looked at her watch, it was just after seven in the morning and Clara was still asleep. She slipped quietly out of bed. It was not yet warm enough in Cairo to warrant air conditioning but even though she was wearing a flimsy nightdress she was comfortably warm. She had packed the travel kettle and teabags. The kettle mainly to boil water for Clara's milk feeds, she didn't need many, just one in a morning and one at night but Juliet needed a cup of strong Assam tea. She boiled the kettle and poured the boiling water over the waiting teabag. There was UHT milk in a small carton on the tray and she made her tea and made a bottle for Clara to cool. She was feeling rather pleased with her timid self. It hadn't taken her long to return to her old form.

They arose and Juliet packed what little she had unpacked and departed the hotel for the airport. It was interesting to see Cairo in the daylight and they sat in traffic for a little way around the ring road. Juliet was beginning to feel at home here. She always had. From the first moment that she had set foot in Egypt years ago she had loved it. She had been fourteen at the time and she had only ever been to Ibiza with her parents when she was twelve. Ibiza in February, Ibiza in the late seventies, when it hadn't gained a reputation as a party Island. She had liked it even though her parents had complained about foreign food. And at fourteen as part of a school cruise, Egypt had enchanted her; the heat, the dust, the rubbish, the honking of car horns, the dry heat of the night and the magnificent monuments and the past, the glorious ancient Egypt that was evident everywhere. Even huge granite statues of Ramses II were standing in the central reservations of dual carriageways. It was like no other place on earth and it never would be. Disneyland had nothing on Egypt.

Juliet sat in the back of the taxi cuddling Clara. Apart from her first little hissy fit on the coach from Oxford to Heathrow, she had been very good and now the little eleven-month-old was taking in everything with all senses. She was actually enjoying herself in a quiet observed way.

They made it to the airport in good time and finally boarded their flight. Much to Juliet's horror, as soon as she sat in her seat on the small aircraft she could distinctly smell the aroma of shit. A young businessman had sat in the aisle seat next to her. Juliet discreetly looked into Clara's nappy. Sure enough Clara had done a poo. "I am really sorry to have to bother you," she said the young businessman sitting next to her, "But I need to change my daughter's nappy."

The young man who was not as young as he appeared, said, "Please, madam think nothing of it, I am a father of two young children, I understand," as he slid out of his seat to make way for Juliet to go to the small cubicle at the back of the plane. Juliet went and changed Clara and came back. The young man was extremely polite and pleasant and enquired about Clara's age. He then showed Juliet pictures of his own children as they taxied down the runway. The flight was only 45 minutes. The trolley dollies came around with complimentary orange juice and fruit and then retired. It wasn't long before they landed at Luxor.

It was distinctly warmer in Luxor, pleasantly so and despite being early March, it was more like a good English June day, only with dry heat. Luckily there was no sign of the sometimes threatening Hamsin wind that could plague Egypt at that time of year. As it was an internal flight they cleared the airport in no time at all and Juliet looked around for a taxi. There were a few waiting as Juliet approached cautiously. An old man sat on the grass in the shade of a date palm, he was shabbily dressed but this did not bother Juliet. He eyed her as she approached pushing the pram and dragging her suitcase behind. "Where are you going Madam?" he said.

"Sofitel Karnak," Juliet replied.

"Pay no more than 40 pounds," he said. 40 pounds? thought Juliet but that is not 5 GBP. However she took his advice but she didn't need to. A taxi man stepped forward and she asked him how much to the Sofitel Karnak.

He had heard the old man and said "40."

"That is fine," said Juliet as the taxi driver began to put the luggage in the car. Juliet took Clara out of the pushchair and started to give instructions on how to collapse it but it was no use, the driver was having great difficulty. The old man came over to help. Juliet could see she was getting nowhere with her instructions and handed Clara to the old man. "Would you mind holding her for a moment?"

The old man looked overjoyed "It would be an honour Madam," he said, and he took Clara while Juliet collapsed the pushchair. He cooed over Clara and Juliet realised that he was not used to Europeans handing him their pride and joy because of his appearance. His was old, he looked like he was 90, but he was probably nearer 65 – 70. He was short, very thin and his face underneath his massive turban was as wrinkled as a walnut. His galabiya was dirty and frayed around the hem but his face radiated kindness. He was the gardener for the little manicured piece in front of the Airport, Juliet knew this because he was wearing wellingtons. She smiled at him. Clara had not complained, and as she took Clara back she said "thank you Sir." The old man looked very pleased. Juliet tried to offer him a tip but he would not take it. A rare thing in Egypt when even 20p would make most ordinary people very happy.

They sat in the taxi as it made its way to the hotel. There wasn't a cloud in the sky and it was as blue as Alex's eyes. Past fields of sweetcorn and the road was lined with date palms. Small children barefoot and happy were playing near the little irrigation channels, wearing nothing but a galabiya. Donkeys stood in the shade with baskets either side of their flanks. It is good to be here, thought Juliet. Thousands of miles away from her little flat, from Alex, although in reality she was nearer. How could he hate teaching English in a foreign land? But then did she really know what he was up to at the moment? She felt sad that he wasn't here but then this was her holiday. He had wanted hippy, pot smoking Nuweiba, staying in a hut on the beach and she was doing what she loved, a four-star hotel in Luxor. She and Clara would have a wonderful time, of that she was sure as the taxi pulled up outside the hotel.

After Juliet had checked in, she was shown to her room. It was a nice spacious room next to the pool. The only complaint she had was that it was a twin bedroom but Juliet just pushed the heavy solid beds together, Clara was so small, she would not be able to separate them in her sleep.

Juliet unpacked the important things, like the travel kettle and the sterilising container and tablets and she put Clara in her pushchair and took her for a walk around the hotel. It was much lovelier than she had remembered. There was a cash point machine just outside the hotel lobby and there was a little shop just outside the hotel at the end of the long driveway. The gardens were very pretty and well-tended and it was peaceful. There was even a little shuttle bus and a shuttle boat that took you into the centre of Luxor for free should you wish. There was a mini bar in the room but Juliet had bought a bottle of gin on the way out of Heathrow and she could buy tonic water at the shop. The room service menu looked reasonable and she decided that she could have an early dinner in the room so that Clara could share. There was no way that Clara would wait for the dining room to open at 6pm, it was nearly her bedtime then.

They quickly settled into a routine. Up early and a cup of tea in the room. Breakfast followed, then back to the room to get changed and then out by the pool all morning followed by lunch which sometimes was just a few things kept over from breakfast and then an afternoon nap for Clara whilst Juliet read a book. They might go back out by the pool for a little while and have a dip in the pool together, which Clara adored. They would have an early dinner in the room and a couple of gin and tonics for Juliet followed by bed. It was a change of scene and Juliet was enjoying herself but she had to admit that she was a little lonely.

She did venture into town a couple of times and walked through the souk, taking in all the sounds, sights and smells. Men often asked where Clara's father was and Juliet told them that he was working in Iraq and that he was supposed to meet them, but couldn't make it. That served the purpose of letting them know that she was not single looking for a quick hook up. She dressed very conservatively when she went out wearing trousers, long-sleeved shirts, and a white cotton headscarf.

All of the staff at the hotel were very nice to Juliet, even the male cleaner had listened to her request and cleaned her room in the morning so that Clara could have an afternoon nap without being disturbed. The only disappointment with all of this was that Juliet would have loved to have gone for a swim but she couldn't risk leaving Clara alone in the pushchair, whether she was asleep or not.

All in all, she was having a lovely time. What was the idiot thinking? Surely it must have been a smokescreen, otherwise, why turn down a holiday like this? She had given up trying to fathom the workings of his mind but curiosity got the better of her and a week into her holiday she logged into her emails on the guest computer in the lobby, to find an email from Alex. He had sent it on the day she had left for Egypt, the 9th of March, just over a week ago;

Hi Juliet

Our vacation has just started - two glorious weeks - after several months of hell, which culminated in a student demonstration outside the front of the building where security forces arrived with a vehicle mounted machine gun. Those demonstrating are students on probation who had eventually been suspended from the university. All but one had failed to make the grade at my summer school class (also from hell). The Dean wouldn't let me go outside to speak to them. The President of the university left via a side-door to go on holiday in New Zealand for three, not two, weeks. I don't think anyone wants him to come back - not even he does - but those above us think it would be a good idea - a face-saving measure.

You would be welcome to come here with Clara, but the security situation is volatile, and will probably get worse if Israel attacks Iran. I hope that you didn't lose much money as a result of cancelling, if that is indeed what you did. I haven't made a firm decision about my own future. I have other job options, but urgent change needs to be made here if teachers are to be empowered to provide the best education possible to a remarkable people.

I would like the opportunity to watch with others the DVD that Bill sent to you, Nature of the Mind. If you could ask Alistair to upload it to soul seek (a file sharing service) then I

91

would appreciate it, and make it right with him next time I
see him. If that is possible, please let me know.

A number of us have come close to breakdowns over the last
few weeks. I also finally got to see the implantologist from
Dubai (sexy and French - you'd like him). It is essential that
I stop smoking within the next fortnight if he is to give me
those implants, and I didn't think that coming to Egypt, with a
smoke available, would have helped with that. I hope you
understand my position as I try to understand yours.

Love

Alex
xxxxxx

Juliet read his email, logged out and shut down the computer. She pushed Clara's pushchair out into the sunshine and ordered herself a beer as she sat by the pool. What on earth was that all about? She thought to herself. How did he have the audacity to send her that email after what he had previously said to her? And after how she had responded to him. She had told him she wanted nothing more to do with him and now he was adopting the tone of someone with whom she was on friendly terms. The only slight nod to what she had said was the last line when he said; "I hope you understand my position as much as I try to understand yours." Nuts! Absolutely fucking nuts. And the worst thing about it was that he had thrown in a casual line, about hoping she had not lost too much money. Then there was the invite to go to Iraq. How stupid can he get? Cairo had been dodgy but she hadn't stayed there apart from overnight but Iraq for God's sake? One would have needed to have lost possession of all of one's faculties to consider that a reasonable proposition.

She laughed to herself. But there was trying the sympathy angle. Talking about how hard it was, and how 'a number of us, have come close to breakdowns.' Just who else had come close to a breakdown? Alex 1, Alex 2 or Alex 3, or all three? She hadn't heard from him for weeks and he knew her flight was on the 9[t h]and yet he had sent that email on that very day. She still didn't have a smartphone, and he knew that. He would have realised that she would not be able to access her emails without effort, if she was in Egypt. It was clear that he thought she had not gone on holiday by herself with Clara.

She sipped on her ice-cold Egyptian Stella and thought. Clara had nodded off. Perhaps his 'shag' had turned cold, or had fled the country and now he was left on his own with nothing to do and no one to do anything with in the holidays. Juliet smelt a rat. He had turned on her suddenly and now he had switched back and behaved as if the loss of the airfare was nothing. Yet, he didn't know she had come to Egypt, he didn't know that she had met Nigel Baker again and that he had lent her £300. Serves him fucking right Juliet thought and laughed to herself again. She caught the barman looking at her puzzled. Oh, shit! I had better not laugh again they will think I am nuts and they will be carting me off soon, she thought. She finished her Stella, removed her sarong and her blouse and lay back on the sun lounger enjoying the warmth of the afternoon sun.

Chapter 11 - Threats

The next few days slipped by very much as the other days of her holiday. Nigel Baker sent her a text asking how her holiday was. She replied saying it was good but she was running out of credit on her phone and would not be able to text him again. She had tried to top it up over the phone but as she was abroad it didn't seem to want to work. He responded, saying he had topped up her credit for her own safety and she could text whenever she liked. He was thoughtful and generous, she had to admit and it made her smile. His kindness and generosity was so unlike Alex who was a first-rate wanker and a tight one at that. She had lent him money at Christmas because he had sent so much money home to his mom to put into his building society account, and had then spent a large amount of the money he had set aside for the Christmas period on a hard drive for his computer.

Her holiday was nearly over and her birthday was coming up. She didn't care that she was alone except for Clara, she was having a nice relaxing time and it was good to be away from home. On the day before her birthday she logged on to the hotel guest computer once more, to see if she had received any emails from Alex. She suspected that as she hadn't replied to his last email he would be getting angry by now and would have fired off another nasty one. She was beginning to predict his behaviour and she was curious to see if she was right. It would not have occurred to him that she had gone to Egypt by herself. He would have assumed that she had cancelled the flights.

Sure enough, there were two new emails from him. The first said:

Hi Juliet

Just a quick email to say that Clara's maintenance should be transferred to your Coventry Account on 30 March 2012. It will be for the balance of the period Jan to March, i.e. £600 less £300 = £300.

Hope you are all well.

He did not sign off in that email and it was dated the 14th March. Then there was another one dated the 18th, this time the tone was not friendly;

I understand why you have not replied to my last two emails, but I want you to know that unless I get confirmation of successful transfer to your Coventry account of 300 pounds at the end of March, I will not send you another bean. It is important that I know that the money has reached your account.

*I also require you to arrange the upload of the Nature of the Mind to a file-sharing service like Soul seek. If that does not happen within three days, you may find that any further payments to you start becoming erratic in their arrival, and may even stop altogether. **I will play ball with you only if you play ball with me**. And do you really want a fraud investigator from the DWP paying you a visit, as well as continued regular visits from the boys in blue? See, even if you are not prosecuted for benefit fraud, you will have to pay back everything that has been sent to you. And given that I imagine that you have already spent it on everyone and everything except Clara, you are going to find that a rather onerous experience.*

I trust that the full import of this email is clear to you.

There was no "Hi Juliet" or "Alex" at the end. As she needed the £300 to pay back Nigel, she thought she had better respond, if only briefly and factually.

Alex

Clara and I are on holiday in Egypt as per our original flights, so that is why I have not replied to the last two emails.
Will reply in full, on my return.

Juliet

She logged out. She was not angry, it was as she had expected. She had to laugh to herself when she thought about it. He had just made a tit of himself. He certainly wasn't expecting her to go on holiday without him. What was slightly worrying however was his blackmail threat. Although she wasn't that worried about it, she had all of his personal documents back at the flat and she could threaten to shop him to the tax man, checkmate. And he supposedly played chess. She laughed out loud. He couldn't think his way out of a paper bag. In any case she hadn't received very much maintenance from him so she wasn't worried. But she was going to go through all of his documents and scan them all when she got home, by way of protection against him in the future. And what was all that "I require you to upload the Nature of the Mind file to soul search within three days?" What on earth was it? Nature of the Mind, my arse, the nature of his mind would take up a series of documentaries. It was all just a way of yanking her about a way of manipulating her to do his bidding. That is what she thought to herself as she made her way to the poolside for the morning. After the events of the recent months, she would treat him with a lot more caution from now on and play him at his own game if that is how he wanted it. However she had a little dilemma and he might just be the solution.

The day passed and she awoke and it was her Birthday. She received texts from each of her children, wishing her a Happy Birthday. The sun was shining and that was enough of a Happy Birthday for her, she didn't need anything else. The sun always shone in Egypt. No wonder the Ancient Egyptians were happy, who wouldn't be when you could guarantee the weather? Then her phone pinged again this time it was Nigel wishing her a Happy Birthday. How had he remembered? She had told him it was going to be her birthday on holiday but not the date. He must have looked it up from the old personnel files she thought to herself. She replied Thank you.

They didn't do anything special on her birthday but Juliet decided to take a taxi into town and walk through the souk. The local people were lovely and the taxi driver was a middle-aged man who had driven her before. He had said he would wait for her, even if, she didn't know how long she was going to be. He would sit, and drink coffee with other men of his age and he showed her where to find him. She walked along the Corniche first, the pavement beside the Nile and looked at the Felucca's moored on the banks. The vast expanse of Nile stretching to the West Bank, dark blue with the silver sparkles of the sun glinting on the water, rising up to the golden yellow sand with the hills of Thebes in the distance. How she loved the Nile. She knew that by walking along the Corniche she ran the risk of being harassed by touts and soon enough one man of her age was upon her. "Good morning," he said in excellent English.

Juliet decided to be sociable, "Good Morning," she replied in Arabic.

"Ahh Madam, you speak Arabic?" he responded.

"Shwi, Shwi," she replied, meaning 'a little.' They were soon engaged in conversation after Juliet had established that she had been here before and that she didn't want to see anything over on the West Bank because of Clara.

"Madam, can you tell me why no one comes here anymore, is it because of the fundamentalists?"

"Well I am here, as you can see," said Juliet."I think it has dented the tourism a little for Egypt but for people who know the place, then they will not be put off. Everyone back in England is feeling the pinch and they don't have as much money as they used to. My father religiously takes a holiday each year but last year he didn't because of the lack of money." They chatted some more and it was pleasant, Juliet told him about how she remembered the car ferry before they had built the bridge. He laughed and said it would be back in use soon as the bridge needed repairs. Juliet laughed too and wondered whether the old ferry would hold out or if there would be some catastrophic accident and the loss of many lives. The Egyptians had a laid-back approach to life. "God willing," was one of their favourite phrases, when you asked if they could do something, or asked if the train was on time. It doesn't matter, was another favourite of theirs. You just had to admire their gung-ho approach to life but they were warm in general and they were kind, you could accept that sometimes they tried to hassle you for something, it was their livelihood, their income, and their families depended on it. Juliet felt sorry for them that tourism was so bad at the moment. She had managed to come here on the cheap and she was loving every minute of it even if she was restricted in what she could do because of Clara. She said her goodbyes and wished him luck in finding someone to take a tour and carried on her way. A little way further along the Corniche there was a woman selling scarves. There was something about the woman that struck Juliet as sad and odd. It is unusual to see women selling things in Egypt it is usually the job of a man, and she stopped to look at her scarves. The woman cooed over Clara and Juliet asked her if she had children "Yes, I have four, replied the woman,"

Juliet knew that something was wrong. "Where is your husband?" asked Juliet.

"He is sick," replied the woman. Juliet's heart went out to her. Even if she was lying about her husband being sick, she was out here selling and she had children, it was not usual for a woman to be selling.

"I will take two scarves," said Juliet, they would make suitable presents for the girls, and they were only 20 Egyptian pounds each, that was just over 4 English for two and the woman could probably feed her family on that for three days at least maybe a week. She turned and went back to walk through the Souk. She felt truly blessed. Despite her problems with Alex, she had Clara who was healthy and happy and she might have very little money but she had a lot more than the average Egyptian. She wondered who was the happiest? Her money was on the Egyptians.

She enjoyed the souk. The early morning, or late at night were the best times to enjoy the souk. Both offered different aspects to the souk. Early morning, you had less hassle, the shopkeepers were drowsy and sleepy and they had only just opened their shops after getting out of bed, sitting in the doorways to their shops, sipping coffee, or dousing the sandy pavement outside the shops with water, so the dust would not spoil their goods hanging outside. In the evening, the place was alive and the shopkeeper's senses were sharpened like a knife straight off the stone waiting like a cobra to strike the next victim that walked by. The scent of burning incense filled the air and the array of wares on display was a visual feast. They were waiting for tourists, bellies filled and satiated with alcohol to pass by and fall prey to their sales patter.

She bought some Egyptian festival fabric after some hard bargaining with the shopkeeper. She had plans to make a gazebo in her tiny back garden and was happy with her purchase. After stopping for a baby photo shoot several times (the Egyptians are a crazy photo and mobile obsessed nation and they adore children), she went back to the hotel and

99

relaxed by the pool. Today was her last day in Luxor, tomorrow she would fly back to Cairo for one last night and it was making her anxious.

Juliet was fine. She made it back to Cairo and sat in the taxi on a late Friday afternoon as it made its way from the airport around the ring road to her hotel which was in Giza. The traffic was horrendous and there were queues for petrol stations that stretched for miles. "Why is everyone queuing for petrol?" she asked her taxi driver.

"Since the military has been in control there has been a shortage of petrol Madam," he replied.

She sat in the back of the taxi in the Friday traffic and wondered if she would ever come to Egypt again. The political future of the country was uncertain but that was not the reason. Juliet wondered whether her love affair with the country was exhausted as it was so intertwined with Mark. She somehow doubted she would ever return and despite loving the country, she did not feel sad at that thought.

Two hours after leaving the airport, they finally made it to the hotel. Clara was exhausted. Juliet ordered room service and ordered a wakeup call from reception. She set her phone up with an alarm as a backup although she doubted she would sleep soundly that night. Her flight was leaving at 9am and she had to catch that flight. She had no money and would be in hot water if she didn't make it.

Juliet awoke to the alarm on her mobile and then the phone rang in the room. At least they had been reliable thought Juliet. She climbed her sorry little ass out of bed and made tea and looked at Clara lying asleep. She was thankful, she had a lot to do, a lot to prepare and pack before they left, and it would be easier if Clara slept. It was 4 am and the taxi was scheduled for 5.30am.She needed to cater for all eventualities and she knew that the taxi would take at least half an hour to get to the airport which would make it 6am, and then she needed to clear check-in, and passport control. It was cutting it fine but it was early morning. That was the problem when you hadn't any spare money, no credit cards, no one else to ask or to rely on if things went wrong, it was fraught with dangerous possibilities. Juliet put that to the back of her mind as she set about packing. She made Clara a bottle and packed her hand luggage with everything, and anything that Clara might need. After a shower and getting dressed and a final look around the room she woke Clara and gave her a bottle and got her dressed. Thankfully, Clara was not difficult. She phoned reception to ask for a porter. Thank God, she had chosen to do decent hotels. As she was on her own she couldn't have managed otherwise.

It was still dark but the taxi was waiting. Ham dilil eh, (praise be to God) thought Juliet. The taxi driver was grumpy, Juliet observed as he loaded the pram onto the roof rack. It may be an old second-hand pushchair but it was necessary thought Juliet, as she and Clara climbed into the back of the taxi. She had been expecting a bigger car and hoped the pushchair would be safe, she would have preferred it in the boot but it was on the roof rack.

He drove like a madman. There was no traffic on the road but he was manic. Was he cross with someone? Juliet thought. They went over speed bumps before they got to the ring road and he didn't see them, or he didn't care because he was going way to fast. Bang, Bump, Clang. Juliet saw the sunshade fly off over the back of the boot and land in the road, but she said nothing. What was a second-hand sunshade? She needed to get to the airport on time and she was a woman, what point was there in arguing with an overwrought taxi driver about a sunshade? Nothing, nothing at all, so she kept quiet. She wanted to get on the BA out of Cairo in one piece although with his driving, it was looking unlikely. Thankfully there were few cars on the road. She saw the sun creeping up over the horizon and clung onto Clara for dear life. There is no such thing as child seats in

Egypt and the way the taxi bloke was driving, Clara would be dead if they had an accident, of that Juliet was sure.

Finally they pulled up at the airport and the taxi driver unloaded the pushchair and Juliet's suitcase. A man came rushing up to them from outside of the airport, a young man, who obviously wanted to act as a porter for a tip. He looked friendly enough and Juliet didn't trust her taxi driver so she handed Clara to him whilst she assembled the pushchair. Her luggage was safely on the pavement and she got out her purse, to pay the taxi driver. She handed him the 70 EGP that they had agreed upon. He looked thoroughly pissed off. "What about my tip Madam?" he said in a stern voice. Juliet may have been intimidated had she been alone, but there were other vultures circling, namely the young man who was holding Clara. Juliet was bold "You drove like a madman on the way here with no regard to me or my child's safety, and you lost my sun canopy. You should think yourself lucky I am not going to report you." The young man nodded in agreement and started an argument with the taxi driver. Juliet plucked Clara from his arms, put her into the pushchair and marched into the airport, leaving them to argue but she had slipped the young man an Egyptian five-pound note. It sounds grand but it wasn't. It equated to 50p.

The morning's theatre was well behind her and soon enough, she found herself on the plane and she breathed a sigh of relief. They had made it. They had been to Egypt with very little money, her darling little daughter and herself and they had had a good time and now they were on their way home. After breakfast, she ordered herself two celebratory gins, tonic water, and a coca cola. The BA trolley dolly looked confused "I have never heard of gin and coca cola." She said "The coca cola is for after the gin and tonics," Juliet winked.

Chapter 12 - Home

She put the key in the front door and was relieved to be home. Alistair had met her at the coach stop to help with her luggage. She changed Clara and set off for Headington to get some groceries. When she arrived back home she started to unpack, and there was a knock on the door. A delivery man stood on the paved area outside her flat with a huge bouquet in his arms and he asked her to sign for them. She knew there was only one person they could be from and it wasn't Alex. She looked at the note, it said;

Happy Birthday, Juliet. Nigel x.

It was a nice surprise. She hadn't had flowers for years. Alex used to buy her a bunch of supermarket lilies when they were in the cottage but apart from that she hadn't had a bouquet delivered to her since Alistair was born 18 years ago. She messaged Nigel,

Thank you so much for the lovely flowers, Juliet.

She wondered how he had got her address. She hadn't given it to him.

It had quite made her day, the bouquet of flowers and she opened a bottle of wine to celebrate and sipped the chilled liquid as she admired her flowers and contemplated Nigel. He had money, he was essentially a nice person but no way did she fancy him. She knew he would want a relationship with her but she didn't want one with him. Anyway, no matter how much she vowed to have nothing to do with Alex again it was not going to be that easy and she knew it. Underneath it all she hoped that he would change, that he would come out of this fucked-upness and behave like a normal person. She wanted him to be a father to Clara. She had thought that having a child might help him overcome his problems but it didn't seem to be helping at the moment, and she knew her patience was wearing thin. He was chipping away at her love, little by little and if it carried on, then one day there would be nothing left.

She turned on her computer to look at her emails. She had promised Alex she would reply in full when she was home. She had at that time intended to give it to him with both barrels but when she read her emails, she held back. Alex had handed in his notice and he had written this email;

i am flying back to the uk on 18 april. i should have clara's money then or transfer it before then. i will try and find a birthday present for her from amazon or elsewhere by 11 april. do you have any ideas?

i hope to find accommodation in oxford for a couple of days, and that you will let me see my beautiful daughter.

i hope you'll forgive me for thoughtless things that i've said. the work situation has been the worst i have ever experienced. they don't want me to leave - but i know that my health will suffer if i stay

She had received a letter that day, stating that her operation was scheduled for the 27th of April and she knew she would be in the hospital for three days and she needed someone to look after Clara. This was an opportunity for Alex to step up to the plate. She had no one else she could ask, the situation was dire. She composed an email setting out her dilemma. She knew he was angling to stay at her flat and that was fine if he looked after Clara whilst she was in the hospital. She emailed him with her proposal. It was simple, he would have to look after Clara for two to three days whilst she was in the hospital and then for about a week after whilst she convalesced. Of course she would be on hand during her convalescence to advise and help but there was no doubting she needed another competent adult there, one who cared for Clara. But was he a competent adult? That was another question entirely.

He emailed back quickly with a definite yes, he could do what Juliet had asked. Juliet was relieved, she had so many worries, least of all how he would look after Clara. She was about to throw Alex in at the deep end as far as looking after a small child was concerned but she was his own flesh and blood. Surely, he would make sure that no ill befell her? Just to make certain Juliet wrote up a guide on how to care for Clara. She had a little over a week to get Alex up to scratch on his parenting skills. She thought and hoped that he would come through. After all, if he cared about Clara he would try. She made a stipulation in her email that he should not smoke weed. The last thing she wanted was to have a stoned man looking after Clara even if he was her father. He agreed.

In true Alex style he said he was stopping off in Istanbul for a few days holiday. He certainly indulged himself, thought Juliet but still he arrived on the 18th and as she expected he did not kiss or embrace her. She had told him that she didn't want a relationship with him and they were back to square one again. She was pleasant with him. He was there to do a job for Juliet. He was to look after Clara so Juliet would just have to not let him get to her.

"Istanbul was absolutely amazing," said Alex, "It is a pity you couldn't have joined me," he continued.

Juliet wanted to say something sarcastic but she bit her tongue. "Yes, I am sure I would have enjoyed it but it wouldn't have been much fun with Clara. A city break is not exactly suitable for towing around a one-year-old," Juliet replied, as diplomatically as she could. He was a father but he was not a parent and had no comprehension of the complexities and sacrifices it took when caring for a young child.

"I bought a couple of antique rugs, eventually for the place in France," he said, "I couldn't miss the opportunity, as I was in Istanbul. They were an absolute bargain."

Juliet picked up her ears on hearing this, an antique Persian rug was truly a sight to behold and Juliet had long coveted one but she had never had the money to buy.

"Oh, let's have a look then Alex," Juliet said excitedly. Alex gestured to a gaudy looking bag on wheels which appeared to be rather effeminate. It would have been too girly for Juliet to have considered using it. Still she was getting very excited about looking at its contents. It has to be said that Juliet had imagined a beautifully patterned rug with rich colours and of a decent size that would grace any normal sized sitting room rather handsomely so she was waiting with bated breath as he undid the zipper on the bag and got out the rug. Juliet was speechless. Rug! Rug! That was no rug! It was only big enough to put by the front door and it was ugly enough to only want to wipe your feet on it. It was a rather dull, dark red, with only one other colour as contrast and as for pattern, there was a very simplistic one but it was not like any Persian rugs she had seen. It was in fact, a prayer mat. Juliet knew that the instant he laid it out on her carpet.

"It is a genuine antique," Alex said, "the man in the shop said so," and he looked rather smug as he said it.

"Do you have a certificate of authentication?" Juliet asked tongue in cheek, for she knew he had been had.

"No, it had been in his family for years," said Alex, rather proudly, "He left the shop to get it for me."

Juliet had to stop herself from spitting out her wine. She swallowed hard and thankfully the urge to laugh was under control. "What do you think?" asked Alex proudly, expecting praise.

Juliet had to be careful in her reply so as not to offend, "well, it's certainly very old, you can see that," she said. What she meant was; it has been used thousands of times, not, it is an antique.

"How much do you think I paid for it?" said Alex. This was now becoming tortuous. What the hell could she say? 5 quid? Any more than that would have been daylight robbery but she knew he had paid much more. She herself would not have bought it at all. She sipped her wine in contemplation. She did not wish to offend him so she decided that she would say an outrageous sum and hoped he had paid far less, letting him think he had a bargain. "200 quid," she said. Alex went quiet and suddenly she knew he had paid more. "Well Alex, I have no idea how much these rugs cost, I am no expert, so I could be way off the mark. "How much did you pay?"

Alex paused and then said, "500 quid." What did he just say? 500 quid? Surely she had misheard him. Tight-fisted Alex had paid 500 quid for someone's old prayer mat. The bloke must have been laughing all afternoon and he is probably still telling the story of the sucker who came into his shop and paid 500 quid for his old prayer mat.

"Well," said Juliet rather seriously, "I can see that it is obviously a rare antique at that price." Alex looked relieved "I have bought another one like it, but he is sending it on to me," he said. Was there no end to his madness? Thought Juliet. God, he really had been taken for a mug.

"Oh Alex, you didn't pay for it did you?"

"Yes, I did" he replied.

"How can you be sure that he will send it on to you?" But of course at that price he would quite happily send Alex some other old prayer mat. After all, the bloke had made the sale of the century.

"Oh, I think he was genuine enough, I have no reason to doubt him." Juliet was gobsmacked, absolutely gobsmacked. Here was the man who didn't trust her an inch, yet he had allowed himself to be taken in conned and robbed of 1000 quid for two old prayer mats, one not yet in his possession. It just didn't make any sense. "Bill knows about these things, I will ask his advice," said Alex.

"Yes, I would," said Juliet. She knew exactly what Bill would say. Bill would tell him that he had been had good and proper.

Chapter 13- Troubled Waters

The days drifted by but Juliet had her eye on Alex. He slept in her bed, that was a given as there was no room for him to sleep elsewhere but they were strangers. Like an old married couple who co-existed but had nothing intimate to do with each other. She cooked, he slept, and when he was awake he sat in the lounge with his laptop on his knee. What was he doing? thought Juliet to herself.

He had done little to try and learn about how to care for Clara and Juliet was growing increasingly agitated. He was meant to stay for two to three weeks whilst Juliet convalesced but it was worrying Juliet. Clara had just learned to walk and she was exploring her new world. She had come close to knocking over Alex's hot coffee twice and despite Juliet's remonstrations, all he had said was, "we should have a shelf at four-foot-high around the room." This was disconcerting at best. He seemed to take no heed of Juliet's warnings. Did he not care for Clara? It would appear that he did not.

They had ventured into town together to buy a college tie for one of his former colleagues. Alex had said that he had been so kind to him that he thought he should do this for him. Juliet thought it was kind of Alex and indulged and helped him. Later that day they sat on the sofa together as usual and Alex had his laptop in his knee "What do you think of this?" he said, and handed Juliet his computer. She read an email he had composed. It said; "I am staying in Oxford until September and I can offer English language tuition if you are interested. Email me at this address." September? She hadn't said he could stay with her that long. She had said he could stay until she got well. How could he be so callous? He knew he couldn't stay here with her for five months. Her benefits would suffer and so would her ability to see Guy. She was angry to say the least but she said nothing. She now knew what his intentions were and that was enough. She would sit tight.

"Yes Alex, that sounds alright," was all she said. He had her over a barrel and both he and she knew that. But it didn't stop her worrying all the same.

Two days went by and he still didn't show the slightest sign of being able to look after Clara. "Alex," said Juliet "Have you looked at the manual I have written about looking after Clara? I am quite worried that you are not going to be able to do it. I know you love her and she is your daughter but I have enough on my plate with the surgery without worrying about you two, and I will not be here to help." Alex, didn't look up from his computer, "it will be alright Juliet, stop worrying," but she didn't. He had given her his old computer. It was not more than twelve months old and it was a high spec Dell but he had a new computer that had been delivered shortly after he had arrived and was busy with playing with it.

The problem was that Alex was utterly and completely self-absorbed. He was in his own little bubble. The problems of the past had faded entirely from his memory and now he was all about himself. He did not see or comprehend Juliet's anxieties. He seemed to care little about the surgery she was facing, indeed he had asked her nothing about it. It could have been as trivial as minor surgery for all he knew, he didn't ask and when Juliet broached the subject, he had a glazed look in his eyes. He wasn't in the room, he wasn't listening.

This did not help Juliet's anxieties and she asked him repeatedly about how he was going to look after Clara over the next few days. Her surgery was just over a week away and she was far from happy with the way Alex was approaching looking after Clara. He had given her no firm, or satisfactory answers.

Finally on Sunday, a week after he had arrived, things came to a head. Juliet cooked lunch and was sipping red wine. Whilst stirring the gravy, she had an epiphany. She was not happy and he could not be relied on. She would have it out with him after lunch.

They ate lunch and he returned to his usual space on the sofa. How she resented him occupying a space on her two-seater sofa. It was hers and he was an intruder, not a father, not a lover, and he was only here for himself. It all became very, very apparent. He was not going to look after Clara properly in her absence and the thing that worried Juliet the most, was not that he would neglect Clara because Alistair was there and he would not let that happen, but, if Clara made him angry because she was crying for Juliet, or was hungry or needed a cuddle. Alex would get very, very angry, in fact, she feared for Clara's safety.

All of a sudden, Juliet's fears, thoughts and anxieties were crystallised. There was no way she could leave Clara in Alex's care and go and have the operation. She would rather have a pathetic excuse for a vag for the rest of her life, than subject Clara to his care, wanting that it was. "Alex, I am worried that you are not going to be able to cope with Clara. You haven't read the manual and you have done little with Clara over the past week." She said. Alex barely looked up from his computer, "Oh, we will be ok," was all he said. "But Alex, that does little to allay my fears. What time does Clara go to bed? And what does she have to drink before she goes to bed? And what else do you do before she goes to bed?" Said Juliet worriedly. Alex didn't look up from his computer. "Oh, I am sure she will go to bed when she is ready and I will find something for her to drink," he said. "What about changing her nappy? And if you let her go to sleep when she wants, she will take all night. Children need a routine and proper sleep, otherwise you will have the devil to pay with her the next day. Alex, I haven't written the manual to be a dictatorial parent, I wrote it for you to make it as easy as possible for you and you have thoroughly and totally disregarded it."

Alex didn't look in the least like he had been listening to Juliet, "Have you seen this?" he said laughing pointing at his computer. Juliet's blood boiled. He wasn't listening to her, or taking this conversation seriously. Juliet snapped. She had had enough. "Look, Alex, you are not here to look after Clara, are you? You are here because you gave up your job and we are more convenient than your mother and you need a place to stay. I have tried my best with you but I doubt seriously you are up to the job of looking after Clara and she is my primary concern right now, so I want you to leave."

Suddenly Alex sprang into life. The words "I want to you to leave," resonated in his ears.

"What did you just say Juliet?" he asked.

So he hadn't been listening. Not properly. "I want you to leave and now," she added emphatically.

"But I can't," he said "I have no money. Juliet you have been drinking and this is all because you are drunk." Drunk! Drunk! How dare he, thought Juliet. She was not drunk. She had just enough Dutch courage to throw the bastard out. After everything she had been through, after Christmas and him letting her down over Egypt, she had finally come to her senses." I want you to go," she said "and now. You have taken my hospitality and my good nature and you have abused it. You are not interested in Clara, all you have done, is busied yourself with your new computer. I am very, very upset and I think you will not be able to handle Clara whilst I am in the hospital."

Instead of contradicting Juliet, he said nothing for a while and then said again, "I have no money."

Juliet was incensed. He had come here on a wing and a prayer and she had looked after him. He had spent his available money on a new computer and presents for his friends. He hadn't offered her a penny and he hadn't bought her so much as a bunch of flowers. He had sat on her sofa and let her cook and wash up, look after him and wash his clothes. Juliet was beginning to see red. She had no cash in her purse but she wanted him gone and now. She went to see Alistair who was in his room. She knew he had cash. "Can you lend me 35 quid to get rid of that wanker?" she said.

Alistair had heard all of what had been said between them and he had witnessed all of what Alex had failed to do over the past week. "I have 35 quid," said Alistair.

"Thank you, Alistair, you can have it back tomorrow when I go to the cash point," Alistair nodded. He knew how his mom was feeling. Juliet took the money and threw it at Alex. "You have half an hour to get your stuff together and get out" she said and walked out of the room and the flat. She went next door to her neighbours who she had never spoken to. She couldn't stay in the flat, he might talk her round and she couldn't have that. She had made up her mind. She was shaking like a leaf as she carried Clara out of the flat to her neighbours but it wasn't sexual excitement that made her shake, it was anger, pure anger.

Juliet's neighbours were surprised to see her, but they invited her and Clara in. It was calculating of her, but she knew he would try and sweet talk her, if she stayed in the flat and she was such a sucker. It was better if she removed herself whilst he left. She messaged Alistair. "Let me know when he has gone." It hadn't gone 45 minutes, and Alistair texted her to say that Alex had left. Juliet breathed a sigh of relief and excused herself from the neighbours and went back home. The flat seemed different. Happier and less repressed. He had cleared out, thank the lord. She gave Clara a bottle and settled her for bed. She didn't give a shit where Alex was, or what he was going to do. She had given him a chance and he had blown it and it had left her with a big headache in more ways than one and a really big problem but she would face that in the morning. For now she was happier than she had been in a long time.

The next morning, she texted Nigel and arranged to meet him for lunch at Café Bonjour, she had the £300 she owed him. The cheque of Alex's had cleared.

"I don't want the money back," said Nigel when she offered him the wad of cash. "I was glad to help you out, you need it more than I do."

Juliet was amazed, "Nigel, that is so generous of you, thank you so much."

"But I do want to you to come out to dinner with me soon," he said.

So that was it. Juliet knew he wanted more than friendship from her. What would it hurt to go out to dinner with him? "Ok Nigel, I will have dinner with you. Once I have recovered from my operation."

"What are you going to do about that?" said Nigel.

"Well Charlotte is going to ask her boss if she can have a few days off, to look after Clara whilst I am in hospital," and I shall just have to muddle along as best I can after by myself." Although Juliet had to admit to herself that she didn't know how she was going to manage.

"If there is anything I can do to help Juliet, then you only have to ask. I am only too happy to help," Nigel said and he put his hand on hers on the table and squeezed it gently. He was safe at least Juliet had to acknowledge that and he was secure, very secure.

Chapter 14 - Hospital

The day of the operation soon dawned and Juliet was very apprehensive. Charlotte dropped her off at the hospital. Juliet had told her to go back to the flat instead of waiting with her as there was no point, it was enough that Charlotte was going to look after Clara. Juliet had never left Clara with anyone else and she feared that Charlotte was not going to have an easy time of it and it worried her, but not as much as it would have worried her if Alex had been looking after Clara. She wouldn't let him look after a dog.

It was awful not being able to have a drink, or anything to eat. The worst was not being able to have even a sip of water. Juliet just hoped they wouldn't be too long in taking her down to the theatre as she wanted to get it over with as quickly as possible. Juliet had had surgery before but she still didn't look forward to it.

It was just after 10am when they came to get Juliet for theatre. She lay on the table in the ante-room next to the theatre, lying on her back in her gown with no pants on. She was cold and she could hear them next door finishing off the previous operation. She hoped she would wake up afterward and everything would be ok, she worried about Clara. The poor child had only her to rely on. Alex was not up to the job of being a parent. She lay there for a while alone and considered why she had been so in love with him, when he clearly didn't give a damn. Still she thought to herself, it didn't matter. She was doing this for herself. Suddenly, the anaesthetist and a couple of nurses came into the room. "We are just going to put a line into your hand," said the nurse, and the other one held her other hand. There was no turning back and she didn't exactly feel safe but she knew she had to have the surgery. The anaesthetist put the needle in the back of her hand and she felt the cold liquid travel up her arm, she would be unconscious in a minute and no sooner had she thought that thought, she was out cold.

Juliet came around. At first she didn't know where she was and she struggled to keep her eyes open. She was wearing an oxygen mask and she was very disorientated. It took her several minutes to ascertain what had happened, and where she was. The sun was shining and she was on the recovery ward although she was very groggy at first, and was finding it difficult to wake. A nurse came over to see how she was and checked her blood pressure. Juliet was very drowsy and she had a line in her arm, that she realised was feeding her painkillers intravenously. Her mouth was very dry. "Can I have a little water please?" Juliet said to the nurse and the nurse offered her a glass. It was wonderful, but Juliet sipped gently at first.

After an hour they transferred Juliet to the ward and they brought her a cup of tea. When she felt a little more human she messaged Charlotte to say that she was ok. A nurse came over to Juliet. "Shall we see if you can stand up?" said the nurse, and she took Juliet by the arm to help her up. Juliet gently swung her legs over the side of the bed. The anaesthetic was wearing off and Juliet's bottom was in pain. It felt very, very bruised as Juliet gingerly tried to stand. She managed it but not without a great deal of discomfort and she was relieved to be lying in bed again.

She lay there for a few hours and then dinner came. Juliet was famished but it hurt to sit on her bottom. Hunger overwhelmed her and she gently raised herself into a sitting position, or more accurately half reclining, so that she was not putting any weight directly on her bottom. She ate the meal and drank water, she had the thirst from hell and the pain was not good.

After dinner, the ward sister came around and drew the curtains. "I am going to take your catheter out and I want you to visit the bathroom to pee. Have you been drinking enough?" Juliet sighed, well that was bloody rich, they hadn't told her to keep drinking, it was a good job that Juliet had taken the initiative and drank a lot of water. But she was in a lot of pain. The ward sister said as much, "how is the pain?" Juliet looked her in the eye "Well it is not good, especially in the bottom region," quite frankly, she felt like she had been the victim of some horrendous sexual torture. "I have a solution for that," said the buxom black ward sister. "I have some pain-killing suppositories, if you would just lie on your side and relax, I can slip one in," Juliet was willing to try anything, she was in that much pain. So she did as the Sister requested and then she pulled her nightgown down and lay on her back closing her eyes and trying to relax.

Juliet didn't expect any visitors, she had no one who cared, apart from her children and she knew Charlotte would we be having a hard time with Clara. Charlotte was only 22 and it was a lot to ask her to look after Clara so Juliet had told her not to visit. Juliet was dosing as the visitors started to come in. She shut her eyes and then she heard a friendly voice. "Hello, Juliet. How are you?" It was Nigel.

How she wished he hadn't come, she felt like shit and not at all like being sociable. "I have seen better days," she said not opening her eyes.

"Can I get you anything Juliet?" he said. Juliet had to give it to him, he was sweet but Juliet was in pain and far from feeling sociable. Nigel for once sensed she was not in good spirits and reached out and held her hand. Juliet lay quietly for a while saying nothing and then she said "I am sorry Nigel, I am in a lot of pain at the moment.

"I understand, I just wanted to see you. I have bought you some chocolates."

"Thank you," Juliet said weakly.

She lay there with her eyes closed. "Nigel it is really lovely you came to visit me and I do appreciate it but I am very tired and in a lot of pain," She never even opened her eyes to look at the chocolates.

Nigel kissed her hand and then her cheek and said: "I will come and see you tomorrow, is there anything you want?" Juliet lay quietly, "I want nothing," she said "but thank you for coming, I am sorry I am not more sociable," And with that Nigel left.

Juliet dozed but the ward was a hive of activity, they had bought some young women in. An emergency and from what Juliet gleaned in her half-drugged haze, she knew it was serious. People buzzed about the young woman's bed. Juliet felt sorry for her, whatever it was she was in a bad way.

Juliet had the urge to pee. She carefully sat up. God it hurt, her bottom felt like she had been ganged raped, if that was what it felt like but she felt very, very much in pain. At least she could stand and she steadied herself on the bed head. After a few moments in an upright position, she felt able to take a few steps. She was ok. She was in a lot of pain but she was walking and she made her way slowly to the bathroom. She sat on the pedestal and to her horror, she couldn't pee. She tried to relax and still nothing. She got up from the toilet and turned on the tap in the hand basin letting the water run, but still nothing. It was agony, she wanted to pee but it wouldn't come. She sat on the toilet and thought about it. She tried to relax but she was worried, and then she reasoned with herself. She had been for a pee since the catheter had been removed, hadn't she? She was so drugged up, she couldn't remember. It was the pain from her vag repair that was stopping it. And the pain was overwhelming. She patted herself dry even though there was nothing to pat dry and made her way out of the bathroom to the desk where the ward sister sat. "I have a problem," Juliet said to the buxom black woman on the desk. "I know you have a lot to deal with at the moment but I can't seem to pee and I want to."

The ward sister looked at her. "Get into bed, I will come over." Soon enough the sister came over and drew the curtains around the bed. She had an ultrasound machine with her and she commanded Juliet to lie on her back. She put jelly on her stomach and glided the ultrasound scanner over her bladder area. "Your bladder is three-quarters full. I don't know why you can't have a pee. It is not full, but it is worrying," Juliet knew that health professionals didn't always say what they know.

"But is there a possible problem? What happens if I am not able to pee?" Juliet said, and then finally she got the answers she knew were the plain truth.

"Well it could be that your urethra has been damaged during the operation," Said the sister.

Suddenly Juliet realised what the implications were. "So, if I don't have a pee, what is the next step?" said Juliet. "Well," said the ward sister gravely, "you will have to have a catheter fitted."

Juliet was shocked, "for life?" she asked.

"Yes, for life, if the urethra has been damaged in the operation," the ward sister replied. The things they didn't tell you before the operation, thought Juliet but there was no way in hell that was going to happen to Juliet. She hadn't gone through all of this shit to be left half a woman.

"I will try again," said Juliet, and she did. She made her way to the bathroom and all in vain. She sat on the pedestal, and tried to pee but she couldn't. She cried, tears stinging her face and sat there and then she rationalised it. She couldn't pee because of the pain in her bottom. And then she formulated a plan.

She walked out of the bathroom slowly because of the pain, and up to the desk where the ward sister sat. "Hello," she said "look I know I am a pain in the arse but quite frankly I have one big pain in the arse going on right now and I think I know why I can't pee. It is because of my extreme bottom pain. I think if I have one of those painkilling bottom suppositories, then I might be able to go."

The ward sisters' face illuminated. She held up her hand for a high five "I think it is worth a go," she said and Juliet met her high five with her hand. So that is what they did and sure enough within half an hour after inserting the painkilling suppository Juliet had a pee, relieved that she didn't have to wear a catheter for the rest of her life.

She sank into bed and slept.

The next morning Juliet was still in pain but things looked rosier. She was holding her own and although far from well, she felt she was on the mend. She was taking codeine, paracetamol, and ibuprofen, and the pain was manageable. She slept a lot and awoke when it was lunchtime and ate a cottage pie. It wasn't the worlds best but it was food and she hadn't had to cook it. Then it was visiting time. Juliet had messaged Charlotte to ask how Clara was and had told her that she shouldn't bother visiting. It might cause Clara anxiety if she saw Juliet and no matter how much Juliet wanted to see Clara, she knew it was not very wise. Charlotte messaged back and had said that Clara was fine, and that she was glad to hear that Juliet was ok. Just like Charlotte, thought Juliet, she is probably going through hell but she wouldn't want to worry her mom.

But she had an unexpected visitor. It was Nigel. Although he had said he would come Juliet had forgotten all about it. Juliet felt embarrassed that she wasn't wearing makeup. He didn't care. He was kind to her, a kindness she had'nt know for a while. "I am sorry Nigel, I am not much company at the moment," she said. And then for the first time, she looked at the chocolates he had bought her yesterday. They were the best champagne truffles from Waitrose. He was a sweetie, really he was.

"Thank you Nigel for visiting me. I am sorry I didn't say so," He just looked at her, and said "You are truly beautiful, I hope you get better soon. I want to have dinner with you. When are you coming out?" and he put a magazine on the side table for Juliet. Juliet smiled weakly.

"Thank you for the magazine, I never buy them as I consider them to be a luxury I can't afford. As for coming out, I don't know Nigel, I feel like shite but I want to get out soon because Charlotte has had to look after Clara and it is costing her financially as well as mentally. I hope they say I can go home tomorrow, they did say it would only be three days."

"Well let me know if you need a lift and I will come and get you. I can come out of work. It is only five minutes away." "Thank you, Nigel, you are truly a gentleman," said Juliet. He kissed her lightly on the cheek and left.

The next day she felt a little better and wanted to go home. She was still on a lot of painkillers and she asked the nurse to prescribe some of the painkilling suppositories, once the doctor had said she could go home. She texted Nigel and he came and took her home. Juliet's prescription wasn't ready, but he said he would fetch it in the morning. When she got home, Nigel left quickly as he had to return to work. "Thank you, Nigel for all you have done," she said.

"No problem," he replied, "I will get your prescription tomorrow and bring it to you."

Clara was pleased to see her and so was Charlotte. The doctor had said not to lift anything and Charlotte was worried about her mother. "I will stay tonight Mom just to make sure you are ok." She was so thoughtful, but the next morning Juliet shooed her off in the nicest possible way. "You have done more than enough for me Charlotte, I cannot thank you enough. I know it wasn't easy."

Juliet was making slow progress, it had been over a week since the operation and she still wasn't feeling any better. She couldn't walk very far and the pain in her vag and her bottom was not lessening. She started to think it was not right and she phoned the doctors for an appointment. Perhaps she had an infection. There was no smell but she should have been feeling much better. It was her father's birthday party in a week and they all were going to travel up to the West Midlands for the occasion. The doctor said that she didn't appear to have an infection but, she took a swab. Bloody doctors thought Juliet and then remembered she had some antibiotic tablets in the cupboard. When Juliet had come back from Egypt she had a fearsome toothache. Fearing she might have an abscess that would prevent her operation she had visited the dentist and explained the situation. The dentists had prescribed antibiotics but low and behold the pain had disappeared that afternoon so Juliet had never taken the antibiotics. She decided to start taking them now. She couldn't wait for the tests of the swab to come back. Within two days Juliet started to feel better. So, she was right, she did have an infection. Five days after the visit to the doctors, they phoned her to say the test results had come back and she did indeed have an infection and there was a prescription ready for her to collect. Although still far from 100%, Juliet felt better and was able to do something without feeling in intense pain, and she didn't need the painkilling suppositories although she was still taking ibuprofen, and the occasional codeine.

Chapter 15   Recovery

It was a full month before Juliet was back to her old self. The consultant had said that although it was keyhole surgery it was still a major operation and Juliet should consider it important to take care of her recovery. But, she was relieved one sunny Sunday morning that she could take Clara out a walk in her pushchair without feeling any pain. She came home and started to finish staining the fence that Alistair had started six weeks ago. He had got bored and had not finished the staining. The world looked a sunnier place all of a sudden. Juliet was a doer not a couch potato and it had made her depressed when she found every physical activity an effort.

She had gone to her Dad's birthday party a week before with some effort. She had been living on painkillers and strong ones at that. She didn't relish going, it was her father's 75th birthday and all of her extended family would be there and it was the first major party since her mother had died. Truth be told she didn't like her extended family very much. They were sycophants, hangers-on. People who had been happy to live off her father's largesse but Juliet hadn't forgotten how they had deserted her mother at the hour when she had most needed visitors. Cowards, all of them, couldn't handle it when it got "sticky." But Juliet was expected to attend and although she was still not very well, she went.

They had received some unexpected good fortune. Although Alasdair had a car (that he could not drive, because he had not yet had the money to insure it) someone had rolled into the front of his parked car and he had been given a courtesy car whilst it was repaired. Juliet was the person who had insured the car in her name so she picked up a virtually brand-new Seat estate. It was just as well as besides Juliet,

Clara and Alistair, Alistair was bringing his friends, Adam and Roland. They all had fitted neatly into the car and it was a dream to drive.

Juliet was having good and bad days but she managed to drive all the way to Aston Burf easily enough. It was good for her to be out and about. She had spent the last three weeks cooped up with no one for company and Alex had gone very quiet on the email from since she had thrown him out. So much for caring about her. So much for loving her. Juliet knew he didn't give one jot about her and that hurt, but she wasn't even thinking about that now. She just had to get better. That was her major concern

The weekend had gone well but there were some old ghosts to contend with, least of all Phil. It was hard enough to keep it all together even at the party. Louise, (Phil's wife) had come up to her and said "I think you should say something Juliet,"

Juliet was horrified, she was in pain and not in the most sociable of moods, Chris, Katie's partner had persuaded her to put on a nice dress. Juliet couldn't be arsed, that was how much pain she was in. Where was her brother Lee? Couldn't he make the speech, after all, he had been his father's right-hand man for years? Or was it some sick joke of Louise's, to ask Juliet when she knew she was really unwell? Louise had always had it in for Juliet, it stemmed back thirty years and although Juliet did not give it a thought anymore, clearly Louise did. Juliet really couldn't be bothered with all of this shit. "Yes, Louise, I will say something," said Juliet. "She clinked the side of her glass and cleared her throat "Everyone I would just like to say a little something. I would like to wish my father a very happy 75th Birthday, and I hope you will all join me for his 90th, For he has a good many more years in him yet. Happy Birthday Dad and I look forward to seeing a good many more." Everyone cheered and Juliet felt relieved to be out of the spotlight, she felt absolutely rotten, and every step she took hurt. She was far from well although she never let the mask slip. Although those who really knew her, knew she was not herself.

But she had got through the weekend and the week after she had turned a corner. Nigel had texted her often to ask how she was, but she had kept him a bay. Of course Alex occupied her thoughts. No matter how badly he had treated her, she still loved him and he was Clara's father. She could not give up hope although she was severely pissed off with him, and his lack of care was quite unforgivable. True, she had turned him out on his ear but quite frankly he had deserved it. He had behaved appallingly over the last few months and the final straw had come when he had failed to prove that he could look after Clara adequately. But despite all of that she couldn't let him go. There was something that didn't sit right about it all.

And, then as if manna from heaven, she was given an answer to all of the mysteries.

It was mid-June and about 8pm in the evening. Juliet opened up the computer that Alex had given her, to log into her emails but she noticed a small icon at the right-hand corner of the screen. Alistair must have been using it to log onto Face Book something Juliet did not subscribe to and then she noticed it had Alex's name on it. She clicked onto the icon and his login appeared. Much to Juliet's surprise his computer logged straight into Alex's Face Book. The stupid shit had saved his passwords on the computer and had not changed them, despite Juliet asking him if he had removed all of his stuff from it.

Juliet had a field day. His Face Book page opened up in front of her and what Juliet saw was a revelation. There was no mention of Juliet although there was mention of Clara, Juliet was just "the mother of my child." The absolute bastard, he was presenting himself as someone who had nothing to do with her. There were no posts about Christmas, or the intention of going on holiday with her and Clara. He had presented himself as being totally single. Then she turned her attention to messaging and low and behold he had been messaging one of his female friends. An American woman named Dinah who he had met in Morocco and who was now married to some Englishman and living in Cambridge.

Juliet looked through the past messages. Her blood boiled. He represented Juliet as someone who had purposefully got herself pregnant to trap him. He had even laughed and said that Juliet was desperate for the money he gave her and that was a way of seeing Clara. She was outraged. She was fuming and went to the fridge for a bottle of wine. She continued reading and he was gaining sympathy from this woman. Then after a glass of wine, Juliet calmed down. She knew why he was representing the situation like this. He couldn't be honest about his feelings now could he? He knew he was fucked up, he knew he had fucked up, and he didn't want to make himself appear as though he was in any way to blame for the situation. But she was still angry that he was going around yet again presenting her as someone she was not. He was such a child. Just then a message popped up from Dinah "Hello Alex, how are you doing?" it said.

Juliet laughed to herself. I will have the bastard, she thought and she started to type a response to Dinah, as if she were Alex:

"Hi Dinah, I am a bit down to tell you the truth. I have really messed things up. I have been thinking about my past and the relationships I have had with women, and I know I am messed up. All I do is flit like a butterfly from one flower to the next. I can't commit to a relationship." She pressed send and then continued writing, she didn't want Dinah to suss out that she was not Alex. *"I have behaved really badly to Clara's mother, Juliet. I stayed with her last summer and asked her to marry me, but when she said that it was too*

complicated at the moment, I flipped. I came back at Christmas and she made such an effort, but I was just using her for somewhere to stay and to see Clara. I asked her to meet me in Egypt and then at the last minute I told her I wasn't going. She had already booked the tickets. After all that, she still allowed me to stay at her house. I was supposed to look after Clara, whilst she had an operation, and Juliet had written a manual for me to help me look after her as she is so young, but I didn't do anything and Juliet got worried and scared and threw me out. Now she doesn't want anything to do with me, I have messed up and I don't know what to do."

Juliet could see that Dinah was frantically typing a response, so she waited and sipped her wine.

"*Alex, you have done some pretty bad things, I am shocked. But I think you need to seek help, it is quite clear you have some issues mentally. I am sure you can mend things with Juliet if you try, she seems to have accommodated you so far. But please, go and get help with your issues. You sound as though you really need it. Dinah x*"

"*Thanks, Dinah, I feel a bit better now, I had better go, catch you another time, Alex x,*" wrote Juliet and closed down the message box.

The wanker she thought, he was at it again, going around giving her a bad press in order to make himself look better. The utter, utter wanker. Then she looked through Maher's past messages and what she found there, confirmed one of her darkest suspicions about Alex. They had been messaging each other like lovers. "*I miss you,*" was the theme on more than one message and Maher had even sent Alex an image of a red rose. It made her feel sick. She wasn't opposed to homosexuals or bisexuals, but to think she had slept with one was truly gut-wrenching.

She shut down his Face Book page. He would soon find out what she had done and he would change the password, of that she was sure but not before she had posted a post. *"I am truly sorry to all the women I have dated. I am messed up. It was not you, it was me."*

She opened up her emails and pressed compose, and wrote;

Alex

I know you have slept with another man. I no longer wish to keep your belongings at my house. I am not a storage facility and you have taken advantage and used me. You go around telling other people that I am manipulating you when it is quite clear you are the person who is doing the manipulating. You will not be welcome to stay here again. I won't prevent you from seeing Clara, but I am no longer willing to put you up here.

I shall package up your stuff and you have two weeks from today to get it collected. Send it now offers a good service and you can organise the collection of the parcel online. Let me know when they will collect. If I do not hear from you within two weeks of this email, your belongings will be taken to a charity shop.

Keep your communications to conveying factual information about seeing Clara.

Juliet

That was it. It was over. She wanted nothing more to do with him. But it hurt, it hurt deeply what he had been saying about her, and what hurt the most was that it was clear he had no feelings for her whatsoever. He had been using her. In his fucked-up way he thought that he had to have some kind of relationship with her, in order to see Clara. It was simply not true. Juliet would still let him see Clara although given his circumstances she had to admit that in order to see Clara it

128

would cost Alex money. Money which he did not want to spend. This compounded the depth of the hurt she felt. His proposal had been a foolish and childish act, to do what he considered to be the 'right thing'. He hadn't really done it because he had wanted to. Christmas had been a sham, He had shown her no affection. And when did he start having a relationship with Maher? It was all too confusing to contemplate. Despite the fact she had tried to protect herself from this hurt she was feeling, she was still feeling it all the same. All she had been through, had been for nothing. She wished she had not told him she had had his child but then she knew that was wrong. He had a right to know and for Clara. Juliet had to at least have tried. Well, she had and it was not going to work. She just had to face up to the fact that if he did love her once, he certainly didn't now and he was too messed up in the head. She drained her wine glass and went to bed. Still she thought to herself, he would have some explaining to do when he found out what she had done with his Face Book page. Serves him right, Juliet thought to herself as she climbed into bed and switched off the light

Chapter 16 -New Start?

Alex didn't respond, so Juliet took his clothes in his effeminate wheelie bag to the charity shop as promised. She had scanned all of his documents onto the computer and then posted them all to his mother. There was enough evidence there to give the Inland Revenue if he tried anymore threatening tactics. She hadn't heard from him but she knew it was only a matter of time and he would be very, very angry. Notwithstanding that he had been deceitful and manipulative and wholly responsible for Juliet's decision, he would not see it like that and he would be fuming. He was like a small child who liked to have his own way and he wasn't getting it anymore. He had given no consideration for Juliet's feelings, or her position. He cared nothing about her situation with Guy, a situation that he was partly responsible for and he appeared to care little for Clara. Juliet did not regret her decision.

Juliet saw Nigel twice a week at Café Bonjour. He was sweet, but he was growing impatient with Juliet. He wanted a relationship with her and although Juliet was holding him at a distance he wasn't giving up. "Juliet, you really need a break, just come out to dinner with me, we could go to Brasserie Blanc, I know you love it there."

Juliet sighed. She knew she was going to have to give in and now she had decided to get rid of Alex there was nothing stopping her. It might do me some good, she reasoned with herself, in any case it was only a meal. "Ok Nigel, I will ask Alistair if he will babysit Clara, he has a girlfriend now, and she seems like a sensible girl. I will let you know later. I will text you." Nigel beamed a big smile, and was pleased with his self.

Walking back to her flat, Juliet wondered if she had done the right thing, saying yes to Nigel. It was no good thinking about it, she could never have a serious relationship with him, or could she? He was kind and he had money and he adored her but she didn't love him. Was that such a bad thing? She thought to herself,and then shook herself from this reverie. Juliet Grosvenor do not even consider it, you are just feeling low and worthless because of Alex, she said to herself. He has given your confidence a bashing and that is why you are thinking this stuff about Nigel. However you could have a little fun with him. She thought to herself. She had warned Nigel she wasn't ready for a serious relationship, she had told him she was damaged goods but he hadn't been put off at all. So, she would go out to dinner with him and she may eventually even sleep with him. After all, she had to road test her new vag. She wanted to know what it felt like. Alex had a lot to answer for.

She texted Nigel later that evening and said:*"Yes, Nigel to dinner on Friday at Brasserie Blanc, looking forward to it."* Alistair said he and his girlfriend would babysit. She would be back by ten and there was no way they were having sex. She had asked Alistair to hang about so that there was no chance of her and Nigel being alone.

She opened up her emails everyday with trepidation expecting to see some vile email from Alex but to her surprise there were none. It was both a relief and a source of anxiety at the same time. What was going on in his head?

Friday came and she dolled herself up, not too much. She wore a black linen halter neck dress with a flared skirt and her little black patent ballet pumps with chiffon bows on them. She was still slim and she looked forward to a meal out. Nigel picked her up in his VW Golf. "Oh, Nigel, haven't you thought about getting a better car? She said.
"I hadn't thought about it," said Nigel.
"I bet your wife has bought a new car?" said Juliet.

"Oh, yes, she has," said Nigel "she has bought herself a Mercedes,"

Juliet laughed "I would love a Mercedes! You didn't think to buy one for yourself?" she added.

"No, I am happy with this car," he replied.

She settled herself into her seat, the sun was shining and it was a lovely evening .Even Juliet had to admit that it felt good to get out. Alex had never asked her if she had wanted to go out. Juliet had assumed that he was saving money for a place in France. A place that he had intimated would be theirs together, although Juliet completely doubted that now had ever been the case. He had just been stringing her along.

"You look gorgeous tonight Juliet," he said, "thank you for coming out."

Juliet smiled "Thank you for asking me," she said. They arrived and parked nearby and walked to the restaurant. Juliet was beginning to enjoy herself for once. They were shown to a lovely table for two. Although Juliet was tired and it was a little crowded, she was unused to going out. They ordered their meal, after perusing the menu and a bottle of wine. Juliet was tired and it had suddenly kicked in and she was beginning to regret her decision to come. "I am sorry Nigel, I hadn't realised how tired I am. I shouldn't have accepted your offer."

Nigel looked at her sympathetically. "Look, Juliet, I am really grateful you came out with me and it doesn't matter if you are tired, or you are not sparkling company. I know it must be really hard for you looking after Clara alone and I know I have pestered you to come out. I am so grateful you accepted. You have had so much to contend with, least of all Alex who has not been very kind at all. I can honestly say that I thought you two never stood a chance with the lack of money."

Juliet sat bolt upright in her seat. It was true what he had just said but even so she didn't like him talking about Alex like that. In the cottage it had been difficult, so difficult, that

132

most people wouldn't comprehend what they had gone through. Although Nigel had designs on her, she decided to pass no comment on Alex. Instead she said "Yes, it is hard being a single parent and especially at my age Nigel and I am still recovering from the operation. The surgeon said it would take three months to get over and it has only been five weeks.

Nigel looked concerned, "Oh, I didn't realise" he said. "Is everything all right, down there?"

He added. Juliet looked at him "Well it seems to be ok, but I have no idea, I have not road tested it and I don't know when I can," and she burst into tears. Juliet didn't know why, whether it was tiredness or hormones, or just being out for the evening, or even being with another man but she was tearful. She had gone through a lot and Alex had fucked her up mentally again. She had only had the operation because of what he had said and then he had gone and deserted her and here she was trying to be normal, on an evening out with Nigel.

She wiped her tears away and tried to compose herself. "Sorry Nigel," she said.

Nigel looked bemused. "Look Juliet, if you want me to take you home now, then I will, but please have something to eat first. I am sorry. I shouldn't have pressed you to come out." Juliet sniffed and took a sip of her wine. "I will be alright in a minute Nigel. Sorry, something must have touched a nerve and you are very kind."

Juliet composed herself and reminded herself that Nigel had good intentions. They ate their meal and she was sweetness and light, even though, inside she was hurting emotionally. When they had drunk their coffees, Nigel turned to Juliet, "I want to buy you a car."

Juliet nearly choked on her coffee, "Nigel that is too much."

"Juliet, it won't be a new car but you have suffered so much and you are so tired, a car would help you. I am happy to spend up to three thousand pounds,"

Juliet looked at him in disbelief. What would she have to do for this?

He read her mind and said, "Juliet, it is a gift, even if you don't want a relationship with me, I want to do this for you." Juliet sat quietly for a moment, and then said: "I cannot accept this Nigel."

"Why not?" He said. I have just told you it is a gift. I never thought I would see you again and I owe my divorce to you. If it hadn't been for you, I would still be with Jackie and I am far happier now that we are having a divorce. You were right I should have done it a long time ago and now I want to make you happy and I think a car will make you happy. If nothing else, it will lessen your burdens." Juliet did not know what to say for once. "Look Juliet sleep on it and have a look around for a car you like if you want. Let me know what you have decided to do in a couple of days." Juliet just said "ok", but, she was still not sure in her mind about the car.

Nigel was a gentleman and he didn't make a move on Juliet when he dropped her off. He kissed her on the cheek, and told her it had been a lovely evening. It was a relief that Nigel had been so kind and not made a grab for her. And the car was a lovely gesture but she just didn't know what to think about it. There is no such thing as a free lunch and Juliet knew that. However, the next morning when she woke, she thought about having a car and all the advantages it would bring.

The next day, as she was walking to Headington, there was a used car lot adjacent to the roundabout and there in amongst the other cars was a Mercedes convertible, for £2995. Juliet fell in love with it but she would have to ask Alistair what he thought about that model and she would need to do a bit more research before she decided. But she liked the look if it and it gave her a thrill to think that she might own such a car. If Nigel was trying to woo her, then he was going about it the right way.

It was the weekend and for Juliet that meant she would indulge herself in a film late Saturday afternoon, although it was a lovely day and Juliet thought once more about owning a car again. It would mean that she could go out and further afield than she had of late. She could even go up to the Midlands and see her daughters.

Guy and Mark would be down for Sunday lunch tomorrow and she always looked forward to seeing Guy. They came twice a week and Mark still wouldn't let her have him on his own but Juliet thought that was because Mark was lonely and he liked the company. He still hadn't given up drinking, although he didn't seem to get completely and utterly pissed in front of Juliet and he genuinely cared about Guy. And although Guy missed his mom for Juliet the pain of losing him didn't lessen.

Juliet had a lovely afternoon searching for cars on the internet and the more she looked, the more she wanted one. Nigel knew what he was doing and he texted her that evening;

"Played cricket today. Have you had a think about the car? xxx"

Juliet smiled to herself and replied;

"Yes, I think I have found one I like. I have Guy coming for lunch tomorrow, but we could go and have a look at it on Monday if you are sure about this. Xxx"

"Yes, I am positive" Nigel replied.

Chapter 17 – A Car

Juliet went and got the car. She was thrilled. It was a car after all and it was lovely there was no denying that but what about the strings attached?

At the garage Nigel had put the registration document in her name. It felt good to own a car again. She thought about the car she had owned when she was married to Mark. He had written it off in a flood and when they had bought another car, she had foolishly let him register it in his name, even though she had half shares and ultimately she had come off with nothing. Losing again? When would she learn?

But this car was hers and although it was old, it was a Mercedes. She put the car seat in the back of the car, and strapped Clara in it. She gingerly drove out of the garage. She did not want to crash her pride and joy, for now, it was. Nigel followed behind. It took a while for her to get used to it, at least twenty miles but as soon as they were on the motorway, she put her foot down and left him behind in his golf. He had no idea. It was thoroughly sad. He was kind gentle and generous but he was not the man for Juliet and she knew it. She felt guilty about the car but men had done nothing but be unkind to her even Nigel when he had refused to act as guarantor a couple of years ago.

Life passed by in much the same way as it had done for the next few weeks.

It was the middle of July when she received an email from Alex, as she knew she would. Every day she had dreaded opening up her emails to find one there from him and finally there it was.

Juliet

I am coming to Oxford on the 26th July and I want to see Clara. I also want to collect my belongings I left at your flat. However, I do not wish to come to the flat. I will meet you in Oxford, I shall be there at 9,30 at the Costa Coffee in the Clarendon Centre. Bring my belongings with you. If you do not agree to this I shall contact the DWP and tell them you have been receiving maintenance from me and not declaring it.

Alex

Juliet was angry. How dare he lay the law down to her. She got up from her chair and poured herself a glass of wine. She was shaking with anger. Why did he have to be so hostile? Didn't he ever consider for once that this was all of his doing? She hadn't received anymore maintenance since he had given up his job. Did he have no ability to self-reflect? Clearly he did not. She knew he was mentally ill but he refused to take any of the blame for the situation his self. She rolled a cigarette and lit it, drawing on it deeply in the garden, blowing the smoke into the night sky, muttering to herself under her breath. After five minutes she had calmed down sufficiently and went back inside and back to the computer. She sat down and composed an email to him.

Alex

Yes, we shall meet you at the Costa Coffee on the 26th July at 9.30.

As for your belongings, I sent you an email months ago telling you to arrange a collection for them, (I will forward the email onto you again), and received no response. I also sent a second email and still received no response, so I did as I said I would, and took them to the Charity Shop. I can't imagine they were of much use to you as you would have arranged for their collection.

As for your threats, I scanned all of your bank statements, building society books etc, before sending them to your mothers. I am sure the inland revenue would be delighted to hear that you were not out of the country for the required time last year to avoid paying tax and would be able to issue you with a bill. So please stop threatening me. I have said you can see Clara.

Juliet

She pressed send. He really was tiresome.

She told Nigel that she was going to meet Alex the next time they met. "Juliet, I wish you wouldn't go," he said to her over lunch at Café Bonjour.

"I have to Nigel, it is only right, he is Clara's father. Anyway, I don't think he will bother me again after this meeting at least not for a long time. It is too costly for him to travel here by train and he is tight with his money."

Nigel sighed "But Juliet, I am worried for you. He is volatile."

"Nigel, it is OK, honestly, we will be in the centre of town and there will be a lot of people about, he won't make a scene and if he does we will be quite safe."

The morning of the 26th arrived, and Juliet was not looking forward to it one little bit. Although she didn't admit it to Nigel, she was scared of Alex and especially worried about Clara but she put this thought to the back of her mind as irrational. It was because of what had happened with Guy that she was so worried but Alex wouldn't snatch Clara. For a start off he was probably living with his mother, he had no house of his own and he definitely wouldn't have any money. He was inherently lazy and looking after a small child was something he would not wish to do but it didn't stop her worrying.

She got off the bus in the centre of town and made her way to the Clarendon Centre. She was going to be reasonable she had decided. That was the correct thing to do. She approached the Costa Coffee and saw Alex sitting in the corner. He looked rough. His hair had been cut too short, and it made his face look stern and angular. He had put on weight and he was not wearing his glasses. She pushed Clara's pushchair inside the cafe. Alex saw her approaching, but he didn't look at her.

"Hello Alex," said Juliet.

Alex didn't reply, or look at Juliet. "Hello Clara," he said, but Clara took no notice of him and seemed not to be aware of who he was or to recognise him. It's strange but small children are quite fickle with their affections and it was as though Clara knew who he was but was annoyed about his absence or was it the aura of hostility that was radiating from Alex towards Juliet? This time however Juliet made no attempt to bridge the gap between Alex and Clara or to make excuses for Clara.

Seeing that Alex still had a lot of coffee left she said: "I am going to get a coffee while you two get acquainted." She went up to the counter, knowing that if he was to leave, he would have to pass her to do so. She watched Alex and Clara out of the corner of her eye. He was just sat there staring out of the window. Juliet actually felt sorry for him. He was so stupid. How did he think Clara would have any recollection of him let alone any affection.

She took her coffee and went and sat down at the table.

"How are you Alex?" she asked genuinely and in a soft tone, for he didn't look as though he was having the best of times.

Alex did not answer her question, "how could you throw all my things away?"

139

Juliet was surprised by this, "I gave you fair warning Alex and you never replied to my emails. And, don't tell me you didn't see them, because I know what you are like about your emails, you are fastidious."

He still didn't look at her and then he spoke: "there was a T-shirt in there that my students had given to me."

Juliet could feel her anger rising. "Well, I am sorry Alex, but you never responded to my email. Anyway what about that coat I bought you for Christmas? The one you gave away to your cleaner. I felt very upset about that, it cost me 45 quid from TK Maxx."

"It was too small" was his response.

You got too fat for it or did you give it to your lover? thought Juliet to herself. He was cold and hostile and this was going to be the day from hell, Juliet just knew it. She was walking on eggshells again.

They finished their coffees in silence. "Shall we go for a walk around the University Park?" said Juliet. Although he didn't want to go to her flat, it was not easy trying to have a sensible conversation with someone out in the open air in the centre of Oxford and they couldn't very well walk around the shops all day. Again, Alex didn't reply, he just got up from his seat in a clumsy manner and pushed the chair noisily and aggressively under the table.

They left Costa Coffee and walked out of the Clarendon Centre and along St Giles. The sun was shining although there was a cold wind blowing. Alex marched on at such a pace that Juliet was struggling to keep up with him. He was angry and she knew it. How dare he be angry with her? He had spoilt it all, he had not fulfilled promises. Juliet was growing impatient with his childishness.

"Look, Alex slow down a little will you? We can do this the easy way and we can be civil with each other, or we can do this the hard way and carry on with this hostility. It makes no odds to me." Alex did not reply. He was in no mood for

140

being civil. They walked along in silence, although his pace did slow a little. They walked into the University Park and traversed the gravel path that circled the park. It wasn't crowded in here and the throngs of tourists in St Giles were left behind and they were quite alone. Alex still did not speak.

"Let's sit on this bench a while so you can talk to Clara," said Juliet. She was desperate to break the icy silence that was shrouding them. So they sat down and Juliet faced the pushchair towards Alex so that he could see Clara. The sun was warm on Juliet's face and she prayed he would stop being so hostile. Alex reached out to Clara but she did not respond to him but instead looked at Juliet for comfort and stretched her arms out towards her.

"She doesn't even recognis eme," said Alex.

Juliet felt sorry for him and said quietly "what do you expect Alex? She has hardly seen you, she is very young and what matters to her is safety and comfort and being fed."

Still Alex did not turn to look at Juliet. "Well, you turned me out of your flat. This is all your doing Juliet."

Juliet tried to remain calm. "Now hang on a minute Alex," she said "you came and visited us at Christmas and you slept your way through the days and were awake at night. You hardly spent any time with Clara. And then you stood us up when we were supposed to have a holiday in Egypt. What was that all about? Just who were you sleeping with?" But Alex said nothing. Juliet continued "and then you were supposed to look after Clara but you did nothing about it. I was worried sick about what would happen when I was in the hospital. You hadn't got the first idea about how to look after her."

"You threw away that t-shirt," Alex said loudly and angrily for the second time that morning.

"Oh God Alex, is that all you are concerned about? a bloody cheap t-shirt that your students had signed. What,

141

were you having a homosexual affair with one of them? I logged into your Face Book page remember. I saw the messages between you and Maher. The red rose. And what about the ice cream in bed in a morning that Maher brought you? Is he why you cancelled the holiday?" Juliet's patience had ran out and she was angry. All the frustrations and hurt came tumbling out of her mouth in a stream of venom.

Alex stood up and said, "no, I was not having an affair with Maher. But if you must know, I slept with my female boss." And he stood up. "I wish you were dead." He shouted. How childish, how bloody childish.

Juliet was fuming, absolutely fuming. After how he had gone on about her supposed infidelity, when she had done nothing and now he was being hypocritical and saying he had slept with someone else. And on top of that he had cancelled a holiday with her and Clara at the last minute. It really was too much.

But as usual in true Alex style he threw up a smokescreen and turned it onto Juliet. "You got yourself pregnant to trap me, and it hasn't worked. I don't suppose you took the computer I gave you to the charity shop, did you? You will get no more maintenance from me."

The steam was literally coming out of Juliet's ears, she was so angry. "How fucking dare you say I got pregnant to trap you? I didn't tell you until after she was born. I moved out. Surely I would have come back if that had been my plan. I turned your proposal down if you remember Alex. And I have never asked for maintenance. But I suppose that is a convenient excuse because you are out of work. All of this you have brought on yourself, so don't turn it onto me. You have made no effort with your daughter, and you expect her to be all smiles and 'daddy' when you see her. You are a stranger to her." And with that Alex marched away up the path.

Juliet followed him. She couldn't help herself. She wanted him to see sense. But as they walked she realised it was no use. He wasn't going to change. He was damaged, damaged beyond belief, as Marieke had said in her letter. Juliet had been a fool.

They walked back into the town, thoughts running through Juliet's head. "I have to get a sandwich," said Alex.

"How long are you going to be?" asked Juliet. "It is Clara's lunchtime, and then she will need a nap." Juliet was beginning to see the futility of all of this. The situation was not going to improve.

"I don't know," said Alex.

"Well, phone me when you are done," said Juliet.

"But I haven't got any credit on my phone," said Alex. Well that was him all over, stupid is as stupid does. He never had any credit. Juliet shot Alex a withering look of contempt, "well that is not my problem, is it now Alex?" Alex looked at her for the first time all morning, and she could see the anger in his eyes although they seemed far away, somewhere else. "Does that mean you are not going to wait?" He said.

"I see little point in continuing this Alex. You are not being co-operative and you haven't changed. Nothing is your fault is it Alex?" and with that, she walked away towards the centre of town and the bus stop.

Thankfully the bus came quickly and she got on. She was shaking with anger and fear and just wanted to get home. She hoped to God he wasn't going to turn up at the flat. She got home and locked the door behind her. She gave Clara her lunch and put her down for her nap. She never, ever wanted anything to do with Alex again, of that she was sure.

Chapter 18 – Decisions

In the days that followed, Juliet played that day over and over again in her mind. Everything he had said, his admission about sleeping with his boss. The odd thing was, she wasn't even jealous. She seriously doubted what he had said was true. After all the times in the cottage when he had driven her mad refusing to believe what she had said, calling her a liar when she had told the truth, she now realised it was because he was a serial liar himself. It was 'projection', as they call it in psychology terms. He told lies when the truth became inconvenient. Thinking back on it he had said he had been unfaithful to Bernadette. And why was he so upset about that T-shirt his students had given him? the one that she had thrown away. He had mentioned it twice that day and was clearly angry about it. He must have been having some kind of relationship, with either a student or with Maher (perhaps Maher had signed the T-shirt. She hadn't bothered looking). And saying that he had slept with his female boss was a cover-up. He had said she was vile in an earlier email. He had made it up, to draw the heat away from the truth.

Julie's head ached with thinking about it all. There was no point she finally thought to herself one morning. No point at all. Just move on with your life Juliet. You have tried your best and done it to death. At least, Clara will not be able to say that you didn't try. Juliet would keep all of the emails to show her when she was older if she was curious about her father.

There was another pressing issue. Nigel Baker. Juliet had been reluctant to sleep with him whilst she still held out hope for Alex. But now, now there was nothing holding her back. She didn't fancy Nigel, of course but she had to road test her new vag. She had hoped it would have been with Alex, but that would never be now and she knew it. They were done, finished.

She messaged Nigel.

Hi Nigel

Lunch today?

Juliet

It didn't take long before Nigel replied and agreed. They met up twice a week for lunch and it hadn't changed. Nigel's divorce would soon be made absolute and Juliet knew he was eager to have a relationship with Juliet. In short he wanted a future with her. Juliet had not encouraged him in this it has to be said. In fact she had done her best to put him off her. She had told him that she had been badly scarred by the mental abuse of her marriage and then by her relationship with Alex. The truth was she doubted if she would ever get over Alex. He had been the love of her life and she knew it. She knew that she would never love anyone like she had loved Alex.

But Juliet had thought about the possibility of a relationship with Nigel. He had money. He was kind. He was reliable. He had no children of his own so he would love Clara like a father. But he was also boring. Juliet did not fancy him. He was not the sharpest tool in the box and he made for uninteresting company. No matter how hard Juliet tried to convince herself that it made for a sensible choice to be with Nigel she simply just couldn't face it.

Nigel was overjoyed when he heard all about what had gone on when Juliet had met up with Alex a few days before. He had been especially pleased when she had told him that she never wanted to have anything to do with Alex again.

"Well, now that you feel like that, how about coming out with me again?" he said to Juliet.

"Oh, Nigel, I am not sure. I know you want to go to bed with me but quite frankly I am not sure if I am ready yet." Although Juliet knew that it was Nigel she was not ready for. If Alex had swooned in and begged for forgiveness, she would be putty in his hands and whipping off her knickers at the next available opportunity. She admonished herself privately for thinking like this. She had to get over him and perhaps going to bed with Nigel might help her to do that.

"OK, Nigel, let's go out again." But she did not want to let him spend the night with her. That was a bridge too far for Juliet. If it all went horribly wrong she could blame it on the operation. That was her let out clause and in actual fact, it might be true. She had no idea what sex would be like now that she had been repaired. The scar on the inside of her vagina was still hard as it was still relatively new.

They went to Brasserie Blanc that Friday. It was a hot summer night and Juliet wore the black linen halter neck dress with a full skirt again. It was quite 1950's but it was classy and sexy at the same time. She liked her shoulders. Not having an ample bosom,she had to make do with nice shoulders, so she tried to make the most of them. On her feet she wore black patent ballet pumps with chiffon bows. It was the same outfit as before but he wouldn't notice, men don't.

It was still warm and light, as they parked in Jericho. The swallows were making their whooping noises, as they darted between buildings in the dying day. How Juliet loved the sound of swallows, how they were so entwined with Summer. Nigel took her arm as they walked along the pavement to Brasserie Blanc, the last rays of the sun dipping behind the tops of the terraced houses.

Raymond Blanc's restaurant was always a delight for Juliet. It was the only thing she loved about Oxford anymore. Everything else had been a novelty that had long since died. The large floor length windows were opened onto the pavement for the diners to enjoy the mid summer evening. As they entered the restaurant Juliet was greeted by mouth-watering aromas. The Maître d' took their names, and a young waiter showed them to their table. The waiters! Raymond knew what he was doing. He always employed handsome young French men to wait on the tables. They were attentive and polite and very sexy and they were a treat for Juliet in themselves.

They started with glasses of Champagne. Juliet needed it. She tried not to think of sex with Nigel and stay relaxed but she was not looking forward to it. He was a complete novice. He had minimum experience with women and he was quite frankly shit in bed. From her few experiences of going to bed with him a couple of years ago she knew if she played it right, it would be over within minutes.

The first time she had slept with Nigel she had been very drunk. Usually being drunk equated to piss poor performance between the sheets but Nigel had loved every minute of it. Juliet cringed and recoiled with horror when she thought of it but Nigel had thought about it differently. Nigel's wife had been frumpy and dowdy, not at all like Juliet. She was the sort of woman who wore a flannelette nightie to bed. When Juliet had turned up with stockings and suspenders it had literally blown Nigel's mind and Nigel's wife had never given him fellatio. In fact he had never had fellatio until Juliet. It was like going from chip shop roe to caviar overnight. Juliet had been careful to wear suspenders tonight. She wanted the experience over with quickly.

They ate their meal which went by far too quickly for Juliet's liking and they travelled back to her flat in his car.

147

Once they were home, Alistair went out and Juliet and Nigel were left alone. Clara was sound asleep.

"Juliet," said Nigel, "you know I want a relationship with you and Clara needs a father. We could have another child. I have always wanted a child of my own."

Juliet recoiled in horror inside on hearing these words. Not Nigel, she could not see a future with Nigel. He wasn't sensitive enough for her. She had thought about it and yes, she would never want for anything. She would never have to worry about paying the bills or how she was going to put food on the table. But she wouldn't be happy and that was the most important thing in the world to Juliet, to be happy. But he had been so kind to her. She couldn't kill his hopes just like that. "Nigel, you are very kind to me and I am really grateful for your friendship and kindness but I am not sure that it would work out between us."

He looked crushed "But, but, I love you Juliet."

"Nigel, I know you love me in your way and believe me I want to love you but I am not sure I can. Alex has devastated me. I was on the floor already and he just finished me off. I feel let down and you have to admit you let me down yourself by not being a guarantor. I couldn't understand why you did that."

He looked guilty now. "Juliet, I am sorry about that I just thought that I would have to pick up the bill if you didn't pay your rent."

"But Nigel, you knew I was paying £950 for that house I lived in with Mark and had been for years, why would I have not paid the rent? It would have saved my life. But in the end I went off with Alex so it didn't matter. But I trusted you and I trusted Alex and I have been massively let down. It is my own fault really, I know that. For a start I knew it was just lust with you and I shouldn't have trusted you. You were married. And, I shouldn't have trusted Alex but I did, and look where it has all got me." She sighed.

"But I am not married anymore." He said.

"I know that Nigel and I know you think that you want me but it is not easy to love me. I have been incredibly damaged by it all and then you say you want another child. Well, I don't think I can have one. I am going through the menopause. My periods are scanty and I am displaying the symptoms. The surgeon did warn me that it may happen. And I really don't want any more children. I still haven't sorted out proper access with Guy. It is all such a mess."

Nigel sighed. He wasn't going to give up that easy. "Ok, Juliet, I am listening and I understand but I won't give up. I will give you time and space if that is what you want. But I would like to buy you a ring as a symbol of my faith and I will hope you feel able to love me in the future. It is too soon after Alex I appreciate that but please don't dismiss me straight away."

Juliet was backed into a corner. What could she say but ok? She didn't want to lose him as a friend and she didn't want to hurt him. Perhaps he would grow out of this infatuation after a while. "OK Nigel, if that is what you want. Now, are we going to bed?" His face lit up like a Christmas Tree.

It was over as quickly as she had expected it would be. He was like a small excited boy. Her vag had been alright, she could feel the scar tissue though and she had to use lubricant. Nigel certainly didn't have any complaints. He told her he loved her and she felt absolutely rotten for not being able to say it back but there was no point in lying to him was there? She had felt nothing. No desire, no lust, no emotional response, just empty coldness. It was as if it wasn't her who was naked in bed with him, just her shell, her emotionless body.

He put on his clothes and bid her goodnight. "I shall pick you up tomorrow and we shall go into town and the jewellers" he said, "you can pick your own ring." She shut the door and went to bed. She felt no excitement about the ring. She wished he wouldn't have said he wanted to get her one but she had to go along with it all. After all, she might in time love him. But she doubted it, she severely doubted it.

The next day they went to town. Juliet took Nigel to the antique jewellery shop on The High and picked out an old rose cut diamond solitaire mounted in platinum. It had a slightly yellow tinge to it and it wasn't a perfect diamond, not like the ones you buy today but it was pretty enough and it looked huge on her finger. It was one and a third carat and cost 3 grand. Juliet fell in love with it for its own sake. It had absolutely nothing to do with the way she felt about Nigel.

Chapter 19 – The Unexpected Happens

It was August and Charlotte came to stay for the weekend. Juliet thought it was odd as she hadn't seen her for months. She had a boyfriend and they had been going out for ten months. He absolutely doted on her. Juliet doubted whether this would be good for Charlotte in the long run but she had said nothing, and now out of the blue Charlotte was coming for the weekend. She was arriving that Friday evening. Juliet knew there was something amiss but she was glad she didn't have to see Nigel that weekend and she breathed a sigh of relief as she opened the bottle of wine and poured a glass. She was standing in the kitchen and the light was bouncing off her diamond ring. It was a beautiful ring, she had to admit it, shame it didn't have the emotional attachment it was supposed to.

Around the corner came Charlotte, smiles and waving to her mother through the window. Juliet ran to the door "How lovely to see you, darling. I must say this is a pleasant surprise. You have saved my bacon this weekend. I won't have to see Nigel. Hoorah!" and they both let out peals of laughter.

"Oh Mom thanks for the compliment." Said Charlotte.

"Look darling, you know I love to see you, don't be silly. But it is an added bonus to have an excuse not to see Nigel." And they both laughed again. "Come on let me get you a glass of wine. Clara is in bed. We can have a good old gossip. I have brought us ready made curries from Waitrose." Juliet poured another glass of wine.

"Oh Mom, let me see the ring!" exclaimed Charlotte, as the light bounced off the diamond adorning Juliet's finger. "Oh Mom I say, that is huge and it is beautiful!"

"Isn't it just?" said Juliet, and she twirled her finger so the light played with the stone even more, bouncing light rays over the walls of the room.

They sat down on the sofa, gentle music playing on the CD player. "Well, come on, tell your mother. What is this all about?"

Charlotte took a deep breath. "I have split up with Chris." Juliet wasn't at all surprised and she took a sip of her wine. "That doesn't surprise me. He spoils you and it is no good for you."

"Yes Mom and he is so clingy, I can't cope with it." Juliet nodded, and listened to her daughter. She was too good for him, and he was shorter than her. "But Mom, we were going on holiday to Cuba next month remember? We booked it up in January and we can't cancel, we won't get our money back and I really want to go but not with him. Could you come? You could buy Chris's ticket from him and change the name. Clara wouldn't cost anything as she is not yet two. What do you say?"

Juliet laughed, "and where do you think I am going to get the money from for this young lady?" she said.

"Why Nigel of course," replied Charlotte. "He is crazy about you mom and he has pots of money."

Juliet laughed. The young weren't so concerned as she was about such things but after another glass of wine she felt bold and phoned Nigel and explained the situation. "I can't let her go on her own now, can I Nigel?" said Juliet down the telephone, "she is so young and pretty she wouldn't be safe and she is determined she wants to go." Nigel was sympathetic and he agreed. In any case, it was so late Juliet could offer Chris a lesser sum for his share of the holiday, they were slashing the price of the holidays now anyway, Juliet knew, she had looked on the internet.

Chris agreed to take £850 instead of the £1200 he had paid. The bonus was that he had already paid for a bottle of

Champagne for the flight out. Juliet and Charlotte toasted their forthcoming holiday.

The next weekend, Juliet had to travel up to the West Midlands to go to the travel agents to change the name on the ticket and give Chris the money. He had phoned Juliet every night that week, pleading with her over Charlotte. Juliet had really felt for him but he was his own worst enemy. Juliet had told him not to text Charlotte in the hope that she may be overcome with remorse and change her mind (although Juliet didn't think she would).Only to find from Charlotte the next day, that he had not listened to a word of advice and had been pleading by text every night for Charlotte to go on holiday with him. Finally after a two-hour talk with Juliet, he came to the conclusion, that going on holiday was a bad idea much to Juliet's relief as she was now looking forward to a two-week holiday in Cuba with Charlotte and Clara.

She had decided to combine it with seeing her Dad. He would be at his little piece of God's green earth, by the River Severn in his caravan. All the old members of Juliet's extended family would be there, even her horrendous cousin Louise and her husband Phil. Phil was a laugh but Louise was just a bitch, an obese one at that. She would travel up Friday afternoon and she phoned her Dad to let him know that she was coming. It had the added bonus of another weekend where she would not see Nigel.

She arrived at the caravan a little after 4pm. Ray and Violet were there. Ray was always a laugh and Vi was pleasant. Louise and Phil had not arrived yet. Phil didn't finish until 5pm on a Friday. They were all sitting outside, enjoying the August sunshine and drinking. Juliet had taken her own wine. There were others there as well and the smell of the charcoal from the just lit barbeque was pervading the air. Charlotte soon joined them as did Katie and her partner Marsh and there was soon quite a large gathering, sitting outside in the warm evening laughing and joking.

It was about six pm when Louise and her husband Phil pulled up on the field. Louise towed the caravan and Phil towed his boat. Louise looked in a foul mood but then you could never really tell with her as she had had her eyebrows tattooed on a few years ago, and they were not only green (which didn't sit very well with her pink complexion), they were etched onto her face at such an angle to her puffy eyes that they gave the impression that she was always annoyed and pissed off. However it was apparent from her body language when she climbed down out of the land rover that she was indeed pissed off. Phil climbed out of his land rover and there was a short exchange of angry words between the couple before he unhitched the caravan and wound down the jacks.

"Christ," said Ray "Looks like Louise has got one on her again." Everyone had been watching them and let out peals of laughter.

"What's new," said Katie, "Aunt Louise is always pissed off." And more laughter followed.

Before long Phil came striding over to the crowd of people sitting on chairs arranged in a circle on the grass, wearing a big grin on his face. "Want a whisky Phil?" said Juliet's father, who was fond of Phil.

"Yes thanks, Vic," replied Phil and soon the tinkling of ice in a tumbler was to be heard coupled with the twang of the ring pull on a can of seven up and the gentle pop of a cork being pulled from a bottle of whisky. The sun was still warm and everyone was getting very gently drunk. "What's up with Louise?" said Ray with a laugh. Louise had gone into the caravan and had not been seen for fifteen minutes. "I don't bloody know what's up with her," replied Phil, and everyone laughed.

Just then she appeared at the door of the caravan. Her huge frame filling the small caravan doorway and with a tinny in one hand, she came down the steps and set forth across the field sashaying from side to side as she walked in an attempt to look ladylike. Obviously she thought it was feminine but there was nothing feminine or gamine about Louise. She was fat and bloated and had been for a long time, her face a bright pink from the high blood pressure she suffered from. Juliet felt sorry for her. What had happened to the lovely young Louise with long blonde curly hair? Juliet remembered her as a fourteen-year-old. She hadn't been fat then, she had been rather lovely, at least to look at, she had a propensity to sulk even then and a fondness for lying when it suited her. Juliet and Louise had been the best of friends when they were growing up but for the past 33 years they had been sworn enemies.

Louise looked over to Juliet and said "hello." Juliet responded in kind. It was a kind of ritual they went through when they met. Louise knew she had to put on a show as it was Juliet's father's land that they were on but the two women hated each other with a passion. Well that was not strictly true. Juliet had long since stopped caring about Louise and the past, she had had three husbands and numerous lovers since they had fallen out over Phil and now Louise was married to Phil so why was she still pissed off with Juliet? Juliet couldn't understand this. If anyone had anything to gripe about, it was Juliet because it had been Louise who had told lies all those years ago and obtained Phil through deception. But, Louise obviously still feared Juliet and more so now that she was apparently without a man again. It didn't help that despite only being two years younger than Louise she was in a lot better shape. Louise's hair was thinning, it was cut short and it was still blonde, although she had it coloured a distinctly fake shade of red and it was permed. She had a receding hairline and there was nothing she could do to disguise it. Years of abuse, using home perms may have been to blame but perhaps like Juliet, she was going through the menopause and that was the cause.

Louise pulled up her chair and ripped the ring pull off her can of Carlsberg Special Brew and took a swig from the can. It was to be the first of many that evening.

Phil was on good form. He sat opposite Juliet in the circle of chairs on the grass, the sun slowly setting on the horizon. They had all eaten from the barbeque and it was dusk, Juliet had filled her glass with more wine and wrapped her pashmina around her shoulders to guard against the chill of the evening. She rifled in her bag for her tobacco, a filter, papers and a lighter to roll and smoke a cigarette. Her make-up bag accidentally spilled forth from her bag and Ray who had a fondness for Juliet was taking the piss out of her in a good-natured fashion. Vi his wife was slugging on her gin and tonic and drawing hard on her cigarette. "You desperate smokers," said Ray. Juliet laughed, as she had known he had been a smoker in previous years and there is no one more righteous than an ex-smoker. Vi, his wife continued to puff it up frequently probably much to his annoyance. "Look you have lost your make up bag in your desperation for a fag," but Juliet laughed off Ray's comment and in the half-light, rolled herself a cigarette and lit it, drawing hard on it making the end glow in the dark. Phil eyed Juliet with a gleam in his eye, as Juliet retrieved her make-up bag from the grass. "So, do you wash out your make up brushes regularly?" he said to Juliet, he was already half pissed and mellow, laughing as he said it. Juliet was so taken aback by this comment she laughed heartily. It had only been days ago, that she had inadvertently stumbled across Martine McCutchen's beauty tips on some odd TV channel and she had said to wash out your make up brushes. She drew on her cigarette and exhaled the smoke casually from her lips, the smoke gently curling upwards into the night sky. "Well, actually Phil, I do. Have you been watching Martine McCutchen's beauty tips?" Phil was pissed but without hesitation and with a poker straight face, he said: "Well, as a matter of fact Juliet, I have." Phil eyed Juliet for a split second and they caught each other's eye and then descended into peals of laughter.

It was as though time had stood still. They were transported back in time. 33 years ago, in this same spot, at this time of day. They both recollected all those years ago, but they said nothing to each other.

It was getting late, people drifted off to their caravans. Vic, Juliet's father bid everyone goodnight. Vi had long since gone to bed with a gin and tonic in her hand. Ray remained. He was a player and loved the banter and the flirting. Phil was getting steadily sloshed on Famous Grouse and seven up although the seven up was getting less and less, stayed, bantering with Juliet. She was holding court now and she knew it and she was relishing in the attention. Attention she hadn't had in a long time. Finally Louise had been defeated by her Carlsberg Special Brew and she slipped off to the caravan. She had been outdone and she knew it. In Juliet's absence for the past 30 years, she had reigned supreme. Phil had been under her thumb for all that time and Juliet had been absent but tonight she was back and Phil was entranced.

It was quite dark now and Phil had lit his gas lantern. The moths danced around it in the darkness, drawn to the flame. Ray stayed glued to his chair watching the theatre that was playing out between Juliet and Phil before his eyes but finally he succumbed to his whisky, and went to his caravan. Juliet had run out of wine and realised she was in deep water with Phil. "I must go to bed," she said.

"Why?" said Phil, "the night is still young."

"I have run out of wine"

"Why don't you have a whisky?" he said and before she knew it there was a glass in her hand. She drank the amber liquid, and didn't care anymore. She was having fun and you had to admit that Phil was fun but she had a sense of foreboding and wanted to get away from this scene. She rose from her chair to leave and found herself unsteady on her feet. "Where are you going?" he said.

"I am cold and need to go to bed," said Juliet.

"Oh, don't go Juliet, we are having fun, let's go in the clubhouse, I will put the heater on."

Whether it was the whisky or whether it was because Juliet had not had any fun in a long, long, time, she found herself saying yes to his proposition and they went into the glorified shed that they called a clubhouse. Then something remarkable happened.

Buoyed up by the loss if inhibitions due to the whisky she had consumed, of which she was not used to and the heat of the gas fire in the clubhouse and Phil's warmth, she sat down and started to speak. "This is the first time we have been alone together for 33 years. What happened Phil? Why did you cut me off like that all those years ago?"

Suddenly Phil looked stone cold sober. "What are you talking about Juliet? I did not cut you off. Louise told me your father was after me and that you were pregnant."

Now it was Juliet's turn to sober up and for a moment she did so quickly. "Phil, what on earth are you talking about? I wasn't pregnant, my father wasn't after you. I heard no more from you and then I found out you had gone back to her. For years I avoided you, I didn't know what I had done. But it all fits now, she is a serial liar, she made it all up just to get you back." Tears ran down her face, as she realised that the man who had taken her virginity, the man who had been her first love, had been lied to by her rival. She had been heartbroken when he had not contacted her anymore and couldn't understand why and now she knew. That bitch Louise had twisted the truth to have him all to herself.

Phil looked shocked and angry, and looked as though he was about to cry. Juliet was stunned. Of all the men she had known, she would have never thought that Phil would cry. He presented himself as the personification of everything manly. He was tall, he walked like he had huge bollocks, he wielded a chainsaw, had a large boat which he took out on the sea, he could skin an eel, and took no shit from anyone, least of all Louise and yet here he was virtually crying over some lie that had happened over thirty years ago.

Admittedly it was his wife of 26 years who had told the lie but it was as if suddenly he realised that he had been duped.

"Look, Phil, I didn't know she had lied to you, I thought you had abandoned me. I was so heartbroken. She is one hell of a bitch."

He fell on her, kissing her wildly, begging forgiveness, talking about the madness of it all and how he had been a fool."

Juliet's head whirred with the whisky and she felt out of control. He grappled for her breasts, as they knelt on the clubhouse floor kissing each other and Juliet pulled back. She was very, very drunk but not drunk enough to realise what they were doing was madness. Louise would be on them in an instance. She had obtained Phil by deception and like an old demented harpy, she would be watchful, she could come in at any minute. "Phil, we have to stop, what about Louise?"

"Oh, she will be fast asleep."

"No Phil, she hates me with a vengeance and she will be after you. We shouldn't have done this," and with that she pulled away and tidied herself, regained her composure and staggered out of the clubhouse door. She was very, very drunk. Phil followed her, as he knew she was inebriated and helped her up the steps of the caravan and shut the door behind her. She sank quietly into bed and fell asleep.

Chapter 20 – The cold light of day

Juliet awoke, with the sunlight hitting her face from the overhead caravan opening light. She hadn't closed the night blind the evening before and the sun now shafted brightly through the light overhead. Her head was throbbing and she still felt drunk. As Juliet grappled with her unfamiliar surroundings and the pounding in her head, a stark realisation hit her. What had happened the evening before? She was drunk and disorientated, in a strange bed and an unfamiliar place and then she remembered Phil. The horror of it all! Had it really happened? She retraced her footsteps of the evening before and to her dismay she realised it was real.

She lay there for a full ten minutes trying desperately to recall the events of the previous evening. Her mouth dry, her head pounding and her mind racing. Yes it had happened, and she was horrified. How could she allow this to happen to her? And then she sank gently into the pillow and relaxed. Oh come now Juliet, she reasoned with herself. It wasn't as if Louise had not deserved this. Of course she did. She had treated Juliet like shit for years, lorded it over her because she had won Phil back from Juliet, although not by fair means. She had told him lies. But come on Juliet, she thought to herself, that was a long time ago, so long ago, that Juliet had long since given up caring. Apparently though, Louise had not.

Juliet lay there in pain, although it was easing and thought about it, would she go there again? With Phil? She concluded she would not. Forget it. Forget what had happened last night. It was nothing, she would brush it off, Phil would have been drunk and thought no more about it, like most men, he probably wouldn't even remember. And with that she got up to face the day, albeit still a little bit drunk.

Charlotte came early, as they were going to go and change the tickets for the holiday to Cuba. Thankfully there was no sign of anyone awake over at Louise and Phil's caravan. Juliet cringed when she thought about what had happened. Hopefully no one knew. They had all gone to bed the night before and the last person to leave was Ray. If asked, she would say nothing, except that she was drunk and couldn't remember anything at all.

"Come on Mom, let's go then, we have to meet Chris at 11am to give him the money for the holiday," said Charlotte and they climbed into her car. Juliet was thankful as she was in no fit state to drive. It was a lovely day. "Are you alright Mom? You don't seem yourself this morning."

Juliet laughed, "I am hungover darling. I had too much whisky last night on top of wine, which was not very good and I ended up in the clubhouse with Phil, snogging. But don't say a word to anyone."

"Mother! You just can't throw that out there like that. Snogging with uncle Phil. Come on spill the beans, what happened?" So, Juliet told her the whole story. They were laughing about it and Juliet didn't feel quite so ashamed anymore. "But Mom, would you have an affair with Uncle Phil?"

Juliet sat quietly before speaking, "no, darling, I don't think so, it is not right and it would be messy. Affairs always are." Now it was Charlotte's turn to be silent. "But, you know Aunt Louise is a Grade A bitch. She is vile and she told him lies, lies he obviously still believed until last night."

"Yes, I know, I can't believe he didn't know they were lies and he has believed them all these years. Their marriage is rocky because before your Nan died she told me about an incident when Phil went off drinking with other people in the next field. Louise had woken up in the wee hours and found

161

that he was not in his bed. She went to find him. I don't know what happened but your Nan said that Louise had intimated that she had found him in an embrace with another woman. Apparently Phil walked the twenty miles home that night and didn't come back to the caravan. Louise said he had slapped her face. If you want to believe that, she is a first-class liar, as well as a grade A bitch."

The conversation ended there and they went and completed their mission. They arrived back on the field at midday and everyone had started drinking again. That was all it ever was at the field, one long round of drinking. Juliet had only just started to feel better but Louise emerged from the caravan and shot Juliet a filthy look. Juliet decided that there was only one thing for it. She needed the hair of the dog. Did Louise know what had happened the night before? Of course she couldn't know. Phil certainly wouldn't have told her.

Phil came over and smiled a broad smile at Juliet. He obviously had not regretted last night. He came over to top up Juliet's glass. Juliet whispered, "she is in a foul mood, does she know about last night?"
 Phil whispered back "No, I have said nothing." Juliet breathed a sigh of relief. Thank goodness for that. Louise had just known that they had stayed up late together in the clubhouse. Ray must have been stirring things up or rather Vi had because Ray had surely told her and Vi was best of mates with Louise.

Louise was not quite herself for the rest of the weekend, and she "had one on her" all of the time. Juliet was pleasant with her as if nothing had happened but gave her a wide berth all the same.

Juliet drove home to her flat on Sunday afternoon. She thought about the events of Friday night and she decided to change her mind. It was about time that she had her revenge on Louise. She would have an affair with Phil. It would come to nothing, Phil had too much to lose and she would make sure Louise never found out. But how delicious the revenge would be, every time she saw Louise, she could laugh to herself thinking that she was sleeping with Phil behind her back and she knew nothing about it.

Juliet formulated a plan. It wouldn't interfere with Nigel. They were not really having a relationship in any case. They had only slept with each other once and she was going on holiday in just under two weeks' time. Anyway,Phil was married and lived 80 miles away which seriously limited the times they could see each other. She asked Alistair to phone Phil and ask him to phone Juliet. That way if he was with Louise, she wouldn't know he was speaking to Juliet. Alistair had worked with Phil before and there would be no suspicion about him phoning Phil. If Phil didn't phone Juliet then she would know he wasn't interested. But she had a very strong sense that he was and that he would phone and sure enough, he did.

"Hello Juliet," he said. Juliet was wickedly delighted that he had phoned and after she had replied "Hello," he launched straight in. "I can't stop thinking about you, Juliet. I want to see you."

"Are you saying you want to have an affair Phil? Because you need to know that if she finds out, it will cost you. Half the business, half the house, and the kids will hate you. If you are serious about this then you need to be very careful. Tell no one, I mean absolutely no one that you are doing this and don't phone from this phone again and do not save my telephone number. But I want to see you Phil. Think about it." said Juliet.

"I have thought about it and I want to see you Juliet, it has been too long. I must see you soon. I will pay for a hotel. Can you meet up near Warwick?"

Juliet, was astounded at the speed with which he was moving. He had obviously thought about nothing else since the weekend. This was going to be enjoyable. "Yes, Phil, I can. Let me know a date and I will book one up."

"I will phone you in the morning, when I know for certain, I have to do a job around there but it won't take long." They said their goodbyes and hung up.

Juliet was laughing to herself. They say that revenge is a dish best served cold but God, this was so cold, it was deep frozen. Thirty-three years later and she was getting her revenge. She still remembered the pain of the heartbreak and the embarrassment at having to face the pair of them at family occasions. How Louise had gloated over Juliet. The one Christmas many years later when Juliet had been married and divorced and had children, there had been a party at Juliet's parents' house and Louise had been friendly to Juliet. Juliet had actually thought that the grudge had gone and that they were friends again but she had been wrong and Louise had mixed Juliet, gin and tonic after gin and tonic and had made them all too strong. Juliet was so drunk that she had to stay the night at her parent's house, even though she lived only two hundred yards away. Louise had done it purposefully. Now at last Juliet was going to get her own back. It didn't matter that Louise wouldn't know that Juliet was sleeping with Phil, all that mattered was that Juliet knew. That in itself was revenge enough.

The next morning, Phil phoned just after 7am from a phone box. Juliet was surprised he had managed to find one. "Hello Handsome," said Juliet.

"Hello Beaut," he replied, "Juliet, can you book a hotel for Friday in Warwick? I will give you the money when I see you and I will phone again tomorrow morning. I can't wait to see you."

"I can't wait to see you again," Juliet replied.

Juliet booked a hotel room, in Warwick for Friday. It was a lovely hotel and of course she would have to take Clara, she had no one to leave her with. She arrived on time and found Phil in his land rover on the car park. He knew Clara was coming with her and he had been so sweet with Clara, after all, he had three grown-up daughters of his own.

They checked in and went to the hotel room. It wasn't a day for sex, they sat and chatted. Things that they needed to talk about. What they were going to do, how they were going to conduct their affair. Juliet left Phil in no doubt about what he would lose if it became public, or if Louise found out. She liked Phil and had a fondness for him. She knew that he had worked his bollocks off building up a business and she didn't want him to lose what he had worked for. Louise had done very little to help him. She had dragged her kids up and Juliet found out that she didn't even cook Phil an evening meal. She was appalled at what she heard. Phil often worked till late and didn't come home until 8 or 9pm, only to find that there was no meal. They ate takeaways every night and he often ate the leftovers. He had led a dog's life. Juliet knew from her mom and her kids that Louise's three obese children had been spoilt beyond belief at Phil's expense. Louise didn't work as such. She worked for Phil, one day a week doing the accounts. She gave her kids everything, she was too fat and lazy to do anything for them but money, the latest phones, takeaways and fast food, cash, well she did that. Money flowed from Louise like it was molten lava but she didn't earn it, Phil did.

Phil had built up his engineering business out of nothing, through the sweat from his brow, tenacity and his good nature. He was a likeable man and he had a genuine way with people that bought him business. Nothing was too much trouble for Phil and it showed and that was how he had built his business.

"We have to get new, cheap mobile phones," said Phil. "We need to communicate and I can't use my work mobile, Louise sees the bills and your number will show up. There are very few phone boxes left. If I give you the money can you arrange it please Juliet?" "Of course Phil, it shouldn't cost much, I reckon fifty quid should do it," she said. Phil pulled a wad of notes out if his pocket and handed them to Juliet. "Phil there is far too much here. I only need 100 to cover the hotel room and the phones."

Phil kissed her on the lips. "I want you to have it Juliet, it cost you money to get here in petrol and you will need to buy the phones, pay for the hotel room and then you will need petrol for the next time we meet. Just keep it." He kissed her again and said, "Do you need any money for your holiday?"

Juliet was shocked, and overwhelmed by his generosity." No, I don't Phil, you have given me far too much."

"Just take it Beaut," he said. So she said nothing. He was so nice. He told her all about his life about how he was disappointed, how he felt unloved. Juliet felt sorry for him, but she spelled it out what he had to lose if Louise found out.

"She has hated you for a long time," he said "Every time you were coming up to see your parents, she would mark it in her diary as "her is up," Juliet couldn't believe, that Louise still feared her. But it wasn't surprising really. If you obtained your love by deception then you would always be looking over your shoulder for the real love to take it away. This was going to be better revenge than planned. Although Juliet wouldn't let Louise know, she was not into that kind of bitter twisted revenge. She hoped she would never find out. Phil would have his fling then he would get bored and end it and go back to Louise. Simple. No one hurt but Juliet would be able to sit quietly, and gloat to herself thinking "I have fucked your husband."

They left the hotel at about three pm. They had kissed that was all, Clara was there. It was clear, that Phil had real intentions about an affair. Juliet had warned him of the consequences, should Louise find out and he didn't seem the slightest bit bothered. He had said that he was totally unhappy with his life. There was no love there and he knew he was being used as a cash cow. They (his wife and kids) were taking the piss and Louise was at the forefront of all of this. Juliet wouldn't see him again until after her holiday but he phoned her every day.

Chapter 21- Cuba

It was the night before they were going to Cuba. Juliet, Charlotte and Clara. Charlotte travelled down after work. They had to get up at 4am to leave for the airport. Charlotte was disorganised and had not got travel insurance so after dinner, Juliet bought some online. Juliet was also disorganised and she was tired and had not finished packing. They fell into bed at around 10pm. Juliet had half packed her bags.

The alarm went off around 3am and Juliet awoke with a start. She whirred around flinging things into her suitcase and woke Charlotte. She had never been so unready to go on holiday and she was in a panic. Alistair took them over to the coach stop at 4.30am. Groggy from sleep they stood in the early morning waiting for the coach. Juliet was annoyed with herself but then she relaxed, she had done her best, everything would be alright.

The nine-hour flight was an ordeal and Charlotte was not the best of travelling companions. Still obviously smarting from the split with Chris she was not in a holiday mood and Clara who was eighteen months old was getting on her nerves. Halfway into the flight Juliet remembered the bottle of Champagne that Chris had ordered. Perhaps that would at least go some way to calming Charlotte and after two glasses Charlotte seemed more relaxed.

Juliet's mind was a whirr. Alex, (now disappeared, but still loved) Nigel, (sad but true) and Phil, (thought of fondly but an act of revenge). Everything was madness, she was glad to go away on holiday for a while.

They landed and cleared passport control and collected their bags. It took an hour by coach to get the hotel. It was now 4pm in the afternoon in Cuba but in reality, it was much later. They were all tired. They went to their room, and then went to explore. They walked through the grounds, and down to the beachside bar. The wind was wild. "There are no palm trees," exclaimed Charlotte, as she surveyed the beach.

"What do you mean?" Said Juliet, "I can see two there"

"There are not enough. The brochure had pictures of lots of palm trees," replied Charlotte. Juliet, who was knackered beyond belief, was losing her rag as well as her patience.

"Charlotte, get a grip of yourself. We are knackered. We have been up for over 15 hours and we are all tired. There are plenty of palm trees, it is lovely but I myself am feeling cross, tired and hungry and Christ knows how Clara is dealing with all of this. I suggest we have some food and something to drink and have an early night. Things will look better tomorrow I assure you."

Charlotte snorted in disbelief at her mother's comments, but had to listen and agree and indeed after some food, she admitted she was tired. They went to the room and they all fell asleep on the huge bed, with the hall light on.

The morning broke, and with it a new perspective. The room was nice. It was basic but lovely and there were sliding doors overlooking the wonderfully blue Caribbean Sea. As Juliet arose and looked out on the view one could almost expect Johnny Deppe to come sailing up in a galleon dressed in full pirate costume. But of course he didn't.

Charlotte and Clara slept whilst Juliet showered, and took out her travel kettle, teabags and made tea for her and Charlotte and milk for Clara.

Thankfully after a good night's sleep and tea in bed Charlotte was restored to her usual self. Juliet loved her daughters so very much and it was a joy to be with them on holiday in such a wonderful place.

They went down to breakfast. They were one of the first people to arrive and they ate voraciously; cereal, pastries, orange juice and bacon. They were attended by a lovely middle-aged waiter who was kind and most attentive. Juliet squirrelled away a few pastries in food bags, for a mid-morning snack. They went back to the room, changed, and then went down to the beach. It was very warm and as they approached the beach, they passed through an area that defined the edge of the hotel grounds and the beginning of the beach. There were sand dunes where foliage grew and it smelt of 'green.' There was no mistaking that smell, it was cannabis growing deep in the undergrowth.

Charlotte and Juliet dragged the pushchair over the sand to the sun beds of Charlottes choosing. It was only 8.30am but it was hot. They made camp on the site they had chosen. It was glorious Juliet had to admit. The sea was as blue as can be, the sand was white and soft and they lay beneath an umbrella made of palm. They stripped off and lay on the sun loungers. Despite Clara's age she happily played in the sand in the shade of the umbrella. The beach started to fill with people, groggy from late nights and too much booze and by 10 am music started to boom across the half-filled beach. People were here to enjoy themselves and the hotel was not going to disappoint. The sun climbed higher into the sky and by 10.30 it was scorching hot outside of the umbrella. It really was a paradise to all intents and purposes.

Clara was tired and after a drink fell asleep in her pushchair under the shade of the umbrella. Juliet knew that it was not a safe place even in the shade and slathered her in factor 50 sun screen before retiring to her sun lounger. Charlotte was fast asleep on an adjacent sun lounger.

Juliet lay back and allowed herself some navel-gazing behind her sunglasses. She was lonely and she really wanted some quality sex. Alex was her love and her first choice but he had disappeared. Hostile and probably gay. She still loved him and although she didn't want to give him up, she knew that she should. Nigel, well what can you say about Nigel? He was altogether a thoroughly good bloke and she should probably go with him but he was boring beyond belief, and the clincher was that he was shit in bed. No matter how much money he had, she could not see herself with him for the rest of her life. Phil, now there was a conundrum. He had been her first love, a love unfinished, and he had recently come back but and this was a big but he was married to her arch enemy that bitch Louise. No, thought Juliet, he should be discounted. It was just revenge, a dalliance.

The day passed by very pleasantly. They ate lunch and Juliet and Clara went for an afternoon nap, leaving Charlotte to roast in the afternoon sun. At about 3pm Juliet heard the sounds of Latin American music coming from the pool area. She rose from her slumber and put on her bathrobe and went out onto the balcony with a drink and a cigarette. Clara was still asleep. The music was lively and very sexual and it stirred something in Juliet, something so deep. She felt her soul calling out to her. She was far from dead and wanted to experience all life had to offer.

A while later Charlotte entered the room, she was sunburnt. Juliet was dismayed. Why didn't she listen to her mother? Juliet had warned her about the fierceness of the sun here in Cuba but Charlotte wanted a suntan and she had overdone it. Clara was bathed and Juliet and Charlotte showered and got ready to go down for cocktails.

After several changes of outfit, (Charlotte, not Juliet) they went down to the bar. It was all inclusive. Juliet started off with a Bloody Mary but quickly switched to a Mojito, the loveliness that is mint and lime syrup, with Cuba's very own product, rum. Charlotte had a tea. They were one of the first at dinner at six waiting outside of the dining room. "We are like old aged pensioners waiting outside of the dining room, waiting for it to open for dinner," Charlotte laughed and Juliet saw the funny side. "Well, we have Clara and that excuses us."

They were beginning to adjust to the time difference and their new surroundings. Charlotte was suffering from guilt over Chris but Juliet had known he wasn't right for her, Charlotte needed something else from a man and he hadn't been able to supply it. After dinner they made their way to the bar area where more live music was playing. You had to admire the Salsa Beat of Cuba it was very infectious and catchy and they soon found a table. "Would you like a cocktail?" Juliet said to Charlotte.

"Oh, yes please. I will have sex on the beach."Well, trust Charlotte to like a cocktail with that name thought Juliet as she made her way to the bar, and perused the cocktail menu until she found one that tickled her fancy. The young barman came over "Could I have a Black Russian and sex on the beach please" said Juliet. As soon as the words left her lips, she could have kicked herself. It sounded so, so very wrong. The young barman stifled a laugh although he was used to it a thousand times over and started making the cocktails. Some awful grease ball next to her turned and looked her over. He was late middle-aged and was bald and wore glasses and he gave her a lecherous smile. Juliet looked at him as though he were made of glass and then glanced back at the barman who was serving the cocktails, why on earth did she attract the weirdoes?

Drinks served, Juliet returned to the table where Charlotte was sitting .She started to laugh and told Charlotte about what had happened at the bar. "He is looking at you mom," Charlotte said about the bald-headed man.

"Oh, Charlotte, for God's sake, don't look at him, he looks the sort of man who is pushy and I certainly don't want to give him any encouragement. He will take it like that if he thinks I am talking about him." Charlotte turned away for now. They finished their drinks and went to bed. This holiday was about the beach for them, not the nightlife. Juliet had Clara and she was only 18 months old. Charlotte was nursing a broken heart and even if it wasn't hers, she still suffered from the pain of it.

The morning broke and the light streamed through the windows of the room. Juliet loved the view of the ocean. She put the kettle on and pushed open the doors to the balcony, with a cigarette and lighter in her hand. Charlotte and Clara, were still fast asleep on the enormous bed. The sun had not yet risen, although it was light and she lit her cigarette and gazed at the large expanse of deep blue ocean as she leant on the balustrade, and inhaled her cigarette. She thought of Alex, she knew she shouldn't, he had behaved so badly but she just couldn't help herself. She put him to the back of her mind for now. Then there was Nigel. Well he had been so good to her she couldn't deny that he was generous. But it was like recruiting someone for a job. He looked tremendous on paper, he had all the required qualifications but when you met him in the flesh, he just lacked that wow factor, that personal quality that made him a successful candidate. Then of course there was now Phil but he had broken her heart all those years ago and he was just revenge, he would never leave Louise, he had too much to lose and she didn't want a life with him there were too many complications. She also knew that deep down that there was not the chemistry between them that made for deep passionate love. But he was a good halfway house and he would help her get over Alex. He was a story unfinished, left untold and it needed an end. She stubbed out her fag and went inside and made tea for her and Charlotte and a bottle for Clara.

The day went by in a lovely heat filled haze. They breakfasted early and made their way down to the beach before 9am. Hardly anyone was there. They had their pick of the sun loungers. Of course Charlotte picked one a good way off and not only did they have to carry their bags over the sand, but they also had to drag Clara's pushchair over it as well which made for heavy going on the soft dry silver sand. Juliet was not in the best of moods as they lay on their sun loungers, it would have been easier to have picked a spot nearer the boardwalk but Juliet couldn't stay cross for long in this setting it was too beautiful for that. They lay quietly on their respective sun loungers, Clara in the shade under the palm umbrella playing in the sand. At 10am the music started up and the sun was getting hotter. It really was beautiful here and the only downer was Charlotte. However, it was soon midday and Juliet went and got her and Charlotte a shandy. They ate from the beachside café, burgers and salad for Juliet and Charlotte, and chips for Clara. At 2pm, Juliet took Clara back to the room for a nap. "Don't stay out in this sun Charlotte, the wind is deceptive and it will burn you to a crisp, you can still get a tan in the shade. Are you sure you wouldn't like to come up for a nap?" But Charlotte was determined to stay where she was and burn. Juliet went up to the room and the air conditioning was a welcomed relief from the blistering heat. She lay down on the bed with Clara who quickly fell asleep. Juliet lay there and tried to sleep but she couldn't. But it was nice to have some chill time to herself.

At 4pm, Juliet went for a shower and made tea for herself. She was enjoying her holiday. Clara woke and she gave her a bottle. There was a knock at the door. It was Charlotte. It seemed to take Charlotte forever to dress for dinner. She tried on numerous skimpy outfits and complained that she was bloated. If that was bloated thought Juliet, then Juliet wished she was, however Juliet tried not to show her impatience but she wanted a Bloody Mary. There were not many pleasures in Juliet's life but alcohol was one of them, and it was after

174

four pm, she was on holiday and she wanted a drink. For fuck's sake, the Russian's there were boozing it up at 9am in the morning and on the hard liquor. Juliet had seen them on the beach drinking vodka and coke. They certainly had their money's worth out of the all-inclusive package. Juliet would have to be in bed by 8.30 – 9pm at the latest for Clara so she had some catching up to do.

They finally made their way down to the bar. Charlotte ordered tea and Juliet had a Bloody Mary, well it was halfway respectable, the tomato juice was a tonic in itself and as a pre-dinner drink one could almost class it as a starter. After another Bloody Mary they went up to dinner at 6pm.

The good thing about going into dinner at 6pm on an all-inclusive holiday was that not only did you have the pick of the tables on offer but the buffet had not been ransacked, and was resplendent in all its glory. Juliet and Charlotte had a most attentive middle-aged waiter called George. Juliet guessed him to be the same age as her, or maybe a little older. Whatever he was lovely, nice, kind and very attentive to the three ladies. He adored Clara and he didn't lech over Charlotte which Juliet thought was most gentlemanly of him as most men leched over Charlotte, who wouldn't?

They went down to the bar after dinner and got themselves a drink. The bar was relatively quiet at 7pm. People were either just coming back from the beach to have a shower and get ready for dinner or in the dining room having dinner. So Juliet and Charlotte enjoyed this time. There was a live band playing in the bar and they were rather good. Juliet enjoyed her Black Russian with a small cigar and Charlotte enjoyed her Sex on the Beach.

The bar started to fill up and Juliet was pushing Clara in her pram, trying to eek out a bit more chill time, as Clara was tired. "Don't turn around Mom but that bloke from last night

175

is at the bar and he is looking at you," Oh, for fuck's sake thought Juliet. Don't look and he won't be encouraged and he won't bother you, she thought to herself. But she was wrong.

Juliet had her back turned to the bar and vowed not to turn around and was happily content rocking Clara in her pushchair. The band was playing lady in red by Chris de Burgh and the saxophone seemed to be getting louder. Charlotte was trying to say something to her but she couldn't hear what she was saying the music was so loud. Charlotte had a rather alarmed and amused look on her face that Juliet couldn't quite make out. Juliet became aware that the people on nearby tables were looking at her. Why? Horror came over Juliet. Had she tucked her dress in her knickers after leaving the loo? Was she showing her backside to all and sundry? Juliet was mortified and slowly moved her left hand to her backside to gently feel whether her dress was in place. It was but in doing so she had turned ever so slightly and now she knew why Charlotte looked alarmed and why everyone was staring at her. The greasy old git from the night before had closed in on her and he had the saxophonist accompanying him. He was looking directly at Juliet, as was the whole roo, and he was serenading her to the backdrop of 'Lady in Red'. Juliet was horrified and rooted to the spot. There was no escape and Juliet did not know what to do. She decided in an instant that the best course of action was to do nothing, so with a dismissive wave of her hand and a sneer, turned away from her would be Romeo and continued to rock the pram.

The room laughed and Juliet held her composure but had to smile. Embarrassing? Yes. Mortifying? Yes. Laughable and brave of him? Yes. And she thought it had ended there and breathed a sigh of relief as the song ended. But it hadn't ended there, he hadn't gone away and he approached her "Can I buy you a drink?" he said to her. Juliet had him there

"Well that is not much of an offer as you are not offering something, I would not get myself anyway for free." That did It. Everyone, who had keenly observed this little play burst forth into fits of laughter as did Charlotte and he retreated to the bar. Juliet could feel herself blushing like a schoolgirl and breathed a sigh of relief and relaxed.

The next day passed by much the same as the way the days had before. Breakfast, beach, lunch, except today a young bodyguard called Cory was waiting to carry the pushchair over the sand, only too keen to show off his muscles. Juliet was grateful. He had his eye on Charlotte and wanted to look impressive. Juliet harnessed this to her advantage. Dragging Clara and her pushchair over the sand was not easy to say the least and Juliet knew that Cory would have little change out of Charlotte, although he would be keen to impress her and consequently do anything that they asked.

It was odd. Odd because given Juliet's age and her knowledge, had she been Charlotte, she would have happily given Cory a run for his money but then she knew that she had been young once and like her younger self, Charlotte would never do such a thing.

A little before lunch Cory strode over and stood in front of the sun loungers where Juliet and Charlotte were baking. Unfortunately his crotch was at eye level for them lying on the sunloungers and he was wearing tight swimming trunks. You could not fail to notice his crown jewels bulging in front, thank goodness Juliet and Charlotte were wearing sunglasses. "Hello," he said.

"Hello," said Juliet, "Thank you for your help this morning, you were a star."

Cory smiled, Charlotte pretended to be asleep. "I am only too happy to be of help," he replied, and Juliet knew he would pounce once she went up for her and Clara's nap. Which she did at 2pm.

One had to go through the bar area to get to the lift to go the room, and as Juliet did so she carefully surveyed the bar are, to make sure that her would be Romeo was not there and did not see her. Thankfully he wasn't. So she and Clara went unscathed up to the room and to their afternoon nap.

They followed their routine and after dinner found themselves once again in the bar. Juliet felt relaxed. Thankfully Charlotte's face hadn't turned into third-degree burns and they had enjoyed a nice meal. The would-be Romeo, had faded from Juliet's drink sozzled mind as she went to the bar for her third Black Russian. Sadly, Juliet was too pissed to notice that she was standing next to Mr. Creepy from the night before. The vulture that he was, he did not fail to notice her standing next to him. "Hello Beautiful," he said. On hearing his voice Juliet was rooted to the spot, but despite her lack of response he continued, "lovely ring," he commented on Juliet's hand. Of course, the politeness in her, rose up automatically "Thank you," she said and as soon as she had said so she realised her folly.

And then he started. He was drunk, Juliet knew that. Not so drunk he slurred his words but drunk enough to be cocky and outrageous and that was a danger. He went in straight for the kill "Spend the night with me," he said. He was lucky that Juliet was tipsy otherwise she would have laughed with derision but as it was, she didn't feel she wanted to be really unkind. People are so unkind to others and you had to admire him for trying even if she didn't want him.

"You don't want to go near me, I am damaged goods," she said and turned to the man on the other side "Hello my name is Juliet," she said. He was a geek and so surprised to find her addressing him as was she but she had to go on, afraid of the creepy guy on the other side. But he hadn't given up and as soon as her drink was delivered to the bar said "I have a big schlong."

Did he really just say that? Juliet did a double take. Was he for real? Juliet (quite pissed) turned towards him and looked him dead in the eye and slowly said "good for you, and I hope it gives you hours of pleasure, but I am not interested." And then she casually sauntered off with her drinks.

"Charlotte," she said "we have got to go to the room, I cannot stay a moment longer in this bar with Dracula over there. I like a Bloody Mary but he likes one more than I do and with a shot of rhesus negative and not tomato juice. He is not having my blood tonight or any other."

The next morning as they were going down to the beach very early, as they were used to doing a little before 9am, they had just descended the boardwalk stairs to the beach when Juliet was aware of someone behind her. She didn't turn around but then she clocked him out of the corner of her eye, Dracula. "Good morning," he said.

Juliet couldn't be impolite, she really couldn't. "Good morning," she replied.

He smiled and said, "I shall be on my sun lounger over there if you feel in the need of some counselling." The old dog, he wouldn't give up and you had to admire his tenacity. "Thank you, but I keep my own counsel," remarked Juliet sternly. Hopefully he would find some other prey soon and give up. He walked off down the beach with his stick in his hand. Off for his morning walk.

They settled on sun loungers near the steps that morning, as Cory was not on duty to lend a hand. The next hour passed by relatively quietly with Clara playing in the sand. And then Dracula returned from his morning walk. Juliet was semi-reclining on her sun lounger and Charlotte was spread out. He came over and sat on the edge of Charlotte's sun lounger. He had a hibiscus flower in his hand. Juliet did not want to talk to him but Charlotte seemed to think it fun. "I bought this for you," he said to Charlotte and artfully put the flower in the strap of her bikini top.

Juliet was outraged. "Touch her once more and you will get a slap," she said to him.

"But I might like that," was his retort.

"Oh trust me you won't," said Juliet.

"Is your mother always this acerbic?" he said to Charlotte, and she laughed.

"Oh yes and this is her mild version."

"My name is Vassos," he said to Juliet, "I think we got off on the wrong foot last night, I can see you are a lady, and I apologise." "My name is Juliet," and they shook hands. But Juliet was wary. She spied a wedding ring on his hand even though he was alone.

"Have dinner with me?" he said.

"I don't go out with married men," she lied, hoping this would put him off.

"I am not married, I am separated." Oh, that old chestnut, thought Juliet. But he said no more and wished them a good day and left. Somehow Juliet didn't think that was the last she had heard of him but she could be truly frosty when she wanted to be and hoped this had done the trick. She was still wary and later when she crossed the lobby to her afternoon retreat from the sun, she still checked to see if he was about.

Charlotte came up later as usual and said that he had caught her in the lobby and had asked where her mother was. Juliet sighed she could really do without the amorous advances of a lecherous middle-aged married man on her holiday. "I think he is a complete phoney," she said to Charlotte. "Whilst I was waiting for the lift, I was reading the sign next to it. It says 'Do not take glasses up to your room'. And it is translated into different languages, and 'Vassos' is on there. It is a foreign word for glasses. He has made up his name."

"Oh mother, you are really something else. All that paranoia of Alex's has rotted your brain" "Well that may be, but it is in black and white. How do you explain that?"

Charlotte laughed and went for a shower whilst Juliet made tea.

Juliet decided that she was not going to be prey to Dracula tonight. A few of the hotel guests had stopped Juliet and asked her about Vassos. She had heard conflicting stories from them about him but they mostly had a laugh at his hapless advances towards her. The scene in the bar with the saxophonist was one of their memorable highlights. Juliet took it well but she was determined not to be made a spectacle of again. She had seen a man a bit younger than her on the beach with his daughter, son, and his mother, although Juliet hadn't known this at first. When she had first seen them, she had thought it a curious set up and that the younger man had an older woman. Luckily that evening she was beside him at the bar, and he struck up the conversation, of course, the subject was Vassos. "So, are you going to succumb to Captain Birdseye?" he gestured, across the bar to where Vassos was sitting.

"Not on your nelly," said Juliet and they both laughed "I am Steve," he said "Juliet," she said and proffered her hand to shake, which he did. "Thank you, Steve. I was beginning to feel a bit like prey to a vulture" Steve laughed. "Don't worry love; I think you can handle yourself from what I have seen. Why don't you and your daughter come and join us? There is myself, my mother and my brother and my daughter, we could do with a bit of company."

"I'd love to." Juliet went and collected Charlotte and Clara and they went over to join Steve and his family. They soon made their introductions and found out that the older woman was, in fact, Steve's mother. He had his daughter with him and younger son and the older lad was his brother. His mother was divorced, as was he. "It is all rather complicated," Steve said, as he tried to explain their various relationships.

"Ooh, we like complicated," replied Juliet "because we are also," as she gave a sum up of what was her family life. They had a laugh and a lovely evening, and Juliet was glad to be free from the clutches of Vassos. He would think that Steve had made a move on her and she was glad that it looked like that. "He is very rich you know," said Steve about Vassos, "apparently he comes here every year and he is very generous with the waiters, they don't have a lot of money in Cuba you know."

Tell me about it, thought Juliet, neither do I. "Really? I had put him down as one of those people who come for a week or so and try to grab any woman they can. But it is nice to hear that he is very kind to the Cubans. I know they have a hard time. Our waiter George wanted to buy my pushchair from me as they are expensive here. I have told him he can have it at for free at the end of our holiday, I will just buy another from eBay when I get home but I will have the devil to pay with Clara at the airport without a pushchair." Juliet felt sad that she had given Vassos a bad press but he really wasn't her cup of te, and she was smarting from Alex. She doubted she would ever love again, it was that bad.

It was nearly the end of their holiday. Juliet had enjoyed it and in truth didn't want to go home. She could never grow tired of waking up to that view but go home she knew she must.

They packed their bags and got ready for departure. In the lobby George was waiting with his wife. It was his day off, and Juliet had arranged for the handover of the pushchair. George and his wife like Juliet had had a child late in life, long after their family had grown up and his wife kissed Juliet on both cheeks as she showed them how to collapse the pushchair. She was going to suffer for a few hours due to giving it away, but she knew that she was doing them a good turn and she was happy to do so.

The overnight flight was long and arduous. It was only helped by a bottle of champagne, and the film. Johnny Deppe as a vampire. Juliet had to see the funny side of this. Charlotte was soon asleep and Clara followed too, on Juliet's lap. Juliet was dying for a pee but held onto it for the rest of the flight so as not to wake her daughters.

Chapter 22 – Back home

Nigel picked them up from the coach stop. Charlotte got in her car and left for the West Midlands once they were back at the flat. Juliet didn't worry about her, she had slept the whole flight home unlike Juliet, who felt massively jet-lagged but she soldiered on to the end of the day. She had an early night and fell asleep with Clara at 7pm.

It was mid-September and a weekend. The next day she felt refreshed and as it was Sunday, she cooked Sunday lunch for Guy, Alistair and Mark. It was a happy day if only marred by Mark who on spotting her bottle of Cuban rum asked for a drink. He didn't change, did he? Anything going booze wise and he would want it.

The next day she received a call from Phil at 7am. "Hello Beaut. Did you have a good holiday?"

Juliet soon told him all about it. "I am desperate to see you again, how are Friday afternoons for you? I can get away early. If you book the travel lodge near my work I can be with you at 2pm until 4.30pm. And can you get those phones?" "Yes, that should be achievable but I need to ask Katie if she can mind Clara." And with that they were done. Juliet still had a load of money from Phil. At their last meeting, he had given her 500 quid in an envelope. She had been astounded at his generosity.

Katie was still on maternity leave. She had Alexa who had been born in January and she was only too happy to look after Clara for Juliet while she saw Phil. It was late September and the weather was still warm and lovely and her father Vic was still caravanning as was Phil and Louise. They would probably continue into October. This was the perfect

184

excuse for Juliet. She could see Phil and then collect Clara and go and stay with her father for the weekend.

Friday soon came and she had booked the travel lodge as requested. Phil met her in the car park. He came over and gave her a big kiss "I have a present for you Beaut," he said, and gave her a small rectangle box. Inside was a key ring, a genuine Mercedes key ring. It was a shiny chrome CLK. "I was passing the Mercedes garage and thought of you," he said.

"Oh Phil, it is really lovely, thank you," and gave him another kiss. They went to the hotel room. The time flew by and yes of course, they went to bed. Phil had a shower first. They chatted afterward. It was truly awful to hear the way he was treated at home. He had not eaten a thing all day and Juliet vowed that next time they met she would bring some food for him. She couldn't understand why Louise couldn't be bothered to cook for him but she knew from what her daughters had said that Louise just viewed him as a source of cash.

"I really should have owned my own unit by now," said Phil, "but we are still renting. I work until 7pm or later most days and go in on some Saturdays as well. We have enough money but she isn't interested. She is just happy to spend the money and the kids as well, they always have to have the latest phones and she spoils them. I can't be bothered to put my foot down, I am always knackered when I get home from work. I often fall asleep in front of the TV. Often when I get home they have already eaten a takeaway and I usually pick at the leftovers."

Juliet was aghast, she could see why Louise and her kids were obese "It's not right Phil, not with how hard you work." Juliet told him once again to be very careful and she gave him one of the two matching phones that they were to use. "I haven't saved my name on the phone just in case it falls into the wrong hands. She might suspect but she couldn't prove it. Just deny all knowledge of the phone. And if that happens call me from a payphone to tell me. You will have to memorise my number."

Phil didn't do text messages, so there was no danger of anything incriminating lingering on the phone. Although he did read them so Juliet told him to delete any that she sent him. She couldn't ring him as she was uncertain whether he was alone or not.

It had been a pleasant afternoon and they would see each other later at the field. It added a little excitement to know that she was going to sit with Louise that evening after spending the afternoon with Phil and what they had done together.

She arrived at the field a little after five after collecting Clara from Katie's and her father was pleased to see her. "Did you have a good holiday Juliet?" said her Dad.

"Yes thanks," she replied and she was soon sat outside with the others and a glass of wine. An hour later Phil and Louise pulled up. Phil shot her a big smile as he got out of the car. Thankfully Louise seemed to have gotten over her strop but she did not seem happy to see Juliet. Although Juliet knew from what Phil had said that he and Louise had had a big argument the last time she had come up. Phil apparently had shot her down in flames and told her in no uncertain terms what a silly cow she was being. He was a true Gemini. They both were. So at least today Louise had to put a fake smile on her face when she saw Juliet.

There was a crowd there and the company was pleasant. Phil couldn't take his eyes off Juliet but she was careful not to look at him too often or to talk to him. She made small talk with Louise and the others and they all wanted to hear about her holiday, and she had some marvelous tales to tell which kept them amused. She made sure she went to bed early that night and was not left alone with Phil. It would be stupid to arouse suspicion and there were too many people there. If only one person suspected it could get back to Louise

The next morning, Juliet was alone in the caravan tidying up, it was mid-morning. Louise and Vi were standing on the bank looking at the river and she could hear them chatting. "I don't know what's up with me Vi," said Louise "I keep weeping for no apparent reason and I keep getting these terrible hot flushes. It must be the menopause."

Vi was sympathetic and Juliet knew she was saying this for Juliet's benefit trying to gain some sympathy, just in case she had designs on Phil. But Juliet herself was going through the menopause and there was nothing to it but to brave it out. She had been to the doctors and was adamant she did not want HRT. She felt that it had been largely responsible for her mother's cancer as she had been on it for ten years and it was in its infancy then. Juliet was horrified, when the doctor told her that if you took HRT you still had to go through the menopause when you stopped taking it. There was absolutely no point Juliet thought to herself. To begin with she had been horrified, and had read stuff on the internet but then she had taken herself to one side and had a word with herself. It was life and there was nothing she could do about it, except sit it out. Her periods were scanty and had been since the operation and she also suffered from hot flushes, so she had little sympathy for Louise, even less with what she heard from Phil about her.

Later that morning the girls came down to the field. It was a lovely sunny day and they came into the caravan to hear the gossip from Juliet. They were soon laughing and enjoying a glass of wine. They were not surprised to hear about the life that Phil led "No wonder he is eager to have an affair, Louise has always used and abused him. The only thing she ever cooks is those bloody cupcakes, complete with dog hairs and she thinks they are wonderful." said Katie, "and her three daughters are so overweight but they all keep saying big is beautiful. Like it excuses their appalling overeating."

"Well that is just propagated by Louise, to make them feel better but they all know really deep down that it doesn't. I personally feel sorry for them having a mother like that. She didn't even give them breakfast when they went to school, they used to stop by the pork sandwich shop, and have pork dip which is disgraceful to say the least. Poor old Phil only manages to keep slim by not eating. I don't know how he copes, I really don't." said Juliet.

"And she used to send them off to McDonald's for their lunch in the holidays," added Charlotte.

There was little Juliet didn't know about their eating habits as her daughters and Alistair had often gone on holiday with their grandparents when they were younger and Phil and his family were there also. Alistair had told Juliet how one holiday a few years ago Louise had gone into the caravan and had stuffed two packets of crisps into her mouth out of sight of Phil because she knew he would tell her off. Louise's overeating was obviously some sort of comfort eating and now she was trapped in a cycle that she did not know how, or did not want to break free from. It was quite clear that neither Phil nor Louise were very happy.

The weekend passed by and Juliet returned home on the Sunday evening. She hadn't heard from Alex since their little tiff in the Park at the end of July and she was relieved every time she logged into her emails not to hear from him. But she knew that sooner or later he would rear his head again although for now she was enjoying the peace. She still met with Nigel although thankfully he seemed pre-occupied with his divorce and work at the moment and he didn't ask her out again. He had his cricket on a Saturday and that kept him occupied at weekends.

Phil phoned Juliet every morning at about 7am when he had left the house to go to work and then he phoned her every evening before he left work to go home. They chatted for 20 minutes to half an hour each time and they didn't run out of things to talk about. He always called her 'Beaut', which she adored and she called him 'Handsome.' He said that no one had ever called him handsome. "Well they should have done so, because you are," Juliet had told him. It was sad that two people who were married had so little time for each other or so little affection. A life unlived. Phil was a relatively straightforward bloke and it was a fair assumption to call him a bloke. He was hard-working and clever not academically but he was skilled and had a sharp mind. It was a shame that Louise hadn't got fully behind him with his business and helped him to take it where he wanted to go. He never had a shortage of work these days having built up a reputation over the years and he gained business by word of mouth. He was manly and protective of Juliet and he liked Clara, well he had three girls of his own. "By the Bab some clothes out of the money I gave you," he had said "spend it on what you like. You have struggled for years and it is not right. Someone should have taken care of you." So Juliet did. She didn't spend extravagantly but it was nice not to have to worry and she had not received a penny from Alex since April. And although she knew it wouldn't last, Phil was the tonic she needed for now.

They continued to meet up every fortnight on a Friday afternoon. Caravanning stopped and they were able to spend longer together. Juliet had decided that Phil needed treating. The Travel Lodge was a little clinical for conducting an illicit affair so she looked around for something better. She found that the Copthorne not far from Katie was doing special deals and it was actually cheaper than the travel lodge. She always made a little something for Phil to eat and took a bottle of champagne and two flutes in a plastic container wrapped in napkins. They would meet and she would run him a bath and together they would sit in the bath while he thawed out and drink the champagne and eat the little snack. Phil had no sense of taste or smell so Juliet bought Sushi one time and then she started to buy oysters. She had an oyster knife and bought a plate from home. Phil had no problem opening the delicious little molluscs, and they always had a marvelous time together sitting in the bath eating oysters and drinking Champagne. It wasn't hard to do, to look after him a little and he loved it. It was sad when they parted but it was inevitable that the short time they spent together would fly by and soon be at an end.

It was mid-November and Juliet had gone back to Katie's after her afternoon tryst. She hadn't been there long and her secret phone rang. It was Phil of course. "Hello Beaut, I just wanted to say goodnight."

"Oh Phil that is lovely but really you shouldn't take such a risk." "She has gone to bed and I am outside in the woodshed getting more wood for the burner. I love you Juliet" he said.

Juliet was taken aback. They hadn't been having the affair long and he was saying I love you to her. "I have to go, someone is coming," he whispered into the phone and with that he was gone. Juliet sat there in amazement. Katie sensed there was something amiss. "What's the matter Mom?" she said.

"He just said I love you, to me."

"Oh my god!" said Katie, and then started to laugh. "What are you going to do?" Juliet sat very still for a while. "I didn't think it would come to this. I really didn't. He has been warned. I told him all about what would happen if the affair came out. I never thought in a million years he would say that or that he would fall in love with me. I don't think he knows what it is."

At least Juliet would have a couple of days before she talked to him again. She had time to reflect on what this all meant. Was she in love with him? Well what was there not to love about Phil? Most people adored him, he was easy going, funny and kind, not to mention generous But really, this was getting out of hand.

After the initial shock and thinking about it, Juliet decided that she would tell him she loved him too. Well she did didn't she? Not in the same way that she had loved Alex admittedly. Not that deep, deep emotional angst that accompanies the sort of intimacy that she and Alex had shared. The soul-baring and physical intimacy. Alex knew her and she was deep, very deep. There was the surface Juliet and then beneath it went down, and down like a bottomless well. No one would ever know Juliet as he had done and Juliet didn't think anyone else ever would, she didn't want them to. But Phil? Well it did not hurt to tell him she loved him. He would tire of her she knew that and it would be over. It was as simple as that. These things always come to an end and she had guarded herself emotionally. She wasn't going to make the same mistake twice.

Chapter 23 – Getting Serious

Phil phoned early on Monday morning as usual. Juliet thought, he might have reconsidered what he had said to her on the phone on Friday night, but he had not. "I love you Juliet, and I want to be with you." "I love you too Phil, but it is not as easy as that, you are married to Louise, and as I have said before, you have been married a long time, and she is tied up with your business. She will take you to the cleaners. I don't think, you really realise how bad it will be." Said Juliet trying to put him off. "Look, Juliet, I have to see you this Friday, I cannot wait for another two weeks. I need to see you, can you come up? Have you got enough money?" Enough money? Juliet had an envelope stuffed full of the stuff, every time Phil saw her, he gave her more, despite her protesting. "Ok, Phil, I will have to clear it with Katie, but I think she should be able to do it, I will let you know later." "Ok, Beaut, I had better go and get some work done. Love you," he said "Love you too," said Juliet "Love you more," he replied and she laughed "no you don't," "yes I do," he continued. "Well I am not going to argue with you over that," she laughed and hung up. This little play between them happened every time they spoke on the phone after that.

Juliet was concerned. Phil was quite a determined man when he wanted to be, she had to dissuade him from this. He had been married to Louise for over 25 years; he had never known anything else. Louise would not let him go, and the state of her, meant that she would never find anyone else. If Louise had any sense, she would have gone on a diet, and looked after herself and started to cook for Phil, but she seemed very cocky in her position with him. She had remarked, on one of the weekends when they sat in the clubhouse "He falls asleep every night in front of the TV,"

192

Juliet had laughed "I don't know what you expect Louise, I have been married three times, and men always fall asleep in front of the TV at night. I don't know how they do it." Of course, Alex had never fallen asleep in front of the TV, but then, he did enough sleeping in bed to prevent that. Juliet also remembered, the one evening in the clubhouse that they were talking about PPI, and those wretched cold calls you get, trying to convince you that you have unclaimed PPI. Phil had remarked "Well, I know I don't, because I haven't had any loans." Louise had sat there, and said smugly, "that is what he thinks." A statement, that Juliet would later realise the significance of. Still, it was worrying that Phil had come to this decision. Juliet would have to tell him, all about the horror of divorce.

She saw Nigel two times that week for lunch. He was thinking about moving house, and was fretting about it. He had managed, to be quite crafty in his divorce settlement but, his house was worth over half a million pounds, and he had to sell it. Juliet couldn't understand why, it was nothing special as a house, but it was the area, prices in Oxford were sky high. "Will you come shopping with me at the weekend to buy a sofa? I would really like your help. You can stay overnight if you like?" "I can't do this weekend Nigel, I'm sorry, I am going up to see family, but I will do next weekend if you like, although I am not sure about staying overnight. I am not sure if Clara will settle in a strange house." Nigel was happy enough with that. Juliet had enough on her plate, with Phil at the moment, without Nigel as well.

Friday soon came, and she met Phil at the Copthorne and as usual, she ran the bath for him to bathe and thaw out. He worked in an industrial unit, and the weather was cold, very cold and there was little by way of heating to keep him warm. He was as usual, embarrassed about turning up in work clothes. "Look, Phil, they don't know you aren't my husband, and you are working away, and I have come up to see you. You have nothing to be ashamed about. I am sure hotels see a lot of shenanigans, your work clothes are the least of your problems." Juliet had got Oysters and Champagne, why not? The Champagne was on offer in Asda for a tenner and it was lovely stuff, not too dry like Moet. He soon relaxed and they sat in the steaming water. "Look Juliet I am serious, I want a life with you. I love you, and I adore Clara," Juliet sighed, "Phil, I love you too but I don't think you realise how incredibly messy this is going to be. For a start, she will have half the house. I presume your mortgage is paid off?"

"Well I thought it was but then there was all that stuff with Indemnity Mortgages a few years ago and we had to take out a small second mortgage."

Juliet had known that they had bought their house very cheaply well over twenty years ago, and the mortgage couldn't possibly be very much. "And then there is your business Phil, you will have to pay her off, of course you deal in a lot of cash which means undeclared income and so it won't look that good on paper,so you can probably get away with giving her less. But then there are your kids. They will hate you. They will take their mother's side, especially if you leave her for me. Can you handle that? They may come around eventually but it will take a while."

"Yes, I can," he said, "She hates you. We were coming out of the pub the other night and there was a convertible Mercedes CLK like yours in the car park and a woman got out of it. Louise and the kids were making bitchy comments about the woman and the car. I knew they were having a pop at you."

Juliet sipped on her champagne. "Oh Phil I know they hate me and probably always will, that is something you have to be prepared for. I myself can handle it, it is not a problem for me. That side of the family is dead to me. It has been since mom died. But can you cope with that?" He leaned over and kissed her, "To be with you Beaut I will do anything." That is easy enough to say thought Juliet, but doing it is another matter entirely. Although she knew Phil to be a strong person so she was inclined to believe him, however, time would tell.

Juliet climbed out of the bath and dried herself. Phil continued talking. "Look, Beaut I have it all planned out. We will have to rent somewhere at first whilst I divorce Louise, and then we can buy somewhere. We could always go abroad. I have always fancied fixing boats in the South of France. What do you think?" Juliet laughed as she inhaled her cigarette. "Oh Phil, you make it sound so easy. I don't mind where I go but presumably we will have to move somewhere within commuting distance of your work until the divorce is settled." Phil was actually seriously considering this and he had been formulating a plan. It didn't look like he was going to be put off it easily either.

"I have always wanted to go abroad, but Louise didn't want to," said Phil.

"Really," said Juliet, "I thought it was the other way around. Louise has always said it was you who didn't want to go."

"It bloody well wasn't."Well that was a turn up for the book. She really was a serial liar. Juliet had known it from an early age. When Juliet was thirteen, she had been given a leather clutch bag for her birthday and she hadn't even used it, when Louise had asked her to borrow it. Juliet had said yes but it seemed to be taking Louise a long time to give it back to Juliet. Some weeks later Juliet saw Louise with the bag and asked for it back. Louise had turned to Juliet and said, "But it is not your bag Juliet, it is mine." Juliet was flabbergasted and stunned and said nothing. What could she say to a statement like that? Needless to say she never saw that bag again.

Juliet put on her black silk corset and her stockings and went to the bathroom doorway. "Come on then Handsome, get yourself dry and make me a happy woman." He didn't hesitate and arose from the tub and grabbed a towel. "You're one hell of a sexy woman Juliet," and he chased her into the bedroom grabbed her and pulled her onto the bed, kissing her passionately.

Sex between them was good. Not Alex and Juliet standard but it was good. He didn't try to make her come and she didn't care. She never wanted a man to be master of her pleasure again like Alex. She was not going to be a slave to anyone's love like that ever again.

"Why don't you get yourself a vibrator? Louise has one." Juliet knew that Louise didn't just have one, she had several and what's more, they weren't just vibrators. They were dildos, big, black dildos. Her daughters had told her. Louise made it public knowledge along with her use of Tena lady's. It really was quite repulsive. Whatever Louise' peccadilloes sexually, they were hers and hers alone. Having big black dildos was definitely not a badge of honour to wear out in public. "No thanks Phil, I really don't want one. I can easily give myself an orgasm if I want to, my finger is an expert, and as for a dildo no thank you. If it isn't a penis attached to a man then I am not interested."

The thing about sex for Juliet was the physical intimacy. Being held, kissed and fucked. Masturbation satisfied a simple need like eating a cheese sandwich. If you were hungry then a cheese sandwich would stop your hunger but it didn't necessarily mean you wanted to eat it. And for Juliet sex was like food. She liked to be delighted by the visual feast, and then to savour every mouthful, every sensation.

Their evening came all too quickly to an end. "I want you to start looking at rental properties Juliet, somewhere for us. I need somewhere to store my boat so bear that in mind when looking." "Ok, I will." Said Juliet but she had little intention of doing so. She hoped that this was just a fad and that it would pass. If she held him off until Christmas then perhaps the cooling off period when they were not able to see each other and he was at home with his family would make him think differently.

She spent the night at Katie's and drove home the next morning. Phil was at work and phoned her first thing. "I want to see you before you go home. I have to see you." So, they met at the little lay by just before the motorway. He was waiting and hopped into the passenger seat of her car. "I really want to be with you forever," he said, as he kissed her tenderly. Juliet hoped he would see sense she really did. She was careful not to encourage him in this folly of his. Instead, she constantly pointed out the pitfalls and dragged her heels.

Chapter 24 – No turning back

Phil and Juliet spoke every day, morning and night. Each time Phil said "Love you more," when Juliet responded with "I love you too," to his "I love you," they had a little battle, as to who loved each other the most. It usually ended with Juliet saying, "I refuse to argue with you over this," laughing and hanging up. However Phil showed no sign of giving up on his idea of leaving Louise. The more it went on the more Juliet was convinced he was serious. However, Christmas would tell.

The next weekend she went to see Nigel. They went out to buy a sofa and he let Juliet guide him then they went shopping for other household stuff. Juliet had taken a look around his house, and it was clean and tidy, but it lacked little finishing touches so they went around TK Maxx and filled a trolley. Nigel got out his credit card. "Are you sure this isn't too much to spend?" said Juliet. "Not at all, I have just made ten grand from Next shares that my father gave me a few years ago. He only paid 65p for them each. "
Say no more," said Juliet. OMG! She thought to herself, why couldn't I be as lucky as that. But she knew she was never going to be. Of course she could have Nigel if she wanted, she knew this but it would never be. He was great as a friend but as a partner, no, that would not work for her, or for him. She would use and abuse him and he would let her. She needed someone stronger than Nigel. She felt bad about the car and the ring but he had wanted to do that she hadn't led him on. She had told him she didn't want a relationship, that she was damaged and that she definitely didn't want/probably couldn't have another child. But he still didn't give up hope. Perhaps this was the problem. The more Juliet backed off from men and gave them their space, the more they wanted her. She had got it all wrong and it had taken her

a long, long time to realise this. She laughed to herself at how stupid she had been, yet she really wasn't into playing games. She had experienced quite enough of that with Mark and Alex thank you very much.

They went back to Nigel's house to arrange the things they had bought. Juliet was rather pleased with her choices. The house looked more like a home and the sofa would complete it. She was making a cup of tea in the kitchen and Nigel was elsewhere in the house. The door opened and she expected to see Nigel but it was a young woman, in her late teens. "Who the hell are you?" she said to Juliet.

"Who are you?" Replied Juliet.

The young woman had anger in her eyes. "What are you doing here?" She said.

"I am a friend of Nigel's and you still haven't answered my question."

The young girl was extremely angry and hostile. "Did he leave my mother for you?"

This was preposterous. Juliet was here to help Nigel. At that moment Nigel came in. The young girl now turned her attention to him and started ranting about Juliet. Nigel calmed her down and took her to the door and then came back. "What the hell was that all about Nigel?" said Juliet, who was rather angry at what had just happened. "How the hell did she get in? I presume she is Jackie's daughter?" "Yes, she is, and the door was unlocked."

"Look, Nigel, I really have had enough drama in my life, and I don't want anymore. Accusing me of having an affair with you and taking you away from Jackie? What the hell is going on here?"

Nigel looked rather sheepish. "Well, I did tell Jackie that I loved you when I asked for a divorce."

Juliet was horrified. "How dare you implicate me in all of this Nigel, I have been through hell with my divorce. Why did you have to mention me? We were through long before you asked for a divorce."

Nigel stood there, wimpishly."Well, when I asked for a divorce Jackie wouldn't let me be and kept asking if there was someone else so I thought of you because I love you."

Juliet stood rooted to the spot. Nigel said nothing. "Nigel, I sympathise but it was such a shock to turn around and see her standing there, I didn't know what to think. But I think the best thing I can do is leave."

"But Juliet, don't go, she has gone." "Yes Nigel but for how long? She has two sisters don't forget and I don't want a knife through the roof of my convertible."

"You have insurance," said Nigel. Insurance! Was that all he could say.

"Yes, Nigel, but it will be a hassle and will put a dent in my no claims bonus. I am sorry, but I am going." She collected her bag and put Clara in the car seat, thankfully she hadn't witnessed the scene in the kitchen. She drove off. Nigel would have to stew. He was a wimp, notwithstanding the car and the diamond ring. Anyway that was peanuts to him, the man had just received 10k in share dividends. She had earned that money in more ways than one.

She drove home and was cross. Cross not angry, there is a difference. Yes, the little scene she had just been an unwilling participant in, was unpleasant and unwelcome to say the least but it had given her an excuse to cool it with Nigel. Men, they were all the bloody same underneath, self-centred and self-interested. Alex, Nigel and even Phil. They all wanted their own way no matter what the cost to Juliet.

She got home, fed and bathed Clara and put her to bed. It was Saturday night and she was alone with a microwave curry from Waitrose. It was what she called her night off from cooking. She settled down with a large glass of wine to listen to music. She felt soothed and relaxed. She would have to put in an application to the court to arrange proper access with Guy, it was well overdue and if Phil kept up with this living with her malarkey, she would need a proper arrangement. She would do it first thing Monday morning.

She opened her emails. And low and behold there was one from Alex. He hadn't contacted her since July and she knew he would appear again.

I will be sending some presents for Clara for Christmas. I trust you will let her have them.

On what planet did he live? Of course, she would let Clara have his presents. She did have to wonder where he was getting this attitude about her from. Was it his past? Whatever the reason, she felt uneasy about it? She replied to him briefly.

Of course, I shall give Clara your presents, you are her father. But I am reminded of the old adage "Beware of Greeks Bearing Gifts" What is it you want?

But she received no response.

Phil's offer was looking more and more tempting. She could make a clean getaway. Alex would not know where she was and neither would Nigel. Yes she was on the run again. She really did not know what to do for the best but she really needed to get clear away from Alex, of that she was certain. She couldn't trust herself not to fall again for his charms. They were far from done with each other of that she was sure and the best way to make sure of that, was a new life. If he didn't know where she was and she would feel safe. She did not feel safe here anymore. It was the old life and everything tied with it, the place, the people. She needed a clean break. But she was still not sure about Phil. Christmas would see whether he was serious or not. She wouldn't push him though, she would sit back and wait and see.

Monday came, and Phil phoned as usual, but she hadn't heard from Nigel and there were no delivered flowers by way of an apology. Wimp, though Juliet, still it suited her purpose. When he did text again, she would be waiting.

Finally on Wednesday he text her asking to meet her for lunch. She replied. *"Nigel, I think after the little scene on Saturday that it would be better if we did not meet for a while. I don't want to come between you and your stepdaughters and until you have moved, I shall not come and visit you at your house. I hope you understand. I do not want to inflame the situation. Juliet"*

She felt that was good enough to hold him in abeyance for a while. He replied saying he understood and was sorry, although she had to prompt him for this, it wasn't of his own volition.

She applied to the court and by the end of the week, a date came through which was just before Christmas. She had warned Mark and he was ok with it. She told him it was a formality if he agreed which surprisingly he did. You could have knocked Juliet over with a feather, although she still expected something to go wrong at the last minute.

She saw Phil once more before Christmas. It was the usual routine up at the Copthorne. It felt very Christmassy. "I would like to buy you a ring Beaut, as when all of this kicks off we shall not have any spare money," Juliet was flattered, "Look,Phil, I don't need a ring, my mother left me three and I have one from Nigel. Save your money, we shall need it in the future." Phil knew all about Nigel, and wasn't the least bit worried about him. Juliet had been honest and open with Phil and he knew the score. That was something Juliet liked about him very much. They both had pasts and present encumbrances and he accepted it.

"Have you done anything about a house to rent?" The truth was, Juliet hadn't. She had taken a brief look on the internet, but not seriously, she was waiting until after Christmas. "Well Phil, I am not sure, there don't seem many properties about that will accommodate your huge boat on a trailer. How much do you want to spend?" Juliet was really concerned that if he left her, she would have to pay the rent and without a job she would have to rely on benefits so she didn't want anything too grand.

"I really haven't got a clue, but I have to house my boat. That is not negotiable. Anyway, I have nearly 20k saved in a biscuit tin. I was saving for a Porsche but then you came along and you are better than a Porsche any day of the week," and he let out peals of laughter making the water in the bathtub ripple.

Juliet laughed, 20 fucking grand in a biscuit tin. "Phil you are not for real. In a biscuit tin? And where do you keep this said biscuit tin?"

"Behind the wardrobe of course." Juliet could not believe her ears. How on earth could, or would, anyone keep a biscuit tin with 20 grand of cash in it, behind a wardrobe. Notwithstanding that his house might be burgled, his wife and children had notorious sticky fingers and surely the biscuit tin was no secret. Although it might be, Juliet couldn't imagine Louise dusting behind the wardrobe. She was notoriously slovenly on the housekeeping front.

They said their goodbyes at the end of the evening, and departed. Phil had been careless with his car in the car park. It was a distinctive black land rover and it bore a private plate, it was parked near to Juliet's very distinctive Mercedes convertible. There were a lot of Christmas Party's being held at the Copthorne but he seemed not to care anymore whether they were found out. "Got to go out to a meal tonight with all of the bloody kids and their boyfriends. Louise is paying but of course, that really means me." Juliet wondered how they would take it when the money tree had gone. It didn't bear thinking about. Still, he might cool off over Christmas and reflect on his idea. Perhaps Louise would make Christmas nice for him but she doubted it. It would be parties thrown at his expense ones where she could showcase her dog hair cupcakes.

Chapter 25 – Back to Court

Juliet was nervous about attending the court hearing for her access application for Guy. Although Mark had agreed in principle and Juliet had partially believed him, she was still nervous nonetheless. Juliet had told Mark that she was not having a solicitor to represent her and there was no need for him to have one either as he agreed in principle to what Juliet had proposed. There was no legal aid available for such representation anymore so neither of them could afford it. However it didn't stop Juliet from worrying. Juliet was proposing that she have Guy every other weekend and for two weeks holiday every year and alternate Christmases. Mark was very jumpy about this but realised that he had very little choice but to go along with it.

Cafcass had conducted a DBS check on Juliet and of course, they asked about the incident when she had been arrested. Juliet was fuming inside. That was his doing not hers and now she was the one who had a blemish on her character. Just fucking typical. The years of abuse Mark had given her and now it was she who was stained and tainted by it. She had hoped of trying to get a GP managers job when Clara was older but this would kiss goodbye to any hopes of that as they would do an enhanced DBS check and would find this out. It really wasn't fair. She hadn't been prosecuted but nonetheless, the fact that she had been arrested was enough to put doubts in prospective employers' minds about the suitability of her character for such a position.

Phil phoned Juliet on the morning of the court case as usual. "I wish I could be there to support you Beaut, I really do. I hope everything goes alright. Know that I am with you in spirit." Juliet was grateful of the moral support, even if it was merely words but she knew he meant it, he was kind-hearted.

She arrived at the court and Mark was there. Unlike last time they chatted. Juliet had earned a degree of trust with Mark over the past 20 months or so since she had been living nearby. A lot had to do with the fact that she cooked Sunday lunch for him and Guy and they came up for dinner in the middle of the week. It was hard for Guy to leave in the beginning and she saw him run around the tree outside when it was time to go, playing his father up. It was heart-breaking to say the least. Juliet bought him clothes and sweets and played with him and he absolutely adored Clara. They would often go into the bedroom and leave Mark watching TV, to play ships on the bed. Guy and Mark would come on a Saturday if the girls were visiting and Juliet would play music and they would all laugh and dance in the living room, despite Mark moaning that he couldn't hear the TV but he was lonely and glad of the company.

The court case went ok. They sat in the Judge's office not in the main court. Mark still had to have his way and said that Guy had music lessons on Saturday morning so Juliet could not have him on a Friday as requested but she could pick him up on Saturday lunchtime. Juliet was not happy but she had little choice but to agree. However she was pleased overall with the outcome it had not been traumatic like the last time she had been in court. Should Phil keep up this relentless idea of them living together, she would have something set in place. Mark knew she was having an affair with Phil as Juliet had told him and he didn't mind in the least, he knew it was over between them. Had it been Alex back in her life, his attitude would have been completely different.

Juliet, Alistair and Clara were going to spend Christmas at Juliet's fathers. Juliet was going to cook for everyone and that made 11 in total. Juliet's brother Lee and his wife

Theresa and their two children were also coming. Juliet went up to see Guy the day before Christmas Eve and she had secretly deposited presents for Guy with Mark the evening before, when he had been in bed. She was sad about Guy not being able to join them, but next year it would be different and she consoled herself with that thought.

They arrived at Juliet's father's early afternoon and Juliet set about decorating the place. Juliet cooked some food for them all and they were settling down for the evening and the doorbell rang. It was Louise and Phil. Why they had to do this pretend round of visiting people at Christmas, was beyond Juliet. She had long moved away from this old-fashioned way of doing things but it was as though Louise was trying to live the kind of life that Juliet's mother had done all those years ago. The fact that Juliet's father had been fairly successful had always rankled with Louise and she saw Juliet as being spoilt. Spoilt! That was a bloody laugh, Juliet was far from it. OK, yes it may have appeared that way when she was a child. She had a pony and piano lessons but if only people knew the truth. It was not easy being a child in that household. There was no love, no affection. Juliet's mother was a cold woman. It was not that she didn't love and adore her children, she did, but she was always dancing a tune around their father Vic. She had never been a physically affectionate woman, probably due to her own upbringing, one of nine children and a twin to her sister Pat. They had been born when her mother was 44 and they were the last children. By this time Agnes, Juliet's great-grandmother was worn down and worn out. Vic, Juliet's father had shown her affection when she was small but as she grew older it ceased. Was it because he thought it inappropriate? Or was it that he had just got conditioned by Dorothy's lack of affection towards him. But Vic ruled the roost and everyone danced a tune around him. Juliet may have had a pony but if she wanted to go riding on a weekend, it had to be on Vic's terms and that meant getting up at 6am on a cold Sunday morning to go. She would return home for 9am, her feet frozen into two blocks of ice and unable to feel her fingers. Neither of her parents had said 'I love you,' to Juliet as a child, it was just not said. Juliet vowed in her teens that if she had children, she would make damn sure she told them she loved them.

And that was how it was. To the outside world Juliet had appeared to have what she wanted, but in truth, it was not like that at all. But it didn't stop Louise being jealous of Juliet and it went back to when they were children. Whilst Juliet had shaken off the trappings of showy wealth years ago as a shallow façade bringing little value by way of happiness, it had left a profound impression on Louise and she sought to emulate Vic and Dorothy as best she could. In the process she was ruining her children and working Phil into the ground but the fact that she herself lacked any work ethic, meant that however hard she tried she would never be like Dorothy and Vic. Her own mother who was fiercely house-proud and a very good cleaner had commented frequently on the state of Louise's house and she would go there and clean it whenever Louise was throwing a party, because she was so ashamed. Juliet was just glad that Phil didn't have a sense of smell. That was probably how he had managed to put up with it for years.

But here they were, Louise and Phil, sat in Juliet's father's lounge. Juliet looked at Louise. She hadn't seen her for a couple of months and she was still as fat as ever. If Louise had suspected Juliet and Phil of being up to mischief, she had done little to make herself more desirable to Phil. She sat on the sofa with her ankles crossed. Juliet was amazed at the size of her calves and she realised that she probably couldn't cross her legs as they were so fat. She had to make do with crossing her ankles. She rested her clasped hands complete with chubby fingers on her apron roll that sat just below where her waist should have been. She was wearing leggings and one of her floaty tops that she was so fond of. Her hair was cut short and was permed. The receding hairline was very noticeable. I would get myself a wig if I had a hairline like that, thought Juliet. Louise was fond of comparing herself to Ma Larkin, the character in Darling Buds of May but the reality was far from it. Louise was not a nice, happy, jolly person like Ma Larkin. She was a nasty, jealous, backstabbing bitch. The only similarities were the size of their bodies.

Juliet sat and listened to Louise holding court. She rarely glanced at Phil, she daren't. He had drunk whisky and she could see him watching her and smiling. Oh the delicious wickedness of it. Did Louise know that he lay in bed next to her on a morning thinking of Juliet? I bet she didn't. She was in her own smug little world.

"Oh we have the biggest tree you have ever seen in our conservatory," said Louise. "It must be nearly ten feet tall." Juliet laughed inwardly .She knew that Phil had moaned about the tree. He had got home from work and had to erect it and cut the top off, so that it would fit into the room. He had also moaned that despite Louise and his three daughters having a vast collective weight they had not bothered to erect the tree themselves, something that had greatly annoyed him when he had come home from work, knackered, starving and faced with the remnants of a cold takeaway. How wicked it is to know the sad, sordid realities of other people's lives whilst they sit and brag about them as though they were wonderful, Juliet thought. Phil had also told Juliet how he and Louise had visited her brother Lee, and Louise had commented, "How can Juliet afford to buy Christmas Cards from Waitrose?"

Of course, if only she knew that they had been purchased with Phil's money. Phil and Juliet had laughed over that "Good for you Beaut," he had commented. Louise would never dare venture into Waitrose. She would have been out of her comfort zone. She preferred Asda. Well, she didn't cook (apart from the cupcakes), and would not appreciate the delights on offer there. The best she did was brisket of beef. She had made some for bonfire night down at the field, but Juliet had blown her out of the water with warm homemade sausage rolls and her stew. Even Louise's daughters had shrugged their mother's brisket in favour of Juliet's delights. How Louise must have hated that. Juliet had to admit to herself, that revenge was definitely a dish best-served ice cold.

The next morning Juliet's phone rang, it was Phil "I have to see you Juliet, you looked so beautiful last night I couldn't take my eyes off you. I need to see you if only for half an hour."Well it wasn't sex he was after in that short a time frame that was sure. He had it bad and she knew it. "I have to go shopping Phil, so I can meet you near to Katie's, just down the road and around the corner, no one will stumble upon us there." "Ok, see you at 10.30 then."

She waited in the car but not for long and his car pulled up. "Oh Beaut I miss you so much, I just want Christmas to be over. I want to live with you. You cannot imagine how horrible it is living with her. She keeps bloody moaning all the time and she is watching me like a hawk. She followed me down to the woodshed last night."

"Perhaps she wanted your body," laughed Juliet.

"We haven't had sex for months," said Phil.

Oh that was bad, really bad. "Really? Come off it Phil, I have been married and had an affair. Of course you are still having sex with her, there is no way of avoiding it. I am not some innocent teenager, you don't have to say that to make me feel better." Replied Juliet.

"No I mean it Beaut. I don't want to touch her. I let her go to bed first and then follow up later when I think she is asleep. The other night she waited that long, I found her asleep in her PVC gear."

Ooh, gross, thought Juliet and let out a laugh. "I bet that wasn't very comfy to sleep in. Sorry for laughing Phil, it was just the thought of Louise asleep in PVC." God, how did the woman do it? PVC, with her figure? No wonder he didn't want to have sex with her. If only Louise knew that Juliet knew all of this, it would kill her, it really would. "No wonder she suspects you are up to no good, if you are not giving her any. For God's sake Phil, don't tell her. I can understand how you must be feeling but if you tell her and you have nowhere to go your life will be hell. You work so hard, you deserve a rest. But if you tell her now, you will have no peace over Christmas at all. Just bide your time. Get drunk if you have too, but don't whatever you do tell her." He seemed comforted by this and they held each other tightly. "I had better go now Beaut, but thanks for that I needed to talk to you and to see you."

"Oh, and Phil, just keep your secret phone in a safe place. If she suspects something, which I think she does, she will be looking for any clues that will give it away. If you want to leave her, then you have to do it on your terms and with a clearly executed plan. Spend your time thinking about that. Christmas will be over soon enough." And with that, they kissed and parted.

Juliet sincerely hoped he would listen to her advice and act upon it. He had been known to act rashly before, especially when he was drunk. But he was also fairly sensible and Juliet had told him what he would experience should he let it slip. That should be enough to make him hold his tongue. Perhaps he would even get over this madness with Juliet, but she somehow didn't think that was going to happen, not after what he had said this morning. He was in deep, very deep.

Chapter 26 – New Home

Christmas morning Phil phoned Juliet early. She went outside to take his call. He was taking a risk but she was thrilled to receive it all the same "Happy Christmas Beaut. I love you." Juliet replied likewise. They didn't need to give each other gifts, they just liked each other's company and they were both grownups. That was how they operated. How they fitted together. They both had kids and their company was enough for them. "Hope you are ok," said Juliet.

"She is being a right Bitch," he replied.

"Well hang on in there Handsome," she said. "I would rather be with you than here, you know that but there is nothing we can do about it at the moment," "You're right Beaut, as always."

"Love you" she said,

"Love you more," he replied,

"No you don't, I love you more."

"No, that is simply not true, I love you more. "

"I L…. But the line went dead. Louise must have found him in the woodshed. Juliet had vegetables to prepare. What would be would be. There was nothing she could do about it, fate would decide.

Christmas Day went off well enough. Juliet worked her arse off cooking for that many people but everyone enjoyed themselves. She phoned Guy and wished him Happy Christmas in the morning. He was pleased with his presents. It was a constant heartache, a pain that would not go away but there was nothing she could do about it, not at the moment. She knew that it must be a lonely Christmas with Mark. He had said he was getting ready meals in for them. Kids are not interested in the food at Christmas, thought Juliet and Mark had bought Guy lots and lots of toys. That was what he did best, being a big kid himself. They would be back home the day after Boxing Day and Juliet would invite them both down for a meal.

January came and Phil resumed his phone calls on a regular basis. He had phoned sporadically while he had been off over Christmas but Juliet knew that Louise was not letting him out of her sight. She had suspicions, that was pretty clear. Phil kept up the pressure about a house for them both and Juliet realised that he was serious. She started to look for a house to rent in earnest and then halfway through January she found one. She was concerned about the monthly rental but Phil wasn't. It appeared to have room for a boat and it was in a very nice part of Wolverhampton, on the outskirts, towards Bridgnorth. There were no pictures of the house but Phil phoned her that evening and said he had been and had a look at it and it fitted the bill, although the gates had been locked and he could not get in. He asked Juliet to arrange a viewing. Juliet protested that if he left her, she would not be able to afford the rental. She asked him repeatedly and he was still adamant that he would not leave her. Juliet would just have to take a leap of faith and trust him.

There were viewing appointments available on Saturday morning, according to the agent. So he gave them an time.. Juliet's father had gone on holiday to Tenerife so she could stay at his house overnight. The weather had been bad and there had been snow although thankfully it had cleared a little on the Friday morning in time for her to travel up to the Midlands. She got to her fathers' just before lunch which was fortuitous, as it started snowing heavily on Friday afternoon. Phil phoned her and said he would pick her up tomorrow morning at around 10.30am. At least he would have no problems with the snow in his land rover. Charlotte was still living with her grandfather and she would be able to look after Clara.

Juliet was up early and it was still snowing. She cleared the snow off the drive before it became too much and caused difficulties. Phil picked her up at 10.30am. "Hello, Beaut. It is good to see you."

They hadn't seen each other since before Christmas, and he leaned over and gave her a kiss on the cheek. "It's good to see you too," Juliet replied and they set off towards Wolverhampton. Thankfully Phil knew the way. Although Juliet used to know Wolverhampton and it's surrounds very well twenty years ago, her memory had faded considerably. They arrived at the house and parked on the car park of the pub opposite and made their way over to the property. The gates were open and they walked up the gravel driveway. It was quite spacious and Juliet could see why Phil liked it, there was indeed room to store his boat here. There was no sight of the house however and then they reached the end of the driveway and turned and the house was tucked away out of sight of the road and not visible from the entrance to the drive. It was an odd house, it had obviously once been a cottage, but had been added onto. The garden was a bit of a shambles and there was a large pile of rubbish on the drive. There was also a tumbledown shed at the end of the drive before you turned towards the house. Someone had obviously laid a few slabs near the house in a haphazard fashion but it was ok.

The landlord met them. Phil talked about his boat and the driveway and the landlord was enthusiastic. He liked them, Juliet could tell. He showed them around the house which again was odd but spacious. It was essentially a dormer bungalow that had been extended and then extended again, all by the landlord Terry. Upstairs was a lovely large bedroom with a Velux window and sloping ceilings under the eaves and there was also a bathroom with corner bath and shower. It was a little dated but it was still nice with a window overlooking the garden. Downstairs there was a large lounge of which Terry was rather proud as he had built it himself. It had laminate flooring and large bi-fold doors overlooking the neighbouring garden, which Terry explained belonged to him as they lived in the big house next door. It was a lovely view and looked as though they were looking onto open parkland. The snowy scene was beautiful. Terry explained it was National Trust Property. There was a small back garden that belonged to the house itself but it was a complete mess, full of building rubble and debris. You would have thought he would have tidied it up, thought Juliet especially for the money he was asking. Although likeable, you could tell he was a cheap snob as he kept talking about the area, saying it was a conservation area and the best area in Wolverhampton.

There was a downstairs walk-in shower and four further bedrooms, although the one had a view of a fence and you wouldn't really want to use it as a bedroom. The kitchen was a little old-fashioned but had once been a good one. But the cooker! Oh my, the cooker! It had a halogen hob with five rings and there were two ovens. Juliet was in love. She would have taken the house on the strength of the cooker alone. They left and went back to the car.

"We'll Beaut, what do you think?'
"Well Phil it is up to you. Can you house your boat here? I can make anywhere a home. I know how to work the magic and I have moved many times." Phil didn't hesitate. "I love it Beaut. I am going to phone Terry," Juliet sat and listened to the one-sided conversation. Phil came off the phone "He said he liked us and the house is ours if we want it. I told him we did." There was nothing more to say. Phil had made his mind up. They were going to live together in Tamarisk.

Juliet drove home to Oxford and they put an application in for the house. Being as it was through a letting agent there were a large number of forms to fill in. Juliet was defeated. The forms were aimed at finding out the creditworthiness of the parties wishing to let the house. Juliet had no credit rating whatsoever and as for Phil, well as he was self-employed they were demanding accounts and a statement from his accountant. That would not happen. Louise did his accounts, and he couldn't contact his accountant as he would tell Louise. When Phil phoned that evening, Juliet had plenty to say.

She explained the situation but Phil was not defeated. "Look Beaut, phone Terry and explain the situation. Tell him that I will pay six months' rent up front. I will get it out of the biscuit tin."

Juliet did as she was told, although it was going to be an uncomfortable conversation. She phoned Terry and his wife Ann answered. She outlined her situation. "Hello, I know this is rather unconventional and I will be plain with you, Phil is married and plans to leave his wife. He is self-employed and we cannot ask for the accounts without his wife knowing. If you are in anyway uncomfortable with this then we fully understand. However in order to overcome this Phil is willing to pay six months' rent, plus deposit upfront in cash. Think it over and let me know." Ann said she understood and would tell Terry when he came home. Juliet was 90% certain he would say yes. There is something intrinsic in human nature that makes people greedy. The lure of 6 grand in cash is hard to resist, for even the most cynically natured individuals.

Sure enough Terry took the bait. The deal was done. He sympathised and said that he understood. He himself had lured Ann away from her abusive husband. It appealed to his inner knight in shining armour but more so to his bank balance and inner greed.

Juliet told Phil "I will drive down with the cash for the deposit tomorrow Beaut. You need to put it into your building society account and have a cheque made out. The deposit needed to be in the form of a cheque. It basically amounted to money laundering. But Juliet would say it was from the sale of a car. They weren't really concerned, her building society account rarely saw a balance beyond 500 quid and they made no comment when she deposited the money.

Everything was sorted and the house was theirs. They were to move in on the 1st of February. Juliet gave notice on her flat and organised a van rental. It was simple. On the morning of Friday the 1st of February Juliet would drive up to the Midlands early in the morning and after dropping Clara off at Katie's she would then drive over to Wolverhampton and leave her car at Tamarisk. She had arranged to meet Phil at 9am on the pub car park opposite. They would then go and sign the lease at the letting agents. They arrived there in time and sat in the office whilst the lease was presented.

"This is like getting married," said Phil. Juliet was busy looking over the lease "We have paid six months' rent upfront and this lease does not seem to represent this," she said to the agent. "I am going to have to cross out this clause as a consequence," she said, "Can you confirm that Terry will agree with this, otherwise we are not signing," The agent looked sheepish and got on his mobile. A while later he said "Yes that is fine Mrs. Grosvenor, do what you asked."

They were out of the letting agents by a quarter to ten and Phil took Juliet over to the van hire place where she hired a long wheeled based transit. "I'll see you about 6pm Beaut," and he gave her a kiss. He was planning to go home and tell Louise and then just walk out. Juliet hoped he had the bollocks to do it but if not, then it didn't matter, she would have six months with no rent to pay and time to sort out herself out.

Juliet drove back to Oxford. It was a little after twelve when she arrived. Alistair was waiting with his friends to

217

load the van. They were away by 3pm. Finally they got to Tamarisk at 5pm. They were met by Ann, Terry's wife who magically appeared out of nowhere when they parked the van. They lived next door and could see everything that went on at Tamarisk. Juliet found this a little disconcerting, but Terry was alright. Ann however was a different kettle of fish. It was the first time Juliet had met Ann and she could tell straight away that Ann did not like her, although she was pleasant enough, there was just something there that made Juliet feel uncomfortable.

Chapter 27- Settling in

They were busy unloading boxes when Phil's land rover pulled up on the drive. He had done it, he had left her. He got out of the car and had a big smile on his face. Juliet was worried about him as leaving your wife of 27 years is not an easy thing to do. "You ok Phil?" Juliet asked.

"Yeah, never been better," and he threw himself into unloading the van. Katie and Charlotte came over and brought Clara. They were being nosy. They couldn't wait to have a look at the house.

"What do think?" asked Juliet

"I don't know," said Charlotte.

"It's a bit of a weird house," said Katie.

"Yes, it reminds me of that film, you know the one Katie, The Hills Have Eyes," said Charlotte, and they both burst into fits of laughter. Juliet had never seen the film and was bemused at their reference

"What do you think Uncle Phil?" Said Katie.

Phil laughed "I know the one you mean, but listen girls, you can't keep calling me Uncle Phil now, just call me Phil, ok."

They sorted out the beds and Juliet got Clara to sleep. Juliet and Phil were in the kitchen. Phil had showered and was wearing a large bathrobe that Juliet had brought back from Egypt and she was wearing her bathrobe too. She had pre-cooked a casserole for them to have that night but none of the kitchen stuff had been unpacked and Phil suggested they just have bacon sandwiches. Phil cracked open a bottle of red wine and poured them each a glass whilst Juliet tried to get to grips with the complexities of how to work the cooker. "So, how did it go then?" said Juliet, when she had finally worked out how to turn on the grill.

"Well, she was crying and saying don't go, please don't go."

"Oh dear," said Juliet, "not well then." What a pathetic excuse for a woman, Juliet thought. If he had been my husband, I would have told him to fuck right off.

"And the kids kept phoning me, especially Tiffa, while I was driving over here."

"Oh God," replied Juliet "You haven't told them where we live have you?"

"No, don't be daft Beaut, of course, I haven't."

Juliet breathed a sigh of relief. Phil could do without a scene this weekend. They would have to know, in due course where he was living but the dust needed to settle first. "Have you turned your phone off Phil? because things will be raw with them tonight. Let them calm down first." "Yes, Beaut, I have."

Phil and Louise had three girls. The eldest was Charlene, who was just like her mother. She was the same age as Katie and like Juliet and Louise they had been friends on the surface but enemies underneath, always in competition with one another, although it was Charlene who tended to copy Katie. Charlene had taken up with some old cast off of Katie's and had soon got herself pregnant trapping Jimmy in the process. To say Jimmy's family weren't pleased was an understatement. They felt that Charlene was not good enough for their son. Juliet had learned all about this first hand from Louise a few months ago. They had bought a house together and Juliet wondered how they could afford it. Charlene was only a dental nurse and Louise had said that she was on family tax credits because their combined wages were so low. Juliet couldn't fathom how they had afforded to buy a house but she suspected that Phil and Louise had helped them out, or more realistically Louise.

Tiffany or Tiffa, as they called her was the middle child. She was bolshie and outspoken and behaved more like a man than a girl. There was a likeable quality about her though and she was a lot like Phil. She was the same age as Alistair and although her bulky frame dwarfed Alistair they had been friends when younger. Like her sister, Tiffa was also a dental nurse.

Then there was Britney. Britney had what Louise called 'learning difficulties'. Her speech was impaired and she could barely read. When Britney was very young Juliet had asked her mother about it. "Louise says she has dyslexia," said Dorothy to Juliet, "and Louise is on the board of governors at the school in an attempt to help Britney." Although she hadn't sought any real help for her and at the time Juliet had been working at a charity that assessed children with complex disabilities and she had described Britney to her boss, who had said that it sounded like Dyspraxia. Juliet felt sorry for Britney. She was 16 and clearly Phil felt protective over her. Sadly they were all overweight and getting bigger. A couple of years earlier, Katie had brought Tiffa with her to Oxford and Tiffa had spoken to Juliet over her sadness at her size. Juliet had talked to her and it was clear that Tiffa wanted to do something about her weight but with the onslaught of Louise saying, "Big is Beautiful" all the time and the poor diet they kept, it was no wonder that Tiffa's weight was now spiralling out of control.

The weekend passed by. Juliet unpacked all of the boxes and the house was resembling a home. She cooked Sunday lunch for Phil and he kept his phone turned off. He went to work on the Monday morning with a packed lunch that Juliet had prepared for him. That evening he had returned home and after a shower and a glass of red wine he was talking to Juliet in the kitchen.

"Have you spoken to Louise today?" said Juliet.

"Yes, she came up the work with the kids. She asked me to come home. But don't worry Beaut, that ain't gonna happen."

221

"Was that all she said?" asked Juliet.

"No, she said she had suspected for a while that I was having an affair with you."

"Oh," said Juliet "hindsight is a wonderful thing. If she suspected then why didn't she ask you? I suspect she is making that up."

"She said she saw us in the clubhouse that first night." This was sounding really far-fetched. Louise knew how to play him. Phil was bright but not what you would call emotionally intelligent and she had obviously played him for years.

"I don't know whether I believe that Phil because if you had been my husband and I had come looking for you and found you in the arms of another woman, I would have flung the door open to the clubhouse and asked what the fuck was going on. But she didn't."

"I don't know about that Beaut but she said she knew." Was Louise really that weak? She portrayed herself as some strong woman, who didn't take any shit. But it would appear that the reality was somewhat different. Juliet couldn't believe that she was still asking him to go home when it must have been apparent that he was determined to leave her. It wasn't as if he had moved into a house that belonged to Juliet, they had taken a lease out on a rental property in joint names. That in itself signified the gravity of his decision to leave Louise.

"She said she had noticed that the biscuit tin had gone," Phil continued.

So, Louise had known the location of the biscuit tin thought Juliet, "Oh, and when did you move that?" "Wednesday" he replied.

"Where is it now?"

"Up the work." Juliet doubted that Louise had noticed the biscuit tin had gone missing, that was unless she was regularly dipping into it. It was more likely that when Phil had left, she had gone to see if the tin was there. She would have been worried about her financial position. But all this hindsight was about saving face for Louise. It was as though she wanted to make it appear that she knew what was going on but was turning a blind eye. She had been humiliated and that was what she couldn't bear, the humiliation. If she had loved Phil that much she wouldn't have taken the piss out of him for years and she would have treated him better. She would have lost some weight for a start off. She knew how he hated her being so overweight.

"Phil I hate to say this but you are going to have to get the books from her. She is in control of your finances and she could do a lot of damage. It is quite clear that she is in shock at the moment as she didn't expect this to happen but when she is over the shock she will seek to protect herself. I know she has always done your books but it has to stop. You do see why don't you?"

Phil looked concerned, "Yes of course Beaut, I do. I will ask her tomorrow."

"Phil there is no ask about it. It is your business and you have a right to see them." Phil was a bit slow, poor love, but then he had never experienced this before. He had trusted his wife of 26 years to act in his best interests. Juliet knew however from her daughters that there was a lot that went on in his house that he didn't know about. A lot of it to do with money. Louise was always feeding her children with cash, so much that they laughingly referred to her as the cash cow behind her back. But it wasn't Louise's cash was it? It was Phil's.

When he came back from work the next day, he told Juliet that he had asked for the books but that they were with the accountant. That's very convenient, thought Juliet to herself, it is more likely that she is trying to keep control of them as long as possible. But she said nothing.

It went on like this for two weeks and Juliet was getting concerned. She had not said much about it to Phil because she didn't want to seem as though she was nagging him. With men if you repeatedly go on to them about something they dig in their heels and do nothing, so Juliet had kept quiet but she was getting very, very concerned. It was about time she said something.

"Phil those books have been with the accountant a long time, it has been nearly two weeks. Perhaps you should go and see the accountant. You do realise that you cannot trust Louise now. You have betrayed her and whatever she is saying and however she is acting, you cannot trust her. You have broken her trust. I am not saying you should cut her off financially, of course not. You need to honour your obligation towards her and the kids and give her some money but you cannot start to sort this out until you have the books."

Phil had obviously been thinking this over too and was also getting concerned. "I know Beaut, I need to know, she controls everything and I am not happy. There wasn't the money I thought I had in the biscuit tin. I counted it the other night." Oh right, it was just as Juliet had thought, they had been dipping their sticky fingers in it.

"Oh, dear?" was all Juliet said, "Could you have been wrong Phil?"

Phil looked deadly serious "No Beaut, I wasn't wrong, I think she have taken some out. But when I asked her she said I must have been using it on you,"

Juliet was fuming. The big fat cow! "Well, it is only what I suspected Phil. I thought she would have been dipping into it. You do know she hands money out to the kids like Smarties. Katie and Charlotte told me years ago."

Phil was angry. He was being made a mug of and he knew it. "This has gone on long enough. I am going to the house tomorrow and getting the books." Juliet knew he meant business, she could tell.

Juliet always cooked delicious meals for Phil. She made sure that every night he had a home-cooked meal. It was just a shame that he didn't have a sense of smell and could appreciate just what a good cook Juliet was. They had settled into life together very well and although it had been only two weeks everything was very pleasant apart from Louise hanging onto the books. Juliet suspected she was just trying to maintain some control. She wouldn't want to be ousted from the business. She couldn't be ousted from the business, Juliet knew that she had been with him since he had started that business, although now she only went in one morning a week. Juliet thought that she could be bought out when the time came.

Chapter 28– Surprises

The next evening when Phil came home he didn't look pleased. He put the books down on the kitchen counter. Juliet was cooking. "Oh, you got them then?" said Juliet. "Yeh, but I don't know Beaut, there is something not right." "What do you mean Phil?"

"Well I don't do accounts but I was looking over them this evening and there is something not right. Will you have a look?"

Juliet was confused, "Ok Phil but I don't know if I can be of any help?" He opened one of the ledgers. Juliet was surprised that in this day and age Louise was still keeping manual ledgers and not using a computer system. She went over to look at the open ledger. It was untidy and there were entries that had been scribbled over and obliterated and a page had been torn clean out. Juliet knew this was wrong. If an error is made in a manual ledger then it should be crossed out neatly to indicate it was an error but you should still be able to read it and pages should never be torn out.

"It's a bit of a mess," said Juliet "she should have crossed that through and she shouldn't have torn a page out."

"No, not that Beaut,"

"What then Phil, I don't understand."

Phil went on to explain. "There are entries in here for suppliers that we stopped using long ago," and he pointed them out. "ACE supplies £250, Brierley Hill Tools £450, and he kept pointing them out.

"Are you saying Phil, that you did not have any goods from these companies in the last month?"

"We haven't had stuff from them in years."

"But there are entries in here as though she has paid them, and the cheque number is next to them. Where has that money gone Phil?" Juliet was beginning to see what had been happening.

"That's what I'd like to know," said Phil," and it has been going on for a long, long time. By my calculations, there is 10k missing over the last six months alone."

"Of course the payee on the cheque need not be the company in question Phil. You have to get the bank statements, cheque stubs and you also need to get the folder containing the invoices because there will be one and we need to cross check the journal entries with the invoices. Whilst you are at it demand everything to do with the business. If I am right, she has been fiddling you Phil."

Juliet couldn't believe that Phil had been so naïve as to never look at his books before. But then she could. He had trusted Louise and he worked so hard. He worked 12-hour days, hard physical labour and not pleasant at that and he was no longer a young man. He was in his early fifties. What a cow she was thought Juliet to herself. She was fat, lazy, pompous, conceited and now it would seem dishonest. Well, that didn't surprise Juliet, she had always told lies. But to diddle your own husband. That was shameless. Their marriage was a pack of lies. Juliet couldn't wait to see what further investigation would yield.

Phil came home that night will all of the documents Juliet had suggested. She had a cursory look through them. What did surprise her was that both Phil and Louise had company credit cards and they were virtually maxed out, both to the tune of 15k. "What the fuck Phil? I can't understand why you are using credit cards as a means of borrowing money for your business. It is not the best way to do it. The interest on them is astronomical." "Oh, Louise said that the accountant had advised it." Juliet severely doubted that was true "Well it would be better to have an overdraft surely?" "We already have one of those?" he replied.

"And, how much is that for?"

"10k."

Juliet already knew because he had told her that he was earning about 50k a year. He wasn't declaring all of that and he was paid a lot in cash but when it was all added up, it came to 50k. Juliet was gobsmacked. "This amounts to 40k of debt Phil for the business. That is shocking. You don't even own your own unit. You are your business. Do you understand that if you had an accident or suddenly got ill and could not work for six weeks, your business would fold? I can't believe that with all the years you have worked and all the business you do, you are operating on credit like this."

Phil looked crestfallen "I didn't know half of this Beaut. But that isn't the end of it, I have uncovered more as well." Oh God, Juliet thought what is it now? She suspected that Louise was helping Charlene pay her mortgage but she would soon get her teeth into the books tomorrow, when she went over them with a fine-tooth comb. Phil started to speak "Well, you remember me telling you how I built the conservatory myself to save money."

"Yes, I do," said Juliet "And very impressive that was too."

He continued, "At the time we could have had a loan to build it. It would have cost about 10k but I told Louise that we couldn't really afford it. I worked my bollocks off in the very little spare time I had to build that conservatory to save money and now I have gone and found out that when we took out the mortgage to cover the shortfall of the indemnity mortgage which was 10k, the mortgage we took out was not for 10k, it was for 25k." Phil had really been taken for a mug.

"Well, how did that happen Phil? Didn't you have to sign the mortgage agreement?" "I should have done but Louise forged my signature." So that was what Louise had meant in the clubhouse months ago, when she had said 'that's what he thinks' referring to Phil not having taken out any loans. "That is fraud Phil." Juliet was amazed. The scheming, devious, deceitful, dishonest cow was in fact little more than a common criminal. Juliet laughed and laughed, tears rolling down her face.

"I don't know why you think this is funny because I bloody well don't," said Phil.

"Phil, I am sorry, I am not laughing at you. This is thoroughly disgraceful, I agree that but there you were feeling guilty about sleeping with me and leaving her when all along she has betrayed you. She has been fiddling the books and doing god knows what with the money without you knowing and for quite a while, long before you and I ever started. In my book sexual betrayal and financial betrayal are equal. They are both as bad as each other and break trust.

It was certainly a revelation. Juliet knew where the money had gone but she couldn't very well say so, not yet at least. It was perfectly obvious. Louise had upped the mortgage on their house in order to provide Charlene with a deposit for her house. It was the least Louise could do. Louise said she had gone to see Jimmy's parents after they had heard about Charlene's pregnancy. Louise must have felt really ashamed as they lived in a nice detached house in a better area. So Louise had hatched a plan. Rather than tell her silly daughter that the best thing she could do was to have an abortion, she aided her. She would have told his parents that she would help them buy a house and she would have pretended that she and Phil were better off than they really were. She effectively helped her daughter trap Jimmy. Women like that give women a bad name. It was sickening, it really was. And of course, Phil knew nothing about it, sap that he was. It was a very sad state of affairs really. All the lies, the deception and Louise had been driven to fraudulent behaviour in order to maintain a lifestyle that neither she nor her children could afford. And then of course, the sad loser in all of this was Phil. He thought he had money and he now realised that he hadn't got a pot to piss in. It was a house of cards.

The next day she pored over the documents. It was bad. Phil's salary was paid into the joint account and all the bills were paid out of that, mortgage included. Louise drew a salary of around 1300 per month which was astronomical for what she did and that was paid straight into her bank account. Louise had not handed over her bank statements, understandably but Juliet suspected that a lot of the crooked cheques went into either her bank account or Charlene's, but looking at the amount she was fiddling each month Juliet knew it amounted to a mortgage payment. The only loser in all of this was Phil. He had nothing. He had a mortgage on a house that he should have paid off by now and was relatively worthless. His business was in debt up to its neck with no collateral. All that debt would have to be paid off before he could retire. The business was worthless as a result of the debt. Then there were probably personal credit cards that Louise had. She loved spending money and shopping. It was her hobby. Probably some of the dodgy cheques were to pay the monthly repayments on them. The only things they had were their cars, his boat and the caravan. The house was in a poor area and it was a shit hole, it wouldn't be worth a lot and someone would struggle to get a mortgage for it as there was something wrong with it structurally.

They sat in bed that evening talking about it. Phil was unhappy to say the least. "You do realise what she has done is fraudulent. If the taxman ever found out it would mean prosecution and possibly imprisonment for her because you knew nothing about this. You could go to the police yourself, not as though you are going to. I bet her mother would love that. Headlines in the Express and Star; 'Local Woman Swindles Husband out of Thousands' the shame alone would kill them."

"I don't know what the hell to do Beaut. I thought I had something to offer you and now I know I haven't. How can we have a life together? I wanted to offer you a better life."

Juliet sighed "We can build your business up again. I can get a job. I can earn decent money you know."

"I know you can Beaut but I didn't want you to have to work, I wanted to be better than the others."

"Oh Phil, I don't mind, I really don't. But the bigger dilemma is this, if you have so little then how is she going to cope? No one will employ her. I don't mean to sound bitchy but they won't. She has worked for you for years and then she can't, Charlene relies on her for childcare. It is a big bloody mess, I know that and it is all her doing. I feel for you Phil, I really do, I warned you this would be hard but it has been harder for you than I thought with all of the shit that we have uncovered. Not in my wildest dreams did I think that would be the case. She has stitched you up good and proper."

Juliet knew Phil was in a hopeless situation and that he didn't know what the hell to do about it. The next few weeks slipped by. His children were still refusing to speak to him, all except Tiffa, who was sent every now and then on little missions up to his work to ask him to come home. Juliet knew that Louise could not survive financially without him. It wasn't because she loved him because if she did she would not have him back after going off with another woman. But then if she had really loved him she wouldn't have treated him like shit for years. No, it was a question of financial survival for Louise. She had even got her mother to phone Juliet's brother Lee and ask him to intervene. When Juliet's father had told her this, Juliet had laughed. Did they think they were children? How could anyone else ask them to stop what they were doing? Of course her brother had done no such thing of the sort and it was her father who told her. They were making complete idiots of themselves, it was embarrassing to say the least.

Juliet had realised in the midst of this that Phil was not really her cup of tea. He was nice enough and he was blokey and protective, but he led a life and maintained a lifestyle that he had been formed for him over years with Louise and his relaxation time mainly revolved around the Pub. This didn't sit very well with Juliet, but she went along with it. There were other little things about Phil that she had found out and didn't care for. He had mentioned PVC to her and Juliet had laughed and snorted in derision at his suggestion. There was no way she was donning PVC like Louise. He was no great shakes in the bedroom department that was for sure. He certainly wasn't sensual like Juliet. What had happened to him over the years? When she had first known him all those years ago when they were teenagers, he had feverishly explored every inch of her body with zeal. Perhaps it was years of living with Louise. Juliet certainly soon gathered that when he and Louise had sex, Phil would watch porn downstairs whilst Louise waited upstairs. When he was suitably aroused, he would go upstairs to do the deed. Louise was quite surprised that it was only the PVC he needed to get him off, she would have thought a paper bag on Louise's head might have been more appropriate. And what was it with the bloody PVC? She could only imagine that it seemed to keep the rolls of fat in check with Louise, although the visions Juliet had in her head was one of a poorly overstuffed black pudding with the contents spilling out.

Phil's mother Rene lived in a static caravan. After his father had died she had sold her house and gone to live in a static caravan on a caravan park. She had been a staunch caravanner all of her life and indeed she still had a touring caravan. She actually looked like a Romany. She was diminutive in height, had a penchant for gold half hoop earrings and twinkling brown eyes and the character of a small sharp little dog. However, there was one downside to living in a static caravan. Every February it had to be vacated for a month and Rene had been off in her touring van since the day that Phil had left Louise. It was now March and she had returned.

Louise and her mother had wasted no time in enlisting the help of Rene to put pressure on Phil. They must have had to tell her all of the nitty-gritty about the financial situation as

Rene went about this newly given task with relish. When Phil came home one night he was most vexed "I have had mom on the phone today giving me an ear bashing about leaving Louise. Maggie has been onto her. Mom has phoned me three times today."

Juliet felt sorry for Phil, he really was quite weak. They didn't speak much about it and Juliet held her tongue but she knew Phil was between a rock and a hard place and he was being mentally tormented by these demented harpies that were his relations. "You poor love," was all she said and gave him a hug. She wished he would make his mind up one way or the other. He was dithering and she knew it. He had moved in with a dustbin bag of clothes and he had not been and retrieved anymore. He said the place didn't feel like home to him and Juliet realised that unlike her, he had lived in the same house for the last 26 years. Although it was a shit hole, it was his shit hole and Juliet supposed that he had got used to it and it felt familiar. The sad thing was that they were messing with his mind. Juliet suspected that Louise had been up to her old tricks and had been threatening him. Phil was in a similar position that she had been with Mark. It was ironic.

Chapter 29 – Déjà vu

Phil was slipping away and Juliet knew it. A slow withdrawal and he was in turmoil about it. He didn't know what to do for the best.

Usually on a Friday afternoon Phil came home early, generally 3.30 to 4pm and this particular Friday was no different. Juliet would usually run him a bath and they would sit in the bath together having a glass of wine. Juliet ran the bath but Phil was nowhere to be found. She opened the bathroom window slightly and could hear his voice on the driveway. The bath water was going to get cold if he didn't hurry up and she put on her robe and went outside. He was messing with his car "Mr. Evans, I am beginning to think I have lost my appeal. I have run a bath for you and it is getting cold."

Phil looked over "I will be in soon," was all he said but Juliet knew that something was wrong. When he did come in for his bath it had long gone cold and Juliet had pulled the plug on it and had got dressed and was preparing dinner. She said nothing about the bath. He was distancing himself. He said nothing about what he was thinking to her and he fell asleep in front of the TV that evening. He went to work in the morning. At least that is what he told Juliet. She herself was not sure that was where he had gone. Juliet was fuming. If he had made his mind up to leave then he should just bloody well get on with it. He came back from work (supposedly) at about 2pm and went upstairs and had a shower but he didn't come down. Juliet went to look for him and found him lying on the bed.

"What's the matter with you?" said Juliet.

"I don't feel well" was his reply.

It was unlike him, he was never ill. "What is wrong with you?" "I don't know. It is all such a bloody mess, I can't sleep and I can't eat."

Juliet looked at him angrily. He was like a little boy lying there. He hadn't got the mental capacity to think his way out of this and Juliet was sick and fed up with it. He should have been decisive weeks ago, mind you, he should have not let her have so much control in his business in the first place, he shouldn't have trusted her but she had him by the balls. "Why the fuck don't you just go back to her Phil? She has got you by the balls."

He had never seen her angry and he didn't know what to say. She was sure he was about to cry. It was pitiful, it really was. "I don't know what to do." He repeated.

"Well I do. It seems to me that you been bullied into submission and you are too much of a coward to tell me you are going back to her. After all the 'I won't leave you Beaut' you said, you have realised that you have got to go back on your word and you have let me down. You do know that if you go back to her, she will never trust you again and after what you have discovered you will never trust her. She will throw this affair at you every time you have an argument. Your relationship will never be the same again. I know, I had an affair. You are a wimp." She said and paused and then she softened. He was going and he felt terrible, she knew that. After all the shit everyone else had given him, she was giving it to him as well.

"Look Phil just go, honestly, just go. Don't worry about me, I am a big girl. I will get a job, I will be alright." She said quietly and he started to cry. She went over and comforted him.

"I don't know what to do," he sobbed.

"Well, only you can decide," she said, and left him to it and went down stairs. There was nothing she could do. He had to make his mind up and she knew which way it was going to go.

He finally came down and did not display any signs of leaving and she started to prepare dinner. She wondered what the hell was going on.

He started to talk about Britney. Apparently she had been upset when he had visited them at the house last Friday. Britney, because of her disabilities was Phil's Achilles heel, just in the way that Guy was Juliet's. He started to talk about her now. "When she was young, about three, we were at the field," they used to go there virtually every weekend and Juliet knew this although for years she had lived in Oxford and had not visited. Mark had hated going there. There were too many people and he didn't like large social gatherings. He considered them to be common, unintelligent people that he did not want to mix with. Juliet knew it was because he found large gatherings of people intimidating.

Phil continued, "any way, the kids wanted to have a ride in the back of the land rover." (Phil had one with a canvas on the back stretched over a frame which could be taken off). "So all three girls got in the back, I was towing the trailer at the time and we went up the track and around the bend to go up the hill, but suddenly, the girls started screaming on the back of the land rover and I stopped. Britney had fallen out while I was going along. My heart went into my mouth and I was worried sick, she must have gone under the trailer and I had run her over. What if I had killed her?"

Juliet felt sorry for him "Oh, Phil, that is truly awful, but she was alright, wasn't she?"

"Yes Beaut, of course she was, just shaken and a few bumps and bruises. But it gave me the fright of me life I can tell you."

Suddenly it all clicked into place. Juliet had wondered why Britney had learning difficulties. Nothing had ever been said about the birth being particularly bad, indeed Juliet seemed to remember that Louise had given birth within the space of three hours, something Juliet marvelled at as her labours always lasted a long time, despite having had so many. But here suddenly may be an explanation. Falling from a land rover whilst it was moving onto a hard stone road or indeed bouncing off the trailer and then onto the road would not have done Britney any good at all, she would most certainly have banged her head and Phil made no mention of them taking her to the hospital to be checked out after the incident. What if that had caused her some ever so slight brain damage? Juliet shuddered. Phil was carrying the guilt around with him over Britney and he had done for years. Of course the real person to blame was Louise. Men always do stupid reckless things, but a mother would not have allowed it to happen. Juliet would never have allowed her children to go on the back of an open top land rover unless they were old enough to be responsible and three years old was certainly not that. But then Louise had dragged her kids up. She never even read to them. Poor Phil, poor, poor Phil.

The next morning Phil lay there asleep. It had been snowing overnight and he didn't stir. Juliet could see the snow on the trees through the velux window. For someone who was having difficulty sleeping he was asleep now. Perhaps he had made his mind up.

She went downstairs and busied herself. But it was not like him, he didn't usually sleep this late. She went upstairs it was nearly 10.30 and he was still not awake. She decided to go and see her father that was if she could get off the driveway with all the snow. But she managed it.

She got to her father's "Oh, Hello Juliet. How are you? How is Phil?"

"I'm fine Dad, but Phil is not well."

"Oh sorry to hear that Juliet. What's up with him?"

"He says he is sick, sick in the yed more like." Juliet was usually quite well spoken, but with her father, she slipped into Black Country Dialect because it was the way he spoke. They chatted for a while and then she said she had better be going. She hoped Phil would be up by the time she got back.

237

Her dad saw her to the door and she was just getting into the car when her phoned beeped with a text. It was Alistair, he said; *Phil has left, he has left a note x.* Juliet breathed a sigh of relief, and looked at her father "he has left me," she said, "well at least that's over."

"Take care Juliet," said her dad, and she drove back home, relieved that he had made his mind up one way or the other at last.

What a bloody coward! Why hadn't he gone yesterday afternoon when she had told him too? He must have thought that she would behave like Louise and be hysterical. How wrong he was. She wouldn't have cried, she would have been relieved. She got home and looked at the note. It said *"I am sorry, very sorry Juliet, but I have to go back. I thort I could give you a better life, but I can't. Phil"*

Oh dear, his spelling left little to be desired, thought Juliet. He really shouldn't have left a note. "He has taken all of his things mom," said Alistair. She went upstairs and there was a wad of notes on the bedside table. At this she saw red. How dare he treat her like a fucking prostitute and leave a wad of notes on the bedside table. And then she calmed down. He was trying to be nice. He didn't want to leave her in the shit. Well he hadn't left her in the shit, he had paid six months' rent upfront and she was in a nice detached five bedroom house in a smart part of Wolverhampton. She had time to sort herself out. But him? He was the one really in the shit. The amount of debt he had on his plate was awful. She may have had nothing, but at least she wasn't in debt up to her ears. He would have to work his arse off just to get rid of the debt.

Juliet messaged Katie and Charlotte and they came over. They were shocked at what they heard, "Oh Mom, you had a close shave there. He wasn't your class at all. And just think, if it had gone on any longer you would have had to have his kids in your house."

"Oh, shit," said Juliet laughing "I hadn't thought if that. Thank God he has gone."

Juliet was annoyed. Annoyed about the way he had gone about it. It had been childish leaving a note. It would have been better if he had behaved like a grown up, and said he was leaving. She would have kissed his cheek and said she understood but he had skulked off and what was worse he had purposely pretended to be asleep and waited until she left before he went. She wondered if Louise had put him up to it but she didn't think so. He was a child as simple as that. He was emotionally immature and he was a Gemini as was Louise and Gemini's are two-faced. They were welcome to each other but one thing was sure. Juliet would never, ever take him back. She had had her revenge and that was enough for her. In fact it had worked out even better than she had anticipated. Louise had to live with the knowledge that not only had her husband had left her for Juliet, Juliet now knew every minute detail of their finances and the fraud that she had committed.

"Lock the gates tonight Alistair, we don't want any of her scruffy kids coming over here tonight. You can never be sure with low life like that what they will do and we will change the locks tomorrow as he didn't leave his keys." At least they will never come caravanning to the field again, she thought to herself.

Chapter 30 – What next?

Juliet didn't sleep well. She awoke at 3am and was very, very angry. She made a cup of tea and went back to bed. It was the way he had done it, sneaking out. After a cigarette she had reasoned with herself, come on now Juliet, it wasn't like you could see it long term. Phil had displayed some characteristics that she was not overly fond of to put it mildly. She had doubted whether he would have ever changed, given his age and she would have missed the intellectual side of life. He wasn't someone you could take anywhere was Phil and she would have grown very tired of the pub. There was something that was making her angry, some underlying cause and she couldn't put her finger on it. She lay awake in the dark looking at the sky through the Velux window. It was late March and although it had been a bitterly cold winter, and it had snowed a few days before, the days were getting longer and the weather would turn soon it had to.

Her mind turned over and over and then she realised what it was that was making her so angry. Alex. It was Alex. She had thought that she would be free of him and now she wouldn't. About a week ago she had received an email from him saying he had got a job in Saudi and would be leaving in April and wanted to see Clara. Juliet had replied saying that she had moved had a partner and lived in a large detached house in a conservation area and she wanted nothing more to do with him. Alex had then replied and said he had written a will and would leave everything to Clara. Juliet had retorted that he had nothing to leave but his bong. This was how she wanted to leave it with him, she wanted nothing more to do with him but Phil leaving had changed that.

Juliet loved Tamarisk. It was a quirky house admitted but there was something about it that had Juliet hooked. It was secluded for a start and was surrounded by a garden. She had fallen in love with the cooker and the kitchen and she felt very at home here. It was even better now that Phil had gone. The upstairs bedroom was spacious and peaceful, with its Velux window looking out on the stars and the trees. She couldn't let the house go, she couldn't give it up, no matter what it took, she had to stay here, she had to afford it. She had until the end of July to come up with a plan of how she was going to afford it and afford it she had too. Apart from anything else she wasn't going to let Louise think she had won. This house was better than Louise's and in an area that was ten times better. Clara had been up-heaved from her home and planted in a new one and Juliet had to make her happy here there was no way she going to move into a council house just yet.

She lay awake for the next two hours and formulated a plan. She was cross, not because Phil had left her but because Phil had left her with a headache, a problem of how she was going to stay in this house. But stay in it she would, she had to. Men, bloody men, untrustworthy bastards, you couldn't believe a word they said. She thought Phil had been different but he had turned out as bad as the others if not worse. He pretended to be a he-man but underneath it all he was just a wimp and a child and a stupid one at that and he severely lacked skills in the bedroom. Still he had made his choice and it was not a good one, he would suffer for it for the rest of his life. But she was free to live hers as she chose. He would never have that luxury.

Early in the morning, she emailed Terry to let him know that Phil had left. Terry replied to say thank you for letting him know. Ann came around later that morning. "I am sorry about what has happened to you," said Ann.

That was a turn up for the book, Ann, sympathetic. Juliet told her all about Louise and the swindling. "He was weak," was all Ann said and so did her father when she next saw him.

"He is not the man I thought he was," said Vic "weak bastard." Juliet laughed as she drove home from his house. Perhaps she should shop them to the Inland Revenue for not declaring income. Then she thought better of it. He has enough on his plate. He is doomed with her to a life of continual work with little to show for it. They would distrust each other and it would eat away at what little was left of their relationship and he would have a 'squeeze' with any woman that made herself available.

Juliet put in a claim for housing benefit as she was now entitled to it and although they would not pay her the full amount of her rent, it was something. She set about sorting out the back garden. It was a bloody mess but Juliet knew what to do with it and in no time at all she had sorted it out. It just needed some turf. When she could afford it and the weather was warmer she would put some down and get some plants. She was messing about in the back garden one day when Terry was in his. He came over to talk to her "Look Juliet, Ann and I have been talking. We like you and you are our sort of person. If you weren't here we would have to pay the council tax on this place so we are willing to accept a lesser rent when the six months Phil paid is out." Juliet knew he didn't have to do this and although Alistair had finished the decorating inside and Phil had cleared the rubbish off the drive (with Alistair's help) and she was now doing up the back garden, it was still very kind of them. "Terry, that is awfully kind of you and Ann, I know you don't have too but I do like it here very much, and I am looking for a job."

"Well what will they pay you in housing benefit?" he said.

"Well I am not sure but it won't be anywhere near the full amount, probably about £450 – £500." Terry stood and said nothing. Juliet knew it was not anywhere near what he wanted and then she said: "How about £750 Terry?"

Terry looked pleased. "Are you sure you can afford that?" Juliet nodded "Yes, Terry, I think I can."

She would afford it, she would get the shortfall from somewhere and she had an idea where it could come from. "That's brilliant," said Terry "Obviously I will have to run it by Ann, but I think she will agree." Terry left and Juliet went back to her gardening. She knew where she could get it from but she would again have to compromise herself but if that is what it took, then she would have to do it.

She emailed Alex that evening.

Alex, I am sorry about what I said in my previous emails. You have every right to see Clara and I want her to have a relationship with you. If you still want to see her then I am happy to facilitate it. I know you are going to Saudi and Oxford is a little out of your way. I can be in the Midlands and meet you at Wolverhampton Train station if that is more convenient for you. We could have a day out at Dudley Zoo. Let me know what dates. That is, if you want to.

Regards
Juliet

Juliet felt pleased with herself. She had played it very, very crafty. She had not alluded to a partner and she did not want to let Alex know where she was living. Let him think she still lived in Oxford and was coming up to the Midlands to see family to make his life easier.

He soon responded to say yes and gave her a date a week away. He was going to bring gifts for Clara's birthday.

The weather had got better and they had finally seen the last of the snow. Although she was not very well off to say the least, she was going to put on a show for Alex. There was

243

no way she was going to let him think that she needed his money. She wanted to appear as though she had someone supporting her. He did not know that she had a car, a Mercedes convertible at that. On the morning she arranged to meet him she was up early and she washed down her car. It was old but he didn't know that much about cars and it looked impressive. She packed a picnic and then at the last minute she went to Sainsbury's and bought a bottle of red wine and some plastic glasses. She could ill afford this but if her plan paid off then she would be able to stay at Tamarisk and she wanted that right now more than anything else in the world. She dressed well and applied her make up with care. She was meeting him at the train station at 10.30am.

They arrived early and she sat in her car in the car park waiting. Just after 10.30 he came out of the station. If he hadn't been so distinctive because of his stature, she would not have recognised him but with his blonde hair, he was unmistakable. He looked awful. He had put on weight and his hair was cut very short, so short that it did him no favours whatsoever and he was wearing his glasses and his jacket was old fashioned. The way he carried himself told Juliet everything she needed to know, he was a broken man and looked a lot older than he had done the previous summer. He stood there looking around. Obviously he didn't know her car, so she opened the door and stepped out and waved to him. He saw her instantly and came over. She opened the boot for his rucksack. "Hello Juliet," he said. "Hello Alex," she replied. "Please, get in" she gestured to the passenger door. He climbed in and looked at Clara in the back seat. She was asleep. "She has grown so much," he said.

"Yes, hasn't she," replied Juliet. She started the car up and set off.

The conversation was a little stilted at first. Juliet decided to let him do the talking. "How are you?" she asked. She was putting on her very polite, caring face as she asked this question.

"Oh, ok. The weather has been very bad this winter in Wales."

Juliet was guarded "It has been bad everywhere Alex, we have had a lot of snow," She didn't want to give away that she lived in Wolverhampton, she wanted to see what he was offering before she even considered letting him know that. The conversation carried on in this vein for a while, neither of them giving anything away.

They arrived at the zoo, parked up and Clara awoke. Thankfully Alex wasn't too gushing with her. "Let her come around first Alex, she can be grumpy when she wakes." "Just like me then," said Alex and laughed. He looked worn out. What had he been doing to himself to get in this state? Juliet thought. Thankfully Clara was ok with him, even interested. They got out of the car and walked to the zoo. Alex asked Clara if she wanted to sit on his shoulders and she had agreed. Phil had taken her on his shoulders so she was used to it, but Alex was much bigger and walking under a road sign, Juliet had to remind him to duck so as not to bang Clara's head. They got to the zoo and Juliet got her purse out. She was prepared to pay for him if necessary, even though it would skin her out but thankfully he intervened. "I will pay for myself and Clara," he said.

"No need Alex, I know you have no money, I am happy to pay," but thankfully he insisted much to Juliet's relief. She only had to pay for herself.

He warmed a little as they walked around the zoo and he started to relax and Clara seemed happy in his company. The morning went by quite quickly even though it was cold. Well it always is in Dudley when the wind blows because it is on a hill. He even pushed the pram. "Is there anywhere we can buy lunch cheap here?" he said.

"No" replied Juliet "You know what these places are like, but it doesn't matter because I have bought a picnic" He seemed pleased to hear it and gratefully accepted the offer. They went to the top of the hill where the picnic area was and the sun came out.

Just as well thought Juliet because otherwise we shall freeze up here. "Would you like a glass of red wine Alex?" she said.

"Yes thanks, that would be nice. I can't remember the last time I had a glass of wine. Do you still smoke?" he said to Juliet.

"Sadly, I do," she said, "I should really give up but I can't, or rather more correctly I don't want to."

"I know just how you feel," he said.

Juliet wasn't sure whether it was the wine, or whether he felt relaxed in her company or a little of both but he started to open up. "I have had the most awful winter Juliet, living with mom. It has been a nightmare. She is getting old and more and more bitter. She has diabetes and has had to give up drinking wine but she has been the bitch from hell to live with. It has really worn me out." Juliet looked at him sympathetically but he was unable or unwilling to return her gaze.

"I am genuinely sorry to hear that Alex, I really am."

He continued "That is why I am going to Saudi. There will be no social life to speak of and it will be hot but they pay the highest salaries. I need to buy a place in France as soon as I can. I cannot return to her house again, I really can't." Juliet understood, she needed a place of her own that was why she was so desperate to keep Tamarisk.

They continued on around the zoo and the afternoon was pleasant. Nearing the end of the zoo was a small playground, Alex played with Clara and he asked Juliet to take a photo of him and Clara together on his phone. He really looked awful and he knew it when he looked at the photo Juliet had taken.

"I have been very down," he said to Juliet. "I have felt so low," he continued.

"I am sorry to hear that Alex," she said. "Things will be better when you start working again." And they left it at that.

When they got back to the car Alex gave Clara her presents; three cuddly toys from Hamleys. She was pleased with them and even let Alex hug her. It made Alex's day. They drove back to the station. Juliet wanted to get away from him as soon as possible. She wasn't falling for him but the mother in her was feeling very sorry for the little,lost boy that he was displaying. Whatever it was, it was not good. She wanted to remain at a distance. "What are you doing for dinner this evening?" said Alex. Oh god no, this was the last thing she wanted. She was not going there, she had to keep up the pretence of being with someone else, it was the only way.

"I have to get home and cook dinner. I am sorry Alex, and Clara has an early bed." Another time she would have accepted his offer, but after what she had recently experienced, Juliet was cautious. She wanted one thing and one thing only from Alex, maintenance.

She dropped him off in the centre of Wolverhampton but she had one cautionary word of advice for him when he left. "Alex, if you intend to be a father to Clara then please make sure you Skype every week. I know it isn't easy trying to communicate with a small child via a computer screen but you must try. You need to maintain contact with her. It is important if you are to have any relationship with her at all." He still couldn't look Juliet in the eye. "I will Juliet, and as soon as I am settled, I will start sending you maintenance." That was all she wanted to hear. "Thank you for a lovely day, you have been very kind to me when I really don't deserve it." He said sadly.

"Take care of yourself Alex and Good Luck."

Chapter 31 – The sun shines again

Juliet drove home. The sun was finally shining. She was pleased with her day's work. It had worked. He would have noticed the car, and the prominent diamond on the third finger of her left hand. How people can be fooled, or make assumptions about someone based on appearances, thought Juliet. He had obviously believed that she was with someone and was being taken care of. Her plan had worked. If she had emailed him and told him that she was broke and in dire straits and needed his maintenance he would have taken an entirely different position, but as it was, he thought she was being very well looked after by another man and had no need of him. He thought that her kindness that day was pure kindness and not driven by some other need. He had been careful not to overstep the boundaries with her and he had not asked about her partner or where she lived, he hadn't dared. But Juliet knew it was driving him mad. He was dying to know all about it.

Later that evening she received an email from him,

Juliet

Thank you for your kindness and generosity today, it was delightful to see Clara. I shall let you know as soon as I am settled in Saudi and have access to the internet. They are giving me my own accommodation, but it may take a little while. Once that is sorted out, we can arrange a mutually convenient time to Skype each week.
Once again, thank you for today.

Alex

All she had to do was sit back and wait.

The weather grew warmer and she continued with her garden make over. It was so peaceful here and so secluded, Juliet loved it. May arrived and with it the warmer weather and Juliet now understood why the house was called Tamarisk. It was like a little villa in the South of France. It even had the fluted clay roof tiles that were so indicative of that region. Alistair got a job and passed his driving test. It was so warm that Juliet would sunbathe in the afternoons and the girls always visited on the weekends. There was plenty of room here to accommodate Juliet's little tribe and she made over the spare room for guests to stay. It was at the end of what Juliet termed the West Wing and overlooked the parkland that was Terry's garden although her neighbours rarely ventured in there preferring instead their small garden at the back of their house as it was south facing.

After Phil had left, Juliet had phoned Mark and told him all about it. Surprisingly Mark wasn't judgmental, he sympathised. He had got over her leaving him at last. It had only taken him three years. It was now late May and Juliet phoned him again "Look, Mark, why don't you and Guy come up for the weekend, or even for half term? This place is huge and you can sleep in one of the spare bedrooms and I can give you some money towards petrol. Alistair and I would love to see you both as would the girls." Mark could have said no but Juliet knew he was lacking in company and he wouldn't be able to resist and sure enough, he agreed. Since Phil had left she hadn't been able to afford to go and visit Guy and she missed him like hell.

Things were looking rosy for Juliet. Her housing benefit had come through and Alex had settled into his job in Saudi and they Skyped on a Friday morning at 11am as it was his day off. Friday is the start of the weekend in the Middle East. He had even promised £200 in maintenance at the end of May when he would first get paid. Skype was a little tortuous as Clara had the attention span of a gnat, she was only two but Alex seemed content to watch her play and chatted a little to Juliet. Although they were careful not to talk to each other on intimate terms and he never asked any searching questions. He was more than happy to talk about himself, about his job and his colleagues and how horrendously hot it was there. He appeared to be getting out of his depressive state and although Juliet tried not to look at him on the computer she had little choice when Skype started up and he was looking better than he had done in April.

Juliet had laid some turf on the back garden that she had cleared of dead shrubs and debris and had bought a few plants at the garden centre which were flourishing. Now it was late May the addition of bedding plants completed it and it was pleasant to look at. The bi-fold doors in the lounge were wonderful when they were open, creating a feeling of space and tranquillity, the outside blending seamlessly with the inside.

It was hot for May, pleasantly hot, just as well after the long cold winter they had endured. Juliet sunned herself every afternoon on her sun lounger in her secluded front garden. It was time she thought to herself, time that she invested in a barbeque. It was fair to say that Juliet had hated barbeques with a vengeance when she had been married, so much so, that she felt she had been scarred for life by them. Every time Mark had mentioned the words "Let's have a barbeque," Juliet would immediately be sent into a black mood. The reason was quite simple. Mark's idea of a barbeque was such that he would spend a good half an hour trying to get the thing lit, only for Juliet in the end to come to his aid, and light it. Then he would proceed to cremate sausages on the outside but leave them raw in the middle. The children would complain and throw their sausages in the undergrowth at the bottom of the garden for the foxes to discover late at night. Why? Why does a man who never normally cook suddenly decides he is an expert at cooking when an open fire is involved? Juliet never understood. It must be something primitive Juliet had decided, going way back to when humans were cavemen. Not content with undercooked sausages, Mark would then move onto beef burgers. Juliet made her own and they were rather good and surprisingly Mark managed to cook them, you can't really go wrong with a beef burger and by this time the fire would have subdued a little from its initial raging. But it didn't end there. An hour later he would want another burger and then another hour later perhaps another. This did not sit well with Juliet. Juliet's idea of a barbeque was that it should be a complete meal, served at once, all of the constituent parts being ready to eat at the same time. It should be like a proper meal with a balance between meat, vegetables and carbohydrates. There were so many wonderful things that one could cook on a barbecue that did not involve sausages or beef burgers. Up until now Juliet could not contemplate having a barbecue ever again.

But the weather had been warm and sunny and it seemed stupid to go inside to cook and eat when the weather and the garden were so lovely. Juliet knew that she had finally been rehabilitated when she decided to buy a barbecue. She went and collected one from Argos and assembled it in the garden. This was going to be barbecuing Juliet's way. She prepared some chicken pieces and made a marinade for them and diced peppers and put her newly acquired wooden skewers to soak in water. She took some corn on the cob and generously dabbed it with butter, and wrapped it in aluminium foil. Then she prepared some lovely creamy potatoes by pricking them with a knife and rubbing them with olive oil, sprinkling with sea salt before finally wrapping them in aluminium foil. She did this all to the backdrop of music in the kitchen and sipping a glass of wine. She was in her element and enjoying herself tremendously.

When Alistair came home from work at 5.30 he showered and dressed and they sat in the garden. Juliet put her kebabs on the barbecue to join the already cooking potatoes and corn. Hey presto, it was all ready at the same time and Juliet had to admit it was delicious. Men make such a bloody drama out of barbecuing thought Juliet. "This is lovely mom," said Alistair and Juliet felt rather pleased with herself. She had turned a corner and was enjoying her new single life. For the first time in what seemed like ages she was genuinely happy.

Juliet had settled into life by herself and it was good to be near her daughters and her father again. Phil had done her a favour really. Guy and Mark came up for the weekend every now and then and they stayed for a while in the Summer holidays. They didn't do much; play in the garden, go for a walk by the canal, visit Bridgnorth and the field and of course the girls would come and visit. They would have barbecues and sit outside on the warm summer evenings. It was really rather lovely.

In late July, Juliet received an email from Alex. He was coming back to the UK in September for a holiday during Ramadan, and he was staying in the Midlands and he would like to spend as much time as possible with Clara for the five days that he would be there, he hoped that Juliet could accommodate this.

Juliet couldn't very well say no to him, she needed his money and she felt sufficiently emotionally distanced from him to be able to be in his presence without losing her head. So she agreed. She didn't really have any choice, not if she wanted to stay in Tamarisk.

Chapter 32– Alex

Juliet and Alex had become 'friends' for want of a better term, albeit distant. They spoke to each other via Skype and Alex had said that he was going to go to Ireland for a few days to look at some properties. He had switched his attention from France to Ireland, although Juliet couldn't understand why. He sent her some photos of the properties he had found. He must be on good money thought Juliet for him to be thinking about buying a property so soon. She wasn't overly impressed with the properties he had chosen, but she was careful to keep her criticism to herself.

At some point in August Juliet had felt comfortable enough to give him her address. It was silly not to, he was giving her maintenance and he had a right to know where she was living. She couldn't very well keep it a secret forever. She had been forced into a situation where she had no choice but to let him back into her life for Clara, so it seemed childish to not tell him as he would have to know sooner or later.

Alex had been in touch with someone who he had been to school with, a woman who was married and had kids. He said that she had contacted him through Face Book and she had remembered what an awful time he had at school when his stepfather had left his mother. She now lived in Clent and had a granny flat and had offered to put him up whilst he was in the Midlands so that he could see Clara.

The time came when he returned to the UK. He had been in Ireland and had emailed Juliet from there. The property viewing had not gone well and it was time, Juliet thought to voice her concerns about the properties via email.

"Alex, I was never very convinced about the properties you were viewing to be perfectly honest. The house you showed

me by the sea looked as though the land attached was marshland. This would be wholly unsuitable for growing vegetables as it would be very salty due to its position at the mouth of the estuary. Although the views were idyllic, I think that the fact you would not be able to grow vegetables there is a major drawback. I also think that you would not like Ireland. They are nice people and warm, but they do like to be very friendly to the point of wanting to know all your business and I know that you are a very private person and I think this would irritate you beyond belief."

Alex emailed Juliet to say that he was inclined to agree with her and despite the properties in question appearing to be isolated they were in fact near other dwellings which had put him off. However he remained convinced that Ireland was better than France and had found one and had put an offer in on it. Juliet was dismayed, she shouldn't have voiced her concerns about Ireland. She should have known he would do the opposite to what she suggested. Oh well, it didn't matter to her, she wasn't going to live with him was she?

The day dawned when she was going to meet Alex. She was to pick him up at the Dick Whittington car park on the A449. She couldn't understand why he had arranged to meet her at such a place but she went along. She sat waiting in her car and he came walking over. "Hello Juliet," he said, as she got out of the car to greet him.

"Hello Alex," she replied. He seemed relaxed as he sat in the passenger seat. He was so big he filled up her car. "What do you want to do today Alex?" said Juliet.

"I thought we could go shopping, if that is ok with you, I would like to buy Clara some toys and clothes."

"Ok, Alex." It was threatening rain so Juliet suggested the Merry Hill shopping centre. Alex agreed and they set off.

They walked about the Merry Hill centre for a while and had some lunch at McDonald's, Alex brought some gifts for Clara but that had only taken up about two and a half hours, and Juliet was at a loss as to what to do next. Clara was tired and needed a nap and it was stupid to keep up this pretence as she was the one being inconvenienced by it. "Look, Alex, I don't know how you feel about this but I am at a loss what to do next. We can't very well spend the next four and a half hours here. Clara is tired and needs a nap and I think she would interact better with you if she was in her own home. She is a little wary of you at the moment as she hasn't seen you for so long." The truth was that Alex had tried to cuddle her too soon and to Clara he was a relative stranger, she was only two and a half. "If you don't mind, you can come back to ours, at least the tea and coffee is free."

"That is very kind of you Juliet. If you are sure that is ok with you?"

"Yes," said Juliet.

They drove back to Tamarisk. Whilst she drove, she thought. He is going to realise that I haven't got a partner soon enough and he is going to ask questions about it at some point. She thought about it and came up with a plan. She couldn't very well tell him the truth about what had happened with Phil could she? He would throw it back in her face at some point and say that it was more evidence of her lack of morals and say she was an unfit mother, traipsing men before Clara. No she had been very honest with him before and she had learnt her lesson, she would now tell him a pack of lies.

They pulled up on the gravel drive and she could tell that Alex was impressed as they got out of the car. They walked up the driveway and she opened the door to the house. He said nothing and that told her everything she needed to know, but his mind was whirring, she could almost hear the cogs going around.

As you entered the house there was a little porch and then you entered into a dining hall that was tiled with Mediterranean terracotta tiles. To the left and open plan was the kitchen (and stairs) which was spacious and large and to the right was the spacious lounge with laminate flooring. A sliding glass door separated the lounge from the dining room. It was a bit of a bodge job but it was practical as it blocked the sound from the lounge going up the stairs which led off the hall up to the first-floor bedroom and bathroom. Directly in front as you entered the hall come dining room, was a door that led to the downstairs bathroom complete with walk-in shower and hall with further four bedrooms off that. The west wing as Juliet jokingly called it.

She showed Alex into the lounge. "Would you like a coffee?" She said.

"That would be lovely, thanks," Clara was asleep. She had fallen asleep in the car and Juliet had carried her in and put her to bed.

Juliet was nervous but she hoped it didn't show. She was alone with him and she was feeling very uneasy about it. She made him coffee and herself tea and took them into the lounge and put them on the coffee table. She was careful to sit a distance away from him, at right angle to him on the L-shaped sofa.

"It's a lovely house," said Alex, "the view from here is amazing."

"Yes," was all Juliet said.

"Your partner won't mind you bringing me back here, will he?"

Bang. Straight in there. He couldn't resist, could he? Juliet breathed out, "I don't have a partner, I never have." He didn't look the least bit surprised. "But you said in your email?"

"I know what I said Alex. I wanted you to leave me alone. But I regretted it because it was not fair on Clara."

Alex sat, and sipped his coffee. "Is it ok to smoke in here?" He said.

"Yes, when Clara is not about."

Juliet went and got an ashtray, relieved that for now at least he was not going to ask any more questions. She needed to steer him away from this topic of conversation but she knew, the skilled prosecutor that he was, he would return to the subject another time most likely when she was least expecting it. She returned with the ashtray "Are you ok?" he said to Juliet "You seem a bit edgy."

She sat down on the sofa "What do you expect Alex, it is not easy seeing you again, it has put me a little on edge that is all. I don't want us to end up in a fight. I want us to be friends for Clara's sake."

He nodded "Can I roll you a cigarette?" he asked "Yes, thanks" she replied. Thankfully that seemed to have satisfied his curiosity for now.

"So tell me about this place you have put an offer on," she said as she lit her cigarette and drew on it.

The rest of the afternoon passed easily enough. He asked no more questions and when Clara awoke from her nap she seemed happier to be next to Alex and even enjoyed the attention. Thank God, it had been six months since Phil had left and Clara was young enough. Hopefully she had forgotten all about him and would not say anything or make any reference. You know how kids have the nasty habit of dropping you right in the shit when you need them to keep quiet. At the end of the afternoon, Juliet drove Alex back to Clent.

"Thank you, Juliet, I have had a lovely day. I will see you on Tuesday if that is ok with you." Juliet said yes and he waved goodbye to Clara. Juliet was relieved when he closed the passenger door and she drove off. He was going to Wales for the weekend.

On Monday she had an email from Alex,

"How do you fancy going on a narrow boat trip tomorrow?"

Juliet was thrown into chaos. A narrowboat ride with Clara who was two and a half and couldn't swim? Besides which Juliet hated canals with a passion, they gave her the willies.

She emailed him a reply

"I don't know Alex, I am not sure, phone me to discuss please."

And she gave him her phone number." Within minutes the phone rang. It was Alex. Juliet explained her dilemma. Alex laughed. "Oh, come on Juliet, it will be fun."

"Well, it is not my idea of fun Alex but I suppose it will be ok, I have got a life jacket that Clara can use. Just as long as you are the one driving the boat, I don't want anything to do with it." He was being charming and generous she couldn't deny and it wouldn't hurt. She didn't want another afternoon sitting alone with him in the lounge that was for sure.

The next day she picked him up from Clent and they drove to Oswestry. He was relaxed, happy and good company and thankfully, he didn't ask any more difficult questions about Tamarisk or her non-existent love life. They set off on the canal boat, it was a cold, grey day but, after a shaky start he seemed to be in command of the boat much to Juliet's relief. Thankfully there was a cabin down below that Clara was content to be in, looking out of the window at the fields going by. "Juliet, there is a bottle of wine in my rucksack, will you get it out, please? You should find some glasses in the cupboard, let's have a drink."

Well, this was a pleasant change and Juliet had to admit she was quite enjoying herself. She did as he asked and handed him a glass. "Come up here and join me. Clara will be ok in there for a minute or two."

She joined him at the tiller with a glass of wine in her hand. "Fancy a snog?" he said.

Juliet looked wistfully at the passing fields and thought about it. "Why?" she said.

"Because I want to kiss you," he said, "You look beautiful and I want to kiss you."

She contemplated saying no and then decided against it "I'd like that" she said. He put his glass down on the top of the cabin and then put his hand to her face cupping it and turning it upwards towards his, he kissed her slowly and sensuously in only the way he could. Their lips parted. "You had better concentrate on steering the boat," she laughed and went inside to check on Clara.

The smooth bastard, Juliet thought to herself. He had planned this and she had fell prey to it again. But somehow she didn't mind. In fact, if she was brutally honest with herself, she wanted it. Not all those months ago, no, not then but slowly, inch by inch over the Summer, he had crept back into her heart and she wanted him she really wanted him again. She had grown as a person, she had stood her ground, and not appeased him or bent towards his will and yet he had come back and he had decided he wanted her, nearly three years after they had first resumed contact.

Chapter 33 – Past Revisited

They came to a town and moored up. "Let's go and find a pub and have some lunch. I am absolutely starving," said Alex. They held Clara's hands as they walked along the towpath, Clara in between them.

They found a quaint old hotel and found a little table in the corner of the dining room. It had turned quite chilly and was threatening rain. There was an open fire blazing away, heating the room. "Is there anything that Clara can have on the menu?" said Alex.

"She can have some of mine," said Juliet "she will have chips, she is a bit of a fussy eater and it is pointless paying for a meal for her."

"I am having fish and chips," said Alex "I have really missed them in Saudi not to mention fresh milk in coffee, it is all UHT out there and it does not make for a nice cup of coffee at all."

They ate their meal. Alex had a pint and Juliet had an orange juice. She was driving and she had already had one glass of wine she didn't want to risk it. They had finished their meal and they sat next to each other with Clara in between. Alex leaned over and kissed Juliet on the lips but Juliet felt Clara push her away from Alex. "I think Clara is a little jealous," said Juliet and Alex laughed.

It was spitting with rain as they left the hotel and made their way back to the boat and as they cast off the rain began to get heavier. Alex had a waterproof jacket on but it was no protection from the rain as it began to pelt it down rather viciously. Juliet felt sorry for him out there. She opened the cabin door "Do you want to moor up until it has gone over?" she shouted over the diesel engine.

"I don't think it is going over and in any case, I am already soaked. I will just push on and try and get back as quickly as possible. Go inside and keep dry," he replied.

So she shut the cabin door. Thankfully the return journey seemed quicker than the outward one much to Juliet's relief. It was late September but it had not been a nice day weather wise and Alex was soaked to the skin.

They got into the car and Juliet had to put the heater and the fan on full as they were steaming up because Alex was so wet. She set off as soon as the windscreen was clear. It was nearly four pm and the time had flown by. Her mind was a whir as she drove along. "Look Alex, it is going to take us an hour to get back to Wolverhampton and it will be rush hour. It will be hell trying to get you back to Clent and then I will have to come all the way back again. It will probably be at least 6.30 – 7pm before I get home. Do you want to stay at my house? I have a spare bedroom and we could have a takeaway. It will be too late to start cooking as Clara will need a bath and then bed."

"That would be very nice Juliet, if you are sure you don't mind me staying. I need to phone Sue and tell her I won't be back tonight but it won't be a problem, she won't have started cooking yet." So he phoned Sue.

They got back and Juliet gave Alex her large bathrobe to wear which despite being an extra-large looked snug on him and took his clothes to put in the drier. She fed and bathed Clara and put her to bed. "Right, let's have some dinner," she said, as she handed Alex the menu from the Chinese takeaway. Alistair was delighted, they didn't often have a takeaway and he adored Chinese food. Juliet ordered the food and went to collect it and they all ate dinner on trays on their laps in the lounge.

Alistair went out to see his mates and Juliet cleared away the plates, and came back with the bottle of wine. Alex rolled a cigarette and handed it to her then rolled one for him and leaned forward to light her cigarette for her. "I had better show you the guest bedroom," said Juliet "and turn on the radiator, it is dropping chilly tonight."

She stubbed out her cigarette and got up and turned on the table lamps in the lounge making it very cosy indeed. She then went over to draw the curtains on the bi-fold door. "Will you come to bed with me?" said Alex, in that husky, sexy voice of his. Juliet stood rooted to the spot and said nothing with her hand on the cord of the curtain pull. She didn't turn around. Alex got up from the sofa and came up behind her and took her in his arms and kissed the back of her neck, just as he used to do when they had gone shopping in Morrisons three years ago. "I know you want to," he whispered in her ear. Shivers ran up her spine and her body was on fire with desire, a desire she had not felt for a long time. The desire, that she only felt when she was with him, not with Phil and definitely not with Nigel. He slowly turned her to face him and kissed her slowly and sensuously long and full on the lips, holding her in his powerful arms, pressing her against him. She could feel his erection stirring against her hip and she could smell him. It was futile to resist.

"I want an orgasm," she said, "will you give me one?"

"It would be my pleasure," he said and took her hand. "Show me the guest room then." He said and she led the way.

She turned on the bedside lamp and the radiator and drew the curtains. "Do you have any tea lights?" he said, "and some oil if you have any?"

Juliet went and fetched them and when she returned he was already in bed, lying on his side with his torso out of the duvet, his chest hair on display. He had often Skyped her like that in the Summer as it was hot in Saudi and although she had tried not to take any notice she had found it indecent to say the least. Not because she was a prude, far from it but of because of the effect it had on her. Now he was here in the flesh. He held out his hand to take hers and pulled her onto the bed towards him. He took her in his arms and kissed her on the lips, gently at first and then with more intensity. He undid the button on her jeans and undid the buttons on her shirt, pushing his hands inside to feel her bare breasts. She wasn't wearing a bra, she seldom did, she didn't need to, her breasts were so small. He was playing very gently with her nipple and her body started to buzz with excitement and she felt the heat between her legs.

"Take your clothes off and get into bed, I want to give you a massage," he said huskily. She did what he asked and climbed into bed next to him. She could feel the heat from his body next to hers as she lay face down on the bed. He trickled the cold oil onto the small of her back and started to massage her moving his hot hands slowly up and down her back, each time returning from her shoulders he would go a little lower over her buttocks until finally, he reached the crease between her buttocks and her thighs. He started to gently trace his fingers back and forth along the crease, edging closer and closer to her vagina, and all the while he did this he kissed and licked the back of her neck. He knew she was getting aroused, he could hear her breathing growing harder, and he started to bite the flesh between her neck and her shoulder in between kisses. She could feel herself dripping, oh my god, she was dripping. She hadn't been aroused like this for a long, long time. She turned to face him, and he kissed her hard on the lips and pushed her left hip gently backwards so she lay on her back. His hands found their way between her thighs where he explored her wetness gently with his fingers. She parted her legs, and he held her in his left arm and kissed her while he played with her clitoris, she surrendered herself to him and relaxed. She didn't come easily, she never did but he was a master. He knew how to make her come and he hadn't forgotten how to touch her. How slow or fast to go, how much pressure to apply and every so often, he took his finger away from her clitoris and traced the outline of the entrance to her vagina, increasing her desire further, until she felt she could take it no more, but she said nothing. He knew what he was doing.

He was building the intensity of her orgasm. She could feel herself swelling and he could too. He increased the pressure and kissing her hard on the lips he brought her to orgasm. She moaned a long low groan, as her vagina exploded and pulsed, and her body shook. He was very, very aroused and he was rock hard, he moved on top of her and gently entered her, thrusting slowly at first and then faster and harder until he too burst forth and came. It felt wonderful, his body so much bigger than hers covered her completely and she could feel the power of it as he came. He kissed her gently on the lips.

"I have wanted to do that for so long," he said, as he gently left her body and moved off her and onto his back. "Thank you," she said breathlessly. She was grateful, no matter what had gone on between them, no one, but no one knew how to make love to her like he did, and the pleasure that she felt when he did was the best in the world. It was priceless. No amount of money could compensate for that.

They lay quietly for a while, and then he rolled them a cigarette each and topped up her wine, and they sat up in bed smoking decadently. "You have grown bold," he said, "you have never asked me for an orgasm before but I am glad you did."

Juliet blew the smoke from her lips, "I have missed them, it is not the same when you give yourself one, I know what is coming next but when you do it, there is an element of the unexpected to it, and they are stronger because you are kissing and holding me."

I will never tire of them, she thought to herself.

"Sleep with me tonight Juliet, in this bed. I want to hold you as you fall asleep." How could she refuse?

Alex stayed with them for three more days and then his time would be up and he had to go back to Saudi. They had fallen in love again, if they had ever been out of love. Yes, they had fought earlier last year but their love was so intense, that it only stood to reason that when they fought it would be intense also. As Mellors remarks to Lady Chatterley in DH Lawrence's infamous novel "you have to take the rough with the smooth."

Juliet had slept in his bed every night, in the guestroom, and they had made love with a passion every night. She didn't know where this was going to lead or whether it would go anywhere at all but she didn't care, she had loved every minute of it and she felt happy.

She drove him to the station in Wolverhampton to catch his train to London and then Heathrow, and ultimately his flight back to Saudi. He kissed Clara goodbye and got out of the car to retrieve his bags from the boot. Juliet got out also. He took her in his arms and looked her in the eyes. "I don't deserve you, I know that," he said "I have behaved appallingly, and you have still forgiven me and I know I don't deserve it, but I am so very glad you have. You do forgive me, don't you?"

Juliet kissed him, "what a bloody silly question. Of course I forgive you," she laughed as tears filled her eyes.

"I love you Juliet, so very very much," he said.

"And I love you, Alex, I always have and I always will."

She watched him walk away and disappear into the train station, the tears stinging her eyes.

Chapter 34 – Feelings

The next day she received a little note in the post box and she immediately recognised the handwriting. It was from Alex. She opened it. It was a card of a landscape oil on canvas, inside it said;

Train 4 October 2013

My Darling Juliet

I was chuffed to get your text thanking me for the orgasms. I will do my best to try and make everything right – and to keep you stocked up with orgasms for as long as you want them!

Love Alex
xxxx

Another little billet-doux to add to her collection. She had kept them all in a shoebox under her bed, even when they had fallen out, she had not got rid of them. She would never get rid of them whatever happened. She remembered how Mark had torn up the love notes she had received from Alex all those years ago and how she had wished he hadn't. She was so glad that in this day and age of emails and texts he still sent her little love notes. Emails and texts were just not the same, they never would be.

She sent him an email to thank him for it. She wasn't sure what time his plane would land but she wanted to let him know that she had received his card and had loved it.

There was no denying that Juliet loved Alex. Truly, madly deeply. Whatever had gone on before, however they fought, she loved him to the depths of her heart. Phil? Well she had loved Phil to a degree but there are degrees of love. Juliet knew that from her long history of marriages and lovers. But Alex, there was no love like Alex. It was as high as the mountains and as deep as the deepest oceans and she knew she would never be free from it. She could try to deny it, she could push it to the corner of her heart but there would never be anyone like Alex and she knew that.

He responded to her email that evening.

My darling Juliet

How I miss you and Clara, but you especially. I have been so foolish, so blind. But we start a new chapter, I hope you feel the same.

I had booked a holiday in neighbouring Oman for Ede and I would like it very much if you and Clara would join me. If you say yes, I will book your tickets and send them to you by email. You will fly from Birmingham, I have checked. I hope you will agree to it. You will fly out next weekend on the 10th October.

Love Alex
Xxxxxx

Juliet was gobsmacked and not for the first time. Should she say yes? Her head was still spinning from the few days they had spent together which had rekindled their love but she was cautious. She fired off an email.

Alex

I love you to the depths of my heart, I hope you know that. But my love, I am scared. You have promised so much before

267

*and then let us down (Egypt). I don't know what to do. I have
very little money and being stranded in a far-flung foreign
country with no cash is not top of my wish list, especially
with Clara. I hope you understand. But I do love you and
really want to see you again.*

*Love Juliet
Xxxxx*

It didn't go long before he replied

My darling Juliet

*I understand your concerns, but I am not going to let you
down this time. My emotions are a mixed bag. I feel very sad
and angry with myself that I have forfeited so much time with
you and Clara, although this is offset by the knowledge that
at least I can provide well for you in my current situation. I
am falling deeply and helplessly in love with you, willingly
casting off all the insecurity that has previously held me
back. Like you, I am afraid, but I feel that what can be won
is so precious that it must surely be worth the risk. I also
know that, after all, you have been through, after having so
much reason to feel nothing but contempt for me, you are a
very special person indeed to allow me back into your life.*

Please say you will come to Oman.

Love Alex xxxx

Juliet slept on it. She wanted to see him again and it wasn't
just sex, it was him, his company. He made her laugh and
when he was relaxed it was so easy being with him. He was
being open with his emotions for the first time since the
cottage and he was being honest about them in a way he had
not been before. Should she trust him? She pondered on that

for a while. You can shut yourself down after being hurt, or you can take a blind leap of faith and allow yourself to experience love.

She had a sleepless night but after Nigel and Phil she knew she should trust her heart even if it led her into madness. "Do it to the death," isn't that what she always said? Why was she backing out now? There was nothing to it, she reasoned with herself in the early morning, she had to do it. She just had to. It was 5am and she fired up her computer and opened her emails. Clara was asleep beside her and she could see the night stars illuminating the sky through the Velux window.

Alex

I have deliberated on your email and yes, we are coming to Oman, that is if your offer is still open. I so want to see you again, and I am sorry for being so untrusting. Let's move forward in a different vein. Book those tickets and I will pack my bags.

All my love Juliet xxx

She lay down and went to sleep, soundly and didn't awake until 8am. She felt good. No, she felt better than good, she felt alive as she skipped downstairs to make herself tea. She returned to bed and looked at her computer. He had replied;

My Lovely Juliet

I have booked up the tickets for you and Clara and you will find them attached. I have put 100 pounds in your account so that you can buy anything you need for your holiday. Can we Skype tonight about 8pm your time? If that is convenient. I can't wait to see you again.

Love to the depths of my heart

269

Alex
Xxxx

Juliet was amazed at his generosity. He appeared to have undergone a transformation. Perhaps it had taken him a bit of time to get used to the idea of having a daughter at his age. She had after all thrust it on him rather suddenly by not telling him she was pregnant. Whatever the reason she was happy for the moment and she should just enjoy that. He had not asked her anything else about how she came to be in Tamarisk or where the car had come from and he had not mentioned the diamond ring, which he had undoubtedly noticed.

They Skyped that evening as promised and talked for three hours. Alex talked about his emotions and insecurities and his behaviour in the past. "I realise that I am not an easy person to get along with and a lot of what has gone wrong between us was my fault. But you don't know how difficult it was in Iraq. It was a very unstable environment."

That raised the question of Maher and Juliet had to ask him, she couldn't let it lie. She had overlooked it when he had made advances on her but it had reared its ugly head more than once since he had departed. "Were you having an affair with Maher? Are you bisexual?" she said, "I need to know Alex. Whatever the answer I will still love you but I need to know."

"No, I was not having an affair with Mahe, and I am not bisexual or gay. Maher was married."

"I know he was married Alex but it was an arranged marriage, so that doesn't necessarily rule out Maher being gay."

Alex laughed. "Honestly, really Juliet, we were not having an affair. We were just good friends. We shared a flat together."

Juliet was satisfied. She would have to take his word for it. There was no point in torturing herself over it. She had her secrets, and he probably had his. Perhaps she had taken 2 and ? and made 5. She had a word with herself. You are as bad as him for getting jealous. She had never been the jealous type but now she realised it was because of the depth of feeling she felt for him that made her jealous and he clearly felt the same. She knew that it was difficult for him to feel deeply about someone. It made him vulnerable to allow someone to mean that much to him, to allow them to have so much influence over his happiness or unhappiness. She just hoped that they would continue the way they were now. He seemed to have turned a corner, and to have changed, only time would tell whether he would be able to maintain it.

When she logged onto her emails the next day there was an email from Alex;

My darling Juliet

I got 2 hours' sleep last night and decided to take the day off "sick" today. There's nothing assigned for me today and the most that will happen is that I lose a day's money. I feel so much better having had three hours' constructive conversation with you. I will treat myself to a good wank thinking about you (the photo will help – thank you!), and sleep as long as I want/need to.

I am still smiling incredulously as I think about your question about Maher. I hope you haven't tortured yourself thinking about that, but fear that you have. I am sorry if you haven't had enough sleep today as a result of my insecurity yesterday.

Sweet Jesus, if you only knew how much I am looking forward to undressing you and catering for your every sexual need ... I am motivated by LUST as well as LOVE.

Alex

xxxx

Her heart did a little leap of joy when she read those words.

Chapter 35- Oman

Saturday soon came and Juliet was a bag of nerves. She so wanted to see him again. She had fallen hopelessly in love with him and being apart from him was torture. She had received the fifth degree from her daughters about Alex but she had only half listened. They didn't know, they didn't understand what it was like to be this in love, she doubted many people knew.

Alistair was going to drop her off at Birmingham Airport and her flight didn't depart until 9pm. She was going to Dubai where she would change planes to go to Muscat, Oman. Alex wouldn't be there until 2am in the morning local time so she would have a good 8 hours there alone, but he had given her all the details of the booking at the hotel, and had assured her that it would be alright. She got Clara to have a nap in the afternoon and emailed Alex to tell him that she would soon be on her way and couldn't wait to see him.

Alistair dropped Juliet off at 5.30pm and they had soon checked in. Clara seemed to be enjoying herself and was very well behaved and didn't seem to mind being up after her bedtime.

They were flying Emirates and when they got on the plane and were shown to their seats, Juliet was very impressed. As they taxied down the runway, Juliet breathed a sigh of relief. It wouldn't be long until she would see Alex again. Clara soon fell asleep and Juliet tucked her up with a blanket. It was a long flight and Juliet tried to doze as best she could, but she only managed to cat nap. When they landed at Dubai airport the sun was shining, and it was day. Juliet was on the last leg of her journey, and getting closer to Alex. Later in the day, he too would be travelling through Dubai airport.

Juliet managed to negotiate her way through the airport, she didn't need to collect her luggage, it would be transferred for her. She just hoped it didn't go astray. It was not for herself she was concerned, it was for Clara. It would be a nightmare if her luggage didn't arrive in Muscat when she did.

Alex had said she would love Dubai airport and he was right, it was amazing but Juliet didn't want any of the luxuries on offer there, even if she could have afforded them. There was only one thing in the world she wanted and that was Alex and she thought about him as they boarded the flight to Muscat. It wasn't a long flight, it would be just over an hour and despite having had very little sleep, Juliet wasn't at all tired. She could have a nap that afternoon with Clara.

When they arrived in Muscat, Alex had said there would be a courtesy bus from the hotel waiting but Juliet studied all of the signs and no one there appeared to be from the hotel. She approached one man who was wearing a headdress and a long white robe. "Excuse me, can you tell me if there is a courtesy bus here from the Tulip Inn?"

He looked around "I am sorry madam, but I can't see one, did they know you were coming?"

"Well yes," she said.

The man took pity on her, "I am collecting a couple and we will have to drive past your hotel, I can drop you off if you like,"

"That is very kind of you," said Juliet. She felt that if there were another couple in the car, she would be safe and he seemed like someone you could trust.

He turned out to be a very nice young man and would not let her pick up her suitcases or the collapsed pushchair, even though he struggled himself and said that he had injured his back some months previously. The couple he was collecting were American, Juliet hoped they did not mind her sharing their lift. As they set off, he explained that he conducted desert tours. The wadis in Oman were renowned for their beauty. Oman was different from what she had expected. Everywhere there were modern buildings, roads and restaurants that you would see at home, TGI Fridays, McDonalds etc, and everything looked new and clean. It was pleasantly hot, and thankfully the car was air-conditioned.

When they arrived at the hotel it was indeed a four-star hotel and it looked very pleasant. Juliet thanked the young man who had given her a lift and went to the reception. Thankfully everything was straightforward and she was shown to the room. She relaxed as she closed the door behind her.

The time was slipping by and it wouldn't be long before she would see Alex. She looked out of the window. There was a supermarket across the street. She decided that once she had got organised, unpacked and eaten, she would take Clara and they would have a look. She ordered lunch on room service and signed it to the room.

They went over to the supermarket and Juliet was amazed, there was such an array of things on offer. She brought some fruit, some crisps, and some other little titbits for Clara. There was a fridge in the room and it would be good to keep some snacks in there

They lay on the bed and slept. Juliet awoke to find that they had been asleep for two hours and it was now 4pm. She knew that Alex would not be going to the airport until 10pm and he would still be at work. She had tried messaging his phone but it didn't appear to want to send, so she decided to go and see whether the hotel had a computer for public use. They did and she sent Alex an email to let him know they had arrived safely and to warn him about the lack of hotel bus. She told him, that a taxi would cost him around 10 Omani dollars and that she couldn't wait to see him.

They ordered something else from room service for dinner and Juliet bathed Clara and they watched TV. The time seemed to be dragging but Juliet knew it would pass. Why is it when you are having a good time that the time passes so very quickly and when you are waiting for something or someone the time drags so slowly?

Although their sleep had been disrupted over the past twenty-four hours Juliet managed to get Clara asleep by 9pm. She lay there on the bed thinking about Alex and how she loved him. He had displayed some insecurities but he seemed a changed person. His love for her seemed genuine and the fact that he was admitting to having insecurities was a step forward.

There is something difficult about the relationship between a man and a woman, something as old as time itself. Men are not conditioned to talk about their emotions, it is inconceivable for them to do so and it is something women desire so much. But if men do talk about their emotions, so much misunderstanding between them and the woman is swept away. There had been so many difficulties that Juliet and Alex had to endure and overcome and for a while at the start of their relationship Alex had opened himself up to Juliet and told her his innermost thoughts. Juliet had done likewise which had opened her up to scrutiny and condemnation. But faced with the complexities of the problems surrounding their relationship his insecurities had come to the surface and he stopped communicating. It happens so often and it is almost always fatal for the relationship.

When Alex had done this in the cottage Juliet knew it was the end and for the years that followed, she had wanted him to come back to her, to be like he was before, to open up about his feelings. But men are slow to acknowledge or voice their true emotions through fear of being hurt. But three years later after much struggle, he was hers again, opening his heart to her, and how deeply she adored him for that. Most men would not have bothered, sooner turning their backs on love than admitting their innermost thoughts. He may be a damaged soul but he had displayed more emotional intelligence than most men feel in their little finger. He had apologised for his behaviour and acknowledged his failings. She loved and adored him for that alone.

She dozed and woke, it was nearly midnight. She went and showered and applied her makeup, then settled down to wait for Alex. The hands on the clock went by slowly, despite Juliet taking her time over everything that she did. The room was dimly lit, she didn't want to wake Clara and there were butterflies in the pit of her stomach, as she lay on the bed waiting, waiting for the love of her life to knock on the door. And then there it was, at ten to two, the knock on the door. She leapt off the bed, and ran quickly but silently over to the door and peeped through the spy hole and there stood Alex.

She opened the door and he smiled a big smile and leaned forward and kissed her on the lips. He came into the room and Juliet put her finger to her lips and pointed to Clara asleep in the centre of the huge bed, and Alex nodded. "It is so fucking good to see you," he whispered, and took her in his arms, kissing her long and hard. He took a bottle of wine out of his rucksack and looked around for some glasses,
Juliet went and got a couple of tumblers from the bathroom and they sat on the sofa.
"Juliet," he said "there is something I want to say to you," and with that he moved from the sofa and went down on one knee in front of her. She had been married three times, but not one of her ex-husbands had gone down on one knee. Her

heart was pounding wildly in her chest "Juliet, will you do me the honour of being my wife."

Juliet looked deep into those wonderful blue eyes of his and didn't hesitate. "The honour will be all mine." She said and then continued, "Yes Alex, I want to marry you more than anything else in the world."

This is the second book in the "Alex and Juliet Series" if you liked this book then Book 3 is called "Paris Revisited."

Find out how it all ends in

About the Author

Joanne is a woman of a 'certain age' as the French say. Slightly eccentric and often stressed, she is a self confessed Francophile and loves all things French, especially the food, wine and the men; she just can't resist that sexy accent. Joanne has a collection of berets that embarrass her youngest child, but that are so useful in the winter when she is out walking the dog.

When she is not writing, Joanne has six children and four grandchildren to keep her busy. Thankfully cooking is one of her hobbies. She also likes to 'have a go' at painting.

Why don't you join her on social media? She would love to hear from you.

If you enjoyed this book then please leave a review or get in touch with me.

And don't forget to subscribe to
www.joannehomer.com **to claim your free EBook**

Printed in Great Britain
by Amazon

50579798R00159